THE BIGGEST STORY IN OHIO

Book One of the Cleveland Quartet

Greg Schaffner

Environmental Novels

Insinkrator
Event

CONTENTS

Title Page

Copyright

Dedication

ProloguE

PART ONE   1

Chapter 1:   3

Chapter 2:   8

Chapter 3:   11

Chapter 4:   16

Part Two: 25

Chapter 5:   26

Chapter 6:   31

Chapter 7:   36

Chapter 8:   46

Chapter 9:   55

Chapter 10:   59

Chapter 11:   66

Chapter 12:   78

Chapter 13:   86

Chapter 14:   88

Chapter 15:   96

Part Three: 111
Chapter 16:   112
Chapter 17:   121
Chapter 18:   129
Part IV: 138
Chapter 19:   139
Chapter 20:   148
Chapter 21:   155
Chapter 22:   159
Chapter 23:   167
Chapter 24:   175
Chapter 25:   186
Chapter 26:   200
Chapter 27:   209
Chapter 28:   214
PART V: 218
Chapter 29:   219
Chapter 30:   223
Chapter 31:   231
Chapter 32:   240
Chapter 33:   245
Chapter 34:   255
Chapter 35:   262
Chapter 36:   272
Epilogue   288
Stay in touch   307

PROLOGUE

[March, 2006 – about the time of the raid]

Call me Mouse.

I'm a reporter for the Cleveland Plain Speaker, the best newspaper on earth if you live in Cleveland. Among the reporters, I'm kind of a joke. I'm the guy who writes about nothing in particular and nobody worth mentioning. What I write about is not newsworthy. My colleagues envy me, because my readers love me and theirs don't love them. My twice a week column is the most widely read item in the paper, year in and year out.

Why is that? you ask. I think it's because I am not conflicted in my feelings for this splendid town, the way the others are. I love her with all my heart, and all my soul. I fit this town the way skin fits a teenager. When I look in the mirror I see Cleveland, and when I write about Cleveland my readers see themselves as they are in everyday life, except for one crucial thing: I make them lovable in their own eyes. Because the rest of the country thinks we're a joke, my readers make fun of themselves all the time. I do it, too, but I celebrate it as a strength. We're lovable because of our low self-esteem. If this makes no sense to you, you're probably not from Cleveland.

By way of contrast, Peter Zenger – my editor, my mentor, my friend, my nemesis – is the most respected man in the newsroom. He is a brilliant strategist who decides what we investigate and write about. Because of Peter, our reporters have won more Pulitzer Prizes than any other paper our size. Peter doesn't write for our readers. He writes to us, covering our draft stories with withering comments and suggestions for how to improve them. He writes to me a lot. I console myself with the fact that he has an audience of twenty reporters who fear him; I have an audience of half a million readers who love me.

When Peter first arrived from Boston, he sat down with each of us to figure out what we did, what we knew, and what we covered. By the time he got to me, my name had come up repeatedly as an example of what the others were not; a comparison they thought would make them look good in his eyes. Peter was no fool, and he saw through their posturing enough to take it with a grain of salt. When it was my turn, he didn't dilly-dally around. "They tell me you are out of control, don't know anything, do whatever you want, whenever you want to, have no real deadlines, and are friends with every resident of Cleveland."

"Sounds about right," I said cheerfully.

"I have to confess they have me a little worried about just what I'm dealing with here." He opened his arms wide. "I don't even know your real name. Am I really supposed to call you Mouse?"

"Yes, please."

"All the time?"

I nodded.

He glanced down at a set of prepared questions and decided they weren't the way to go. "When I think of a mouse," he said, "I think of a cute, little, harmless creature with big ears and a twitching nose."

"That sounds more like a baby rabbit," I said.

He looked me over. "Could be," he admitted. "What am I leaving out? The rodent side of things, maybe? Are you a rodent, Mouse? Do you have teeth? Do you like to gnaw at things? Do you scare some people because you turn up unexpectedly and in places you don't belong?"

I had to set him straight before he went down that path too far. "I'm more the cuddly, stuffed-toy kind of critter. People tell me things because they enjoy my company and think I'm harmless."

"I suppose that could be useful."

"You'd be surprised."

Peter waited a moment before looking me directly in the eyes.

"Mouse, are you tough enough to do the job of a real reporter."

"No."

I don't think he expected that. "Well, are you a survivor, at least?"

"We mice are hard to get rid of, and I know every hiding place in Cleveland."

He considered what I said and what it meant. "For now," he declared, "just keep doing what you do—whatever the hell that is—and we'll keep an open mind about how to use your talents..." He paused for a beat. "Whatever they are."

Quite the comic, Mr. Zenger.

That was ten years ago, and Peter still hasn't figured out what I do other than being popular with the readers. He told me once that the more discerning ones don't think much of me. That's okay. They're part of Cleveland, and so I love them without reservation. Our poor city has taken too much abuse for me to turn on anyone just because they are discerning.

He came to us from Boston in the fateful year of 1996 with a mandate to make us edgier and more confrontational. I'm pleased to report that we wore him down in less than a year, and now we all get along just fine. In the beginning, he decided that I would be one of his pet projects. Oh, the rewrites he made me do! Version after version, each one worse than the one before. The problem isn't content, because there isn't any to speak of in my twice-weekly column. I write about the ordinary people of Cleveland, the ones the other reporters push aside to get to the newsmakers. I don't just write about them; I celebrate them. I have been called "the voice of Cleveland" by no lesser a luminary than our mayor Frank Jackson. That endorsement brought me nothing but abuse and ridicule.

Peter just doesn't get Cleveland. I tried explaining this to him. What he didn't understand was that Cleveland is the most self-deprecating city in America, and we like it that way. He caught on to the first half of that pretty quickly, but he kept thinking that his job was to goad our good citizens into striving for this nebulous concept called better, or its odious sibling, the best. If I've told him once, I've told him a thousand times, nobody in Cleveland is against being better or even being the best; it's just that we're from Cleveland, and that means we suck unless you are comparing us to Detroit, which sucks worse. We're not humble, exactly, and we're certainly not pretending we aren't as good as we know we are. Nope. It's just that we're from Cleveland, so what do you expect? Better? Really?

I'm not saying I understand Cleveland perfectly, but there is one thing I can say with utter conviction. Nobody loves Cleveland more than me, including our treacherous mayor. You might say that my beat is what makes Cleveland, Cleveland, or—put another way—what just happened that could only happen in Cleveland. My popularity annoys the hell out of everyone, which means I have to put up with a lot of abuse and practical jokes, which I return with gusto and inventiveness. They really shouldn't be surprised. People like to read about themselves, and let's face it; there aren't that many newsmakers in Cleveland. I'm the guy who writes about the lives of readers—not leaders.

My abiding love for Cleveland means that Peter will never respect me, but he has grown to like me. Do I wish it were otherwise? Sure. I'm only human. We all want respect. I respect him. But I'm from Cleveland, so I don't go around expecting much in the respect category. I'm fine with that. Really, I am.

Peter holds a staff meeting every Monday morning. Usually, I'm the last to wander in. Sometimes Peter snaps at me, and sometimes he just smiles indulgently and makes a note to get me later. This serves as a kind of barometer for the other reporters to predict what mood Peter is in. I regard this as a public service for the journalists.

He calls impromptu staff meetings other times, as well, and

I'm not always invited to these. It may be that there's a topic that just concerns the politicians down in Columbus—a town that should feel inferior to Cleveland but doesn't--or some sports item of interest only to the sports guys. That's fine. But then sometimes, if he's really pissed at me, Peter will forget to invite me and then summon me ten minutes into the meeting just so he can complain about how late I am. The others find it hysterically funny.

Peter and I have been at this for ten years, now. Personally, I don't know what it would take for me to mend my ways. We both know he's not going to fire me, and we both know I'm never going to quit my job, no matter how much he yells at me. If you are into psychological jargon, we're co-dependent. I know that's supposed to be a bad thing. The question is, how bad does it have to get to break the pattern, especially when it is the source of such amusement to the rest of the group?

PART ONE

*[2004 - about two years before
the raid on the commune]*

CHAPTER 1:

The Congressman

Stanhope Chemicals, International had an interesting history that bounced back and forth across the Atlantic Ocean before going world-wide. It began in Switzerland, expanded into America, merged with another American corporation, which gave it the name Stanhope Chemicals, Incorporated. That corporation was then absorbed by a German conglomerate, which kept the Stanhope name, but moved its headquarters to Heidelberg in 1980. As it expanded across the globe, it set up regional groups in Europe, North America (which included Mexico as well as Canada), South America (which included the Caribbean Islands), India, Africa, China, Japan, Asia, and Australia. Each group was headed by a Senior Executive Vice President who reported directly to Hermann Neuman, one of the most powerful and feared men on Earth.

Senior Executive VP Ronald Haskins became head of Stanhope Chemicals, North America in 1988. One of his quirks was that he hated airplanes, and he especially hated to fly internationally. Four times a year, he travelled to Heidelberg for the quarterly meeting of the regional heads, drugging himself with Dramamine and copious amounts of alcohol. The other VPs regarded him as a drunk, but they were wrong in doing so. Back home, he was closer to being a teetotaler than an alcoholic. It helped that he rarely flew anywhere. When he met with others, they came to him.

Today was different. Not only was he flying to Cincinnati to meet with a lowly Congressman, but he was bringing along his chief legal counsel Shira Beck and his head of government affairs Robert Harris. It would be an exaggeration to say that they had been summoned to this private meeting, but their host made it clear that the matter was urgent and confidential.

It had better be, the CEO thought to himself.

"What do we know about this joker?" he asked his lobbyist.

Robert Harris was reassuring. "Ben Wicker is one of our most reliable friends at the Capital. We've supported him for forty years and he's repaid our investment many times over."

"What's his district, again?"

"It's Ohio District 6, one of those gerrymandered districts our Republican friends set up in 2002. It runs along the Ohio River all the way from the eastern border with Pennsylvania, then along the border with West Virginia, then continuing to the border with Kentucky. It's mostly small towns except for Cincinnati."

"So, right across the river from our Parkers Ferry and Mount Washington plants."

"Exactly."

"But you say he's a friend."

"One of our most reliable."

Ronald Haskins huffed. "Doesn't mean he's bringing good news."

That made Shira Beck laugh. "Pretty much guarantees the opposite."

The three executives looked at each other warily. There was a lot of potential bad news involving those particular manufacturing plants. Well, it wouldn't be the first time

4

they'd dealt with these kinds of problems, and they were better equipped to deal with them than any major corporation in the country. Part of being equipped was having people like Benjamin Wicker giving them advanced notice of problems.

By prior arrangement, the three of them took a cab directly from the airport to an eminently forgettable restaurant in the suburb of Mariemont. They were escorted into a private dining room at the back. Fifteen minutes later, Congressman Benjamin Wicker walked in, unaccompanied.

The lobbyist made the introductions. Everyone was pleased and honored to finally meet. They made small talk while the waitress took their orders. As soon as she left them, they got down to business.

"So, Ben, what's coming at us that you think is so urgent?"

"I just got wind of a major class action lawsuit that's about to be filed in Cincinnati." He held his hands up in front of his chest. "I know. Why Cincinnati? Your plants are in West Virginia. But lots of my folks are coming down with cancer, too. The river bottom doesn't care about political boundaries. It's all one big layer of toxic sludge, oozing back and forth between West Virginia and Ohio."

"This isn't news to us or anyone else who's paying attention," said Shira Beck. "What's the big deal?"

Stanhope's Parkers Ferry plant had been discharging the deadly toxin C8 (also known as PFOA) into the Ohio River for over forty years. A second plant in the nearby town of Mount Washington contributed almost as much. Their own corporate scientists estimated the total discharge at 1.7 million pounds. They were chipping away at the problems in the manufacturing process, and these days the discharge was less than half what it had been ten years ago. That was all to the good, but the problem with C8 was that it was one of those chemicals that just didn't break down over time. Most chemicals degrade by gradually breaking down into simpler and simpler components until they are harmless. Not *C8* and a handful of similar chemicals. Back in 2002, some dipshit environmentalist came up with a term for them: forever chemicals. It haunted Stanhope and its competitors ever since. All those millions upon millions of pounds of chemicals dumped in various rivers around the country were still there, polluting the water, killing or debilitating thousands of people who drank it. Even if they stopped manufacturing them, chemicals like *C8* were going to be down there forever. For at least thirty-five of those forty years, Stanhope had been sued for this illegal dumping a hundred times over. Never once did a lawsuit even come to trial. That's how good Shira Beck and her legal team were. She took the Congressman's urgency as a kind of personal affront.

"The big deal is that the plaintiffs have found a real lawyer for a change."

"His name?"

"Her name: Maeve Waldoch."

Shira shook her head. She'd never heard of her. "And when you say a real lawyer, what do you mean?"

"One who is going to take it to trial, all the way."

"That's what they all say."

Ben Wicker stood firm. "How many are asking for a two billion dollar settlement?

"IS SHE OUT OF HER FUCKING MIND?"

Shira put a hand on her boss's arm. "Relax, Ronnie. You know how these things work. Even if they end up with a fraction of that, we'll appeal and get a more reasonable settlement."

"Like ten cents on the dollar? That's still a couple hundred million."

"Or less."

He turned to the Congressman. "Is she stupid?"

"Not from what I hear."

"So, what does she know that makes her even conceive of a proffer like that?"

"That's why I wanted to talk to you," Ben replied. "I don't know what it is, but you know I sit on the Ag Committee, which means that I hear things. All I can tell you is that you have a serious leak in one of those plants. Somebody is talking to one of our staff lawyers, and he let it slip. Just that. There's an inside whistleblower and he – or she – has fed something really mind blowing to this lawyer."

That quieted things down. Robert Harris broke the silence. "Ben, I know I speak for the others in telling you we appreciate your heads up. I think it goes without saying that we hope you'll keep your ears open and let us know anything that filters out."

The others nodded.

"The name of your staff lawyer wouldn't hurt," Shira said.

"You'll be careful to protect my name."

"We protect all our friends, Benjamin."

He gave her a name and a phone number. "You promise you'll keep me out of this."

Shira took a quick, sharp breath, feeling insulted that he asked a second time.

"Thanks again, Ben," Robert said, standing up. "Let me see you out. I believe we have some things to talk over."

CHAPTER 2:

Action Steps

"D o we believe him?" he asked.

"I think we should, at least for now," she replied. "You were right to push him about that lawsuit. If there are leaks, we need to find out what they've got and how they got it."

"Who do we trust at Parkers Ferry and Mount Washington?"

The lawyer shook her head back and forth. "I don't think we can trust anybody at either plant. Not now."

"So, we put Duncan on it?"

He was referring to Duncan Gabardine, the head of digital security for all of Stanhope. He was a busy man, and assigning him to investigate this mere rumor of a leak would automatically force him to delegate other matters that needed attention.

Shira took her time before agreeing. "I think so."

"You don't sound convinced."

"You know as well as I do how many leaks we're trying to plug. I'd hate to see him chasing a ghost."

The thought had been on Ronald's mind as well. "In a way, that could be a good thing," he said. "Right now, I'm choosing to believe our dear Congressman that we have a leaker talking to his committee and possibly sharing his information with this bullshit lawsuit. What I'm not buying is the idea that the leak could only come from one of those plants. It's likely, but there are plenty of other plants. Duncan won't get caught up in keeping his focus too narrow."

"He is a pit bull, that one," Shira said in admiration.

"Good. Let's move on. Who's the judge in Cincinnati?"

"Give me a moment." She dialed one of her assistants and had him find out who had the case and whether they had ever worked with him before.

"Who else do we have in Cincinnati?"

"Besides Ben Wicker?"

"Yeah: legal, news, law enforcement, political..."

"Well, for political, there's always the reliable Senator Courtney."

"One of our best," Ronald agreed.

"Then there's the editor of the Cincinnati Blade, Warren Davis."

"How about the mayor?"

"I wouldn't count on him as an ally," she said. "Neutral, say, at this point. It all depends on how public it becomes. If it becomes a national story, it's hard to predict where he'll come down."

They went through a list of other politicians and journalists they had cultivated over the years. Ronald made a note to check in with his lobbyist to see who they missed.

Shira's phone rang. She listened, made a few notes, and hung up.

"That was quick," her boss said.

"Too quick," she replied. "I don't know how we missed this, but we did. All we had to do was plug in the name of that lawyer, Maeve what's her face. Boom. We got a whole bunch of information, stuff we should have known about months ago."

"So, who's the judge?"

"Finley. Chuck Finley."

"Never heard of him."

"Neither have I," Shira admitted.

"Have we got anything on him?"

"I'm already working on that."

"Good. So, are we done? Can we at least have lunch?"

They realized the waitress hadn't come back. Shira went to the door and flagged her down. She explained that Richard Harris had instructed her to wait until they asked for her.

"I hope I didn't inconvenience you."

"Not at all. Did Mr. Harris say when he would be rejoining us?"

"He said you should go on without him and that he'd catch up with you back at the office."

Shira noted that he hadn't said back in their office in Indianapolis. The man was a pro. "We'll have our lunch now, then."

"It'll be a few minutes, I'm afraid, but I'll put it at the head of the line."

"Thank you, dear."

CHAPTER 3:

And Then Some Good News

Over lunch – which finally arrived, and wasn't worth the wait – Ronald Haskins decided to give his chief counsel some news. "Guess who just retired? Dr. Jeremiah Tennyson."

"No!"

"Yep," he said, pleased to be the one to tell her.

"We should break out the champagne."

"A bit early in the day for that."

"Still. The best expert witness in the country is out of our hair? And just in time before this Parkers Ferry thing bites us in the ass." She savored the moment. "I've got to say I'm surprised. He's not that old. I'd be surprised if he was even sixty-five."

"He's exactly sixty-five. Took his retirement and rode off into the sunset."

"Happy trails to you," she sang.

"And happy trials to you," Ronne replied. "You know, maybe we should send that bottle of champagne to him. A little token of appreciation for his retirement."

"Are you sure it's real?"

"I heard it from the President of Case-Western himself."

"So he's not going to be teaching anymore, but does that mean he's not going to be an expert witness? It's one thing to stop teaching; I can see him doing that. But the courtroom is where he shined. He loved to duke it out with our attorneys in front of the jury, showing off his expertise. I hope this retirement doesn't mean he'll have even more time to slice up my staff."

Ronnie enjoyed her outburst. "Relax, Shira. I guess he had a minor stroke. That's the kind of thing that makes a man look at his life a little differently."

"Well, maybe it's karma. He's almost given me a whole series of strokes. What goes around."

The Senior VP shook his head. "You know, that's pretty cold, even for you."

It was cold, but it was also the truth, and Ronnie was one of the few people Shira could be honest with. That kind of honesty was the foundation of the trust they had between them. Each of them had enough dirt on the other to put them away for decades. It would be a form of mutually assured destruction, and that shared vulnerability was another thing that made them so effective. "Is he in the hospital now?"

"I have no idea."

"Maybe I should look into it."

"By all means, be my guest. I have to admit, I'm kind of surprised. I didn't realize you felt that strongly about him."

"That's because you never faced him in court. You know, face to face, eyeball to eyeball. That man is a killer. There's just something about him that's different from others I've faced."

Ronnie was fascinated. His chief counsel was never this talkative about people, just cases. "You have any idea what made him so different?"

She shrugged. "You know, some people are just snakes.

I guess they're just born that way. I go up against them all the time, and let me tell you, I can spot them a mile off. Not Tennyson, though. He's different." She struggled to find the right words. "Those others we go up against? They all have their price. Not Tennyson. That guy was not for sale."

"Well, I'm glad he's out of our hair," he said. He turned his attention back to his Cobb salad.

She still wasn't ready to let go of this supposed good news. "Let's see if this retirement lasts," she muttered, addressing her remarks to her own salad, an unconvincing mandarin orange and chicken teriyaki combo. "And I wonder who's going to take over as the go-to expert against us?"

"Mmph," said Ronald around a mouthful of soggy lettuce and bacon bits.

She looked up in irritation. Was her boss really that hungry? *Apparently so*, she thought. She readdressed her salad plate. "I've always suspected him of being a kind of spymaster. It wouldn't surprise me in the slightest if those leaks were coming to him first, and that he is the one who has been passing them on to Congress and the news media and all those lawyers who keep suing us."

Now Ronald looked up.

"I mean, think about it," she said. "Over the years, Tennyson has nurtured a whole network of spies who feed him confidential info. Then he gives it to his carefully constructed network of lawyers, who file suit against us, and then turn around and hire him as an expert witness."

"You have any evidence of this?" he asked.

"Not really. I'm just thinking out loud here."

"It's plausible. Not to mention kind of ironic."

"What do you mean?"

"Because we do it all the time."

"Lab 9A."

"Yeah, but now the shoe's on the other foot."

Shira closed her eyes for a moment to think it through. "So, I guess the question becomes what do we do when one of our own experts retires? Or has a minor stroke? I'm outside my wheelhouse here, but I'm guessing this has happened in the past, and when it has, there were loose ends that need to be tied up. Lab assistants who suddenly come into possession of items they're not supposed to see."

Ronald nodded. "It's happened."

"But it's not crossed my desk, as far as I recall."

"I think we've gotten on top of it before we needed to bother you."

She took no offense. "So, following your analogy, we're ... where?"

"We're going to be watching Dr. Tennyson very, very closely for a while. See who tries to contact him. See who he keeps communicating with. If what you're suggesting is right, there's got to be all kinds of on-going communications backing up in his email, phone messaging, regular mail. Some of that could be coming from our own employees."

Once again, Shira found herself appreciating the way she and her boss worked together, extending ideas that started out as mere musings. "When you say you want to watch him closely, what are you suggesting?"

He grinned at her openly. "Best you don't know the details, you being a lawyer and all."

"Fair enough." She paused a beat. "Are you thinking Duncan Gabardine?"

He answered with a slight shrug of the shoulders, which was answer enough for her. Duncan it was, then. Duncan and his team of specialists. It wouldn't be long before Dr. Tennyson's phones were tapped, his email hacked, his regular mail inspected before he received it. The surveillance would last a week or two, assuming nothing turned up, which was indeed possible. But if their suspicions were right, the retired professor's private life was going to belong to Stanhope for a long time to come. Shira suppressed a snort of amusement. It couldn't happen to a better man.

CHAPTER 4:

Leaks

The executive team – with the addition of Duncan Gabardine -- got together one week later to assess the Parkers Ferry situation. The news wasn't good. They went around the table, reporting in to each other.

Robert Harris, the lobbyist, went first. "The staffer on the Agriculture Committee that Ben Wicker was so reluctant to identify? His name is Daniels. New to me. I went through one of the others who has been helpful in the past and set up the meet. Ron (our buddy) meets Daniels for drinks after work. I swing by, Ron and I are surprised to see each other, he asks me to join him, the three of us have a couple drinks, swapping jokes, then Ron says he has to run. I convince Daniels to stick around for one more drink."

"Classic."

"It worked in Moscow, so why not Washington?" Robert agreed. His CIA background was no secret to the people in the room.

"Have you recruited him?"

"No. I'm not saying we can't, but for now, I got some intriguing stuff from him. According to him, we have an ongoing flow of leaked documents coming out of Parkers Ferry."

"Ongoing?"

"I'm afraid so. Not only that, we have at least one leaker in this very building." He looked around dramatically. "Maybe in this very room." Then he chuckled. "Not very likely. Still, somebody here at corporate headquarters."

"One person or more than one?"

"He didn't say. I don't think he knows. Plus, there's this: the leaks that reach him go through an intermediary, someone in the press. That turned out to be a problem because I led him to believe that I was a reporter chasing down a story I'd heard from another reporter. He was willing to confirm that there were leaks and that they came from some reporter, but he wasn't going to tell me anything about where this reporter worked, let alone his name."

"Too bad you didn't know that going in," Ronnie said. "You could have used a different cover story."

"The way it goes."

Shira asked how dangerous the leaked information was.

Robert shook his head. "Damn serious, if I read him right."

"Here's what I don't understand," Ronnie said. "Why would a reporter leak this to a congressional committee? Why not publish it first? Isn't he afraid he's going to lose his scoop?"

"It doesn't make sense, does it?" Robert replied. "I started to ask him, but I sensed I shouldn't go there."

"Best explanation is that his editor is sitting on the story," Shira said. "The reporter is getting tired of it being suppressed." She exchanged one of those famous mind-melding looks with Ronnie. "When in doubt, go with the obvious: do you think this reporter works for the Cincinnati Times Leader?"

Nobody had an answer.

17

"I suppose I could have lunch with Warren Davis," Ronnie said, "but I don't want him getting curious if it's some other paper."

Duncan Gabardine stepped into the conversation for the first time. "Maybe I can help with that a bit," he said. "As you know, I've been monitoring all communications to and from Dr. Tennyson. It wouldn't surprise me a bit if he wasn't the source rather than some reporter. I've got him talking with five of our employees in Parkers Ferry, Mt. Washington, Annabella, and here at Corporate. I've also got him testifying in front of a Senate committee ..."

"Which one?" Robert asked, breaking in.

"Environment and Public Works."

"I'll follow up on that. I've got a good contact in there."

Shira was getting more and more animated. "We should have been all over this guy years ago."

Duncan agreed with her. "He's a dangerous man. You know I have personal history with him."

"You do?"

"Believe it or not, I grew up with his kids, Billy and Gary. This was back when we were in junior high school in the late '60s. I was in and out of his house all the time."

"That's some coincidence," Shira said, suspiciously.

"Not entirely," Duncan replied. "I've never said this aloud to anyone, but one of the reasons I wanted to work for Stanhope was because I had a major falling out with Tennyson."

"He got divorced or something?"

"He killed his kids."

That stunned them into complete silence.

"Never proven," Duncan said.

"What happened?"

"Without going into the gory details, he forced them into having a dangerous surgery that should never have been allowed. They survived, but only for a few months."

"So you've had it in for him ever since?"

"I won't deny it."

"The question for us, then," said Shira, "is whether we can trust you to be objective."

Duncan nodded. "That's why I just told you what I did. I'm going to do my best to find out what's there and only what's there and report it without any spin."

Ronnie steepled his hands together and lowered his chin to rest on them. "It sounds like you've already turned up a lot. Just make double sure it's real. But along those lines, have you got any communications between Tennyson and that class action lawyer, what's her face."

"Maeve Waldock," Shira said.

"No. Nothing between them that I've seen."

"Who else has he been talking to?"

"The usual suspects: Sierra Club, EDF, Isaac Walton League, Greenpeace. Audubon, a bunch of others. Plus, he's constantly getting calls from scientists all over the world."

"Any from our scientists?"

Duncan looked pleased as punch. "Several, as a matter of fact. Nobody who works directly for us, but several of the labs we subsidize."

The concern in the room was snowballing. "Have you got this in writing for us?" Ronnie asked.

"I can do that," Duncan replied. "But there's something new I'm working on that I think will be incredibly useful. It's a software program being developed by DARPA that shows all the interlocking connections between networks of people. Have you seen those maps of airline connections with all those curved lines showing all the flights they offer? This is just like that, except it shows emails and phone calls."

"And you have a copy of that software?"

" I have access to it."

Shira stopped him. "We didn't hear that, and we don't want to hear anything more about it. Understood?"

"But you would like to see that map, wouldn't you?"

"Yes," she said. "Just so there's nothing on it that links it to national defense."

Ronnie asked what Duncan wanted to do with this program.

"Basically, what you do is input a list of names and phone numbers into a spreadsheet and let the computer draw all interconnecting lines. So, let's say Tennyson is talking to a scientist at one of our outside labs, and that scientist is talking to several of ours, and maybe one of those is in touch with Maeve Waldock or her team."

"Or if any of them has been talking to the Times Leader or the Beacon Journal or the Columbus Tribune," Robert suggested.

"Precisely."

"How robust is this software?" Shira asked. "How many names can you input?"

"Far more than we could ever use," Duncan assured her.

"Any chance we can get our own copy of it?"

"You mean legally?"

"I do mean legally," she said.

"Not yet."

Ronnie was becoming interested. "Could you, for example, map out every phone call or text message at Parkers Ferry over a period of months?"

"Now you're getting into territory I haven't actually explored. It's certainly conceivable."

"Alright," said the Senior VP. "Let's get back to action steps. What are we going to do with these leakers? Fire them?"

"I'm not sure I'd do that right away," Shira said. "We don't want to tip anyone off that we're monitoring them. Just because two people are talking, it doesn't mean that they are passing along classified information. They could be talking about their kids, for all we know."

"Better to be safe than sorry," Duncan replied.

"We're already sorry. Now we want to be thorough."

"I can do that."

Ronnie took over. "Be sure that you do." He looked around. "For now, I think we're done with this topic unless you have something else for us."

"No, I'm good. I've got my marching orders."

"Then we'll let you go. The rest of us have another matter to attend to."

Duncan headed off.

When the door closed behind him, Robert asked the others, "Do you find Duncan as creepy as I do?"

"What do you mean?"

"He reminds me a little too much of J. Edgar Hoover."

Once that notion got into the air, there was no going back. "It doesn't matter," said Ronnie. "He's effective."

"I wonder if he's monitoring our phone calls."

"Hey, let it go, Robert. Part of his job is to be paranoid. I don't want you going there."

"Just keep being your charming self," Shira added. "So, what are we going to do about Parkers Ferry?"

"In terms of the lawsuit?"

"Yes."

"For now, we stall and gather as much information as we can. I, for one, am going to be really curious to see this map Duncan says he can produce."

"How about newspapers and tv?"

"I think we keep our ears open and hold our breaths for now. Whoever's sitting on this story is doing it for a reason. They can't have all the story, or it would be out already. I wonder what they're missing."

"So many unknowns," said Robert.

"I think it's time we talk about plan B," said Shira. "We've talked about it before, but now I wonder if we shouldn't get serious."

"Shutting Parkers Ferry down?" said Ronnie.

"That or selling it off."

"It would be easier to just fire a couple of employees,"

"Easier, yes. Long term exposure? Maybe not."

"Remind me: where were we thinking of relocating it to?"

"We were looking at a lot of possibilities, but the way things are shaking out, I'm thinking we need to stay the hell away from the Ohio River."

"So, where then?"

"Great Lakes. We need a river. Why not one that empties into Lake Erie?"

"Or Lake Michigan?"

"Sure."

Ronnie turned to his lobbyist. "From a political point of view, which state do we have the most allies in?"

"Ohio, by far."

"Then, what rivers empty into Lake Erie?"

They exchanged embarrassed looks.

"Well, if you can't name the rivers, what cities?"

Robert was ready for that, at least. "From left to right, there's Toledo, Port Clinton, Sandusky, Vermillion – though that's a stretch – Cleveland, Mentor, Ashtabula, and then Erie, though that's in Pennsylvania."

"Toledo sounds promising," Shira said.

"Too big, I think. Sandusky might be an option. It's about the same size as Parkers Ferry."

Ronnie pondered the whole situation for a moment. "Okay, let's not get ahead of ourselves. I do think it's prudent to look at Sandusky, but let's make it discreet, okay? Robert, you look into it."

"Not Duncan?"

"I don't want to get him distracted. Why don't you sound out Senator Courtney? See what he thinks about a new plant along Lake Erie. It would mean a lot of jobs."

"That it would."

"For god's sake, though, don't mention Parkers Ferry. This would be all about expansion, not relocation."

"Good point."

"See what he suggests. I'm not ruling out Toledo or even, I suppose, Cleveland. But see if he brings up Sandusky or Ashtabula."

The meeting was about over. He turned to Shira. "Any last thoughts before we adjourn?"

"I'm trying to think of the right sequence of things," she said. "I think you might want to bring in some of the financial guys and get some scenarios drawn up. What would it cost to replicate the Parkers Ferry plant in Sandusky? And how long would it take to build it? It sure would be better if we could gradually transition from one plant to the other. Move half the production off the Ohio River before we need to shut it down in a hurry in the middle of a media shit storm."

Robert nodded vigorously. "A lot easier to sell some town on a new plant that's state of the art clean than to move the worst polluter in the country there."

"Alright," said Ronnie. "Let's proceed along those lines. I'll talk to the financial team and get them started. I guess I'll have a chat with Duncan and bring him up to speed. He needs to know that we're talking about this even if we don't want him involved yet. Let's plan to get together in one month. I'll have my secretary set it up. It'll be the three of us plus Duncan and somebody from finance."

After the others had gone, Ronald Haskins found himself musing over Robert's comparison of Duncan Gabardine and J. Edgar Hoover, along with the weird story about his connection with Dr. Tennyson. What the hell had he said? He killed his kids. Who says a thing like that out loud? And why bring it up in the first place? Nobody asked him if he had background with Tennyson. The whole thing was bizarre. Over years, Ronnie had come to appreciate how much personal rivalries or grudges drove business decisions that were seemingly unconnected with them. It made him uneasy.

PART TWO:

The Plain Speaker

[March, 2006 – about the time of the raid]

CHAPTER 5:

Emergency Meeting

On Monday mornings, I aim for 7:05 and generally get there between then and 7:15. The other days, it's more like aiming for 7:15 and arriving by 7:30 – or 8:00 at the very latest. This lovely Tuesday morning, I ambled in on the early side (for me) and noticed that the place was empty. The only other person I saw was Jane Smillens, our science reporter, who was just heading out of her cubicle when she looked back and saw me. "Better get a move on, Mouse. Emergency meeting in the conference room."

I threw my stuff down on my desk and ran to catch up with her. Peter was standing at the head of the table about to start. "Ah, nice of you to join us," he said, looking at Jane. He wouldn't even look at me, as Jane and I took the last two seats.

Peter walked up to the whiteboard and drew a squiggly line that curved downward a bit, then went horizontally until it hit another squiggly line going vertically. "This is the Ohio River," he announced in a tone that said we should refrain from joking around about his drawing skills, "and this is the Mississippi. Who can tell me the name of the town where they meet up?"

"Cairo," said Bucky Spencer, our head sports writer and my best friend except for Arne Price.

Tom Glendenning, one of our political hacks, jumped

on him immediately. "That's *Kay-row*," he said.

The little suck up.

"*Kay-row, Ill-a-noy.*"

Okay, big suck up.

Peter gave Tom a dirty look and began adding some place names. "Here's Pittsburgh; now we come to Cincinnati, Louisville, and Parkers Ferry on the West Virginia side of the river. Any of you ever hear of Parkers Ferry?"

We all shook our heads.

"Well, you are going to start hearing a lot about it, and I want us to be the ones who report on it first."

He turned back to the whiteboard and wrote, *C8*.

"Anyone know what this is?"

Jane Smillens wrinkled her nose as if she could smell the answer. "It's a chemical used in Teflon™.."

"It's actually a byproduct," Peter said, with his usual precision, "not an ingredient, and it's nasty as shit. I'll have Jane research it and send you a memo about it today. Can you do that, Jane? Good. Just the basics: what *C8* stands for, how it's harmful, that sort of thing."

He continued his summary. "It turns out that the Stanhope plant in Parkers Ferry has been releasing *C8* into the Ohio River for decades. There's been some grumbling and a few minor lawsuits that went nowhere. Now there is a new focus. In 1985, Stanhope bought some land nearby from a farmer to have a place to dispose of what they said would be ash and scrap metal. No chemicals. The farmer agreed. Soon after, his daughters and his wife started wheezing and coughing. They moved into town. The farmer continued to hunt and grow crops on his land. He started to find deer carcasses and dead muskrats where he'd never seen them before. He found cattle bleeding from the mouth. He and his brother opened up one of the cattle and said it was bright green inside and had the worst smell they'd ever encountered. So, they sued Stanhope. It took a while to even find a lawyer willing to take the case. Once they finally got one, they got a good one. Her name is Maeve Waldock." He wrote it on the whiteboard and gave them a moment to copy it down and absorb what he had just told them. "I got a tip from, well, a relative of the lawyer, that they are filing a huge lawsuit in Cincinnati tomorrow. I want us up and running before it's even filed."

Terry Trowbridge, our crime reporter, raised her hand. "Peter, excuse me, but why not let the Cincinnati Enquirer run with this?"

"Here's the thing, gang. There are whispers, nothing more, that some prominent names in Cleveland are caught up in this, and not in a good way. There's talk that Stanhope's plant right here in Cleveland is releasing the same shit into the Cuyahoga River. That's why I want you sniffing around. See if any of our underworld players are getting twitchy. Be discreet about this. That goes for all of you."

He turned to the trio of political reporters: Sarah, Tricia, and Tom. "You guys get in touch with the legislators here or at the state level who have anything to do with environmental issues. Keep it vague. Let's see who expresses outrage and who defends Stanhope. And let's dig deep and hard and fast into any sons of bitches who are trying to stall further inquiries."

Sarah, Tricia, and Tom nodded enthusiastically.

That left Lenny Kellerman, our financial guy and me. "Larry, keep an eye on the stock market and see if there's any volatility beyond Stanhope itself. And ask around the banks if anyone seems nervous. We haven't done a feature on Stanhope's footprint in Cleveland in years. That just shows you how effective their PR department is. In 1969 with the great fire, they were the most hated company in Cleveland. Now? They're model citizens. I want to see if that's warranted."

He turned to me. "And Mouse, what are you doing here?"

Oh, shit. I'd been had. "Uh, one of the others told me you wanted me?"

Peter held his look of annoyance as long as he could, and then began to laugh. The others joined in. "You fall for that every time, don't you?"

Now it was my turn to look annoyed.

"How may I assist you, dear editor," I replied as gamely as I could.

"Do what you normally do, talk to everyone about anything that sounds interesting. Just keep this whole chemical spill story at the back of your mind. Don't look for the story; see if the story finds you. And if you do hear anything, let the journalists know."

That was another old joke: calling my peers *journalists* and me a *reporter*. He even went so far as to call Bucky our sports journalist. We're all friends to one extent or another, and there is a fair degree of joking around and putting each other down, and nobody has been more supportive of me in my career than Peter Zenger. Yet, to be honest, it does hurt a bit.

When the meeting adjourned, I lingered behind.

"Yes?" Peter asked, his mind already on other things.

"I have an old connection back from childhood with one of the foremost witnesses against Stanhope in the country."

He looked up. "Who would that be?"

"His name is Dr. Jeremiah Tennyson."

"Rings a bell." Peter's eyes wandered off as he tried to recall where he might have heard the name.

"I grew up with his kids and stayed in touch with him ever since."

"The kids moved out?"

"The kids died."

"Oh. Sorry."

"So, he has been kind of a surrogate father to me, or maybe I should say I'm more like a surrogate son to him. Anyway, if this lawsuit blows up into something big, I'd bet you a thousand bucks that Dr. Tennyson will get involved."

"And you think you should talk to him."

"If nothing else, he can fill me in on some background and maybe give me a heads up as things get rolling."

Peter sighed. "Yes, Mouse, go see your old friend, of course. I just want you to understand that your only role here is to feed information to the others. This will never be your story. I don't want you to get bat shit crazy like a couple of the others. Did you see Tricia's eyes? She's already seeing a Pulitzer Prize with her name on it. Even Lenny looked like he was taking in oxygen."

I'm usually quick on my feet, ready with a snappy comeback. Not when it comes to Peter, though. For some reason, I end up tongue-tied, leaving him with the last word. I consoled myself with the fact that he had given me permission to contact Dr. Tennyson. It wasn't much by way of consolation, but I clung to it like a piece of driftwood forlornly bobbing in the middle of Lake Erie.

CHAPTER 6:

The Burning River

The other reporters – the journalists – raced back to their cubicles like drivers at the Indianapolis 500. Me? I wandered around, woolgathering about the Cuyahoga River catching on fire when I was eleven years old and the possibility – never proven – that the Stanhope plant was its cause. That fire made Cleveland the laughingstock of the nation, the mistake by the lake. I took all the ridicule personally. I had a childhood crush on Cleveland, and here was the hit tv show "Laugh-In" making jokes about her week after week. Not to mention Johnny Carson.

Did you know that nobody has ever drowned in the Cuyahoga River? No, it's true. They dissolve first.

The problem with assigning blame was that Stanhope was only one of a dozen large companies pouring toxic chemicals and waste products into the river. And, of course, there was politics involved. Heavily. I was just a kid, not even a teenager, so what did I know about politics? I sure knew about sarcasm, though.

What's the best steak you can buy in Cleveland?

An all-beef wiener.

I volunteered to help clean up the Cuyahoga through a program run by the Cleveland Natural History Museum. It was my first exposure to environmentalism, and the experience lodged deeply in my young, idealistic mind. Once I became a reporter, I found ways to cover the amazingly successful cleanup of the river over the next thirty-some years. Was all that progress now being threatened?

Peter wanted me to keep my ears open but not pursue the Stanhope story actively. Okay. I guess I can live with that. But that doesn't mean I can't find ways to bump into people who know a lot about the evil corporation and listen to them. Dr. Tennyson was at the top of the list, of course, and I had permission to talk to him. Who else? I tried to recall whether I'd ever met anyone who actually worked for Stanhope and pulled a blank. It shouldn't be hard to do, except that would be a direct violation of Peter's orders.

When in doubt, consult with Arne.

I dropped by his cube to find him lost in thought. This was unusual for him. Arne is more an action kind of reporter than a thoughtful one like me.

That came out wrong, didn't it?

Arne is a deeply thoughtful man, especially compared with myself, mister trivia. It's the way we work I was trying to talk about. I tend to do a lot of woolgathering – what I call being thoughtful – while Arne, ex-military guy that he is, sets a goal and attacks it with a kind of fury. Seeing him staring off into space like he was doing now was the opposite of what I expected.

"I hate to say this, buddy, but you look like me right now."

He jumped and then looked guilty. Guilty? Arne?

"Trying to figure out what I'm going to do about Peter's declaration of war," he said.

I was in the same boat, but I suspected our takes on the situation were vastly different. "You want to grab a beer after work?"

"I want to grab a beer right now."

I hoped he was joking. It was only 10:30, and the thought of a beer right then made my stomach feel like it was working on a dead carp. On the other hand, I did want to talk with him. "How about a cup of coffee in the cafeteria?"

He looked at me seriously. "This isn't cafeteria talk."

"Early lunch at the Buckeye?"

"I'll drive," he said.

Stan was on duty when we walked in. "You guys are early," he noted. "Slow day?"

"The opposite," said Arne.

"Well, if you want to slow down, this is the place. You want the usual?"

"Just coffee for me," I said quickly.

Arne hesitated before opting for coffee as well. We wandered over to our regular booth in the back corner while Stan put a fresh pot on.

"So, what's up?"

"Something I've never told you about," he replied.

"Let me guess: you're opening an Army-Navy surplus store and going for the big bucks."

He shook his head in sadness that he was reduced to talking to a dimwit like me. "I've been working on a book about Stanhope for several years now, and I'm not in the mood to share all my research with Peter Zenger just to make him look good and get ahead of his fellow editors. Not when it's all been done on my own time and initiative."

"How far are you?" I asked, keeping the surprise from my voice.

"Hard to say. Lots of notes, lots of questions, nothing

organized, no outline." He trailed off.

"But, even so, a lot of effort. Am I right?"

"Yeah, you're right."

Stan came over with two mugs of what he called coffee. No doubt there were a few coffee beans in the mix, but it tasted like he'd added the charred stuff he scraped off the grill at regular intervals when he cooked fried eggs or hamburgers at too high a temperature. I asked him about that once, and he said something about not wanting good protein to go to waste. He lingered long enough to give us a chance to ask him to join us, but not so long that it got awkward. Whatever his shortcomings as a chef, he was a great bartender.

"Can I ask what your approach is?"

"It's a look at how Stanhope and the other big polluters fit into Cleveland's racial history."

He was just full of surprises today. "Sounds interesting," I said, speaking honestly. "Probably not so much to Peter, though. Am I right that you approached him and he turned you down?"

Arne shook his head. "I haven't even approached him. It's not newsworthy."

"Don't you wish we could outlaw that word?" I said.

He nodded. We'd talked more than once about the term newsworthy and how harmful it was to the entire news industry.

"So, what are you going to do? You have to give him something."

"I suppose you're right, Mouse, but I think for right now, I'm going to go into a holding pattern: watch what the others come up with and how Peter responds."

"He sounded pretty serious."

"For now, but is it going to last?"

"I suppose that depends on whether we turn up any-thing."

"Does it?" he replied. If we'd been drinking beer, he would lean in close at this point, challenging me to hold my ground. With the hot asphalt derivative bubbling in our coffee mugs, he stayed back, not wanting to burn himself if it spat-tered. "If we find nothing, he's going to drop it. He'll have to. But the question is, what happens if we do turn up something really juicy? Will he run it?"

"He sounds like that would make his day."

"I know, but ask yourself. Attacking Stanhope isn't like exposing some corrupt mayor or city councilman. This is one of the big boys we're supposed to be going after – maybe the nastiest of the bunch. Fifty bucks says if we turn up something major, it will be suppressed before we ever bring it to press."

Good old Arne, the most reliably cynical of all my friends, I thought. But would a true cynic spend years (apparently) working on a book that might never get published? There was a lot more going on here than I could see, some personal his-tory that linked Arne to Stanhope. I wondered what it could be.

CHAPTER 7:

Green Mouth Hogs of Annabella

I n the space of one week, the newsroom and editorial staff at the Plain Speaker changed almost beyond recognition. What used to be a relatively laid-back group of Cleveland underachievers was now a pack of feral pigs rooting around in the rich, fungal loam of documents leaking out of Stanhope's plant in Parkers Ferry, West Virginia. There was too much material to go around, but that simply made the reporters greedier, fencing off large areas of the ever-expanding suit as their exclusive domain and fighting off all challengers. Who were these people I thought I knew? What dread disease had eaten the self-control centers of their brains?

If this Stanhope lawsuit story was a big pizza, my fellow reporters were like kids bickering over who got to slice it up and who got which slice. Tom started arguing that he should cover anything to do with PCBs, which meant that the others could squabble over $C8$ and dioxin and whatever other chemicals might be spilling out of Stanhope's factories. Sarah pushed for turf: "I'll look into Parkers Ferry. You guys can divide up the other plants." Tricia was well connected throughout the state government, so she said, "I know the players in Columbus, so why don't I take anything connected with them? You others can divide up the players in Cincinnati or Cleveland or Indianapolis."

There were two more suggestions. Lenny laid claim to anything that had to do with banks or financial markets. All eyes turned to Arne. I wondered what he was going to say.

"I'm trying to figure out what else those plants are dumping into the Ohio River."

Peter nodded. It was an acceptable answer.

Then my buddy Bucky Spencer, our sports writer (of all people) asked a question. "Has anybody been talking to the plaintiffs?"

Even Peter looked startled. Everyone had been so focused on Stanhope that we forgot about the little people, the victims, the ones who read our paper, the ones we are supposed to be defending. After a short moment of silence, the reporters starting volunteering.

"I'll look at any who live around Columbus."

"I'll handle Cleveland."

"I have family in Cincinnati. I'll check around there."

Peter eventually restored enough order to make people take turns. He went around the table, asking us to cough up one bit of information or story, but not go on and on.

Jane Smillens extremely shy. Naturally, Peter picked on her first.

"You all know that Stanhope manufactures *MowDown*™ herbicide, right? It's one of the most profitable products in their entire line. It came out in 1974, and ever since, there have been concerns about whether it causes cancer. Stanhope's lawyers fought back against any such claims, but eventually, the EPA mandated some tests. One of them was a standard mouse test." She glanced in my direction apologetically and then paused to emphasize what she said next. "Rumors have it that some of the mice developed tumors."

Arne repeated the word rumors, making it sound like established facts.

Jane looked pained; she was always careful with facts.

"Go on," Peter encouraged her.

"The original pathologist said that the slides from the mice showed tumors. A second pathologist, hired by Stanhope, said they didn't. Then, when his credibility came into question, the EPA decided to send the original slides to a third pathologist, except that when Stanhope looked, they claimed that they couldn't find them."

"Pretty convenient," said Tom, the most competitive of our political reporters.

The challenge in his voice alarmed Jane. She looked down and stopped talking.

"Stay on that," Peter said, not waiting for her to look back up. He moved on to Terry, our crime reporter. She said the mood at police headquarters was notably tense, and when she asked about Stanhope, people stopped talking altogether.

"That's all you've got?" Peter asked.

"I'm afraid so."

He looked disappointed, but let her go without further comment. He moved to Tricia, who was sitting next to her. She tried to pass, but Peter wasn't having any of it.

"Parkers Ferry isn't the only Stanhope plant dumping C8 into the Ohio River," she said. "According to my sources, there's a sister plant a few miles from Parkers Ferry and another near Pittsburgh that might be the worst of all."

"Anything we can go to print with?" Peter asked.

"Not yet. I've got one source and a couple of documents, but it's sketchy."

Knowing her, she probably had a lot more than that; she just didn't want to share in case one of the others might steal her story.

Next was Sarah. Of the three political reporters, I like

Sarah the best. Like me, she's a storyteller. The main difference is that she tells stories about greedy and corrupt people,
while I write about people who are fundamentally virtuous.
"Have any of you heard about the green-mouth hogs of Anabella, Alabama?"

The tension broke in a spontaneous outbreak of hoots.

I could tell that Peter was debating with himself
whether to let her carry on or not. Sarah was a talker, for sure.
He allowed her to go ahead.

"Stanhope has a chemical plant in Annabella, Alabama..."

"Home of the Albanians," Bucky Spencer said, unhelp-
fully.

Peter made a growly sound at the back of his throat.

Sarah picked right back up. "There's an old man who
used to work there named Amos Mandan. Like just about
everyone else, he was dirt poor and basically uneducated. To
help make ends meet, he raised hogs on the side. He didn't
have enough land to graze them, so every night he drove them
right past the plant to this patch of meadowland before starting work on the night shift. In the morning, he'd round them
up and bring them back home to his shack. The hogs began to
lose weight and look kind of weird. They didn't move right,
and their mouths began to turn green.

"Green?" said Bucky.

"That's right, green."

"Sounds dangerous."

"That's what Amos thought," Sarah said. "He was beginning to wonder whether he should put them down, but to a
man with his limited resources, this would have been a heavy
hit. Then one day, one of the plant managers came up to him at
work and offered to buy all fifty of his hogs for ten bucks each.
This was a reasonable price for healthy hogs and a great one for

what he had. He didn't want to seem too eager, so he told the manager to throw in a pint of Wild Turkey, and he'd sell them."

By now, Peter had had enough. "If there's a point to this story, I'd like to hear it."

"It's all about PCBs and covering up what Stanhope knew about them," Sarah said quickly. "Turns out there were all kinds of health issues showing up around Anabella, including cancer, reproductive issues, children with learning disabilities. The locals talked about a stream that went through the poor side of town that would be clear one day, red another day, purple sometimes, and even gave off a kind of foggy steam. The EPA got involved and determined that many of the citizens had increased levels of PCBs in their blood. Stanhope denied it all. The locals weren't buying it. They held a town meeting. Among the speakers is our hog farmer, Amos Mandan, wanting to know why a chemical plant wanted to buy fifty green-mouth hogs. The lawyer for Stanhope demanded to know who this plant manager was."

"Wait a minute," Peter said. "Are you saying Stanhope's own lawyer didn't know?"

"Apparently not. He was a new hire from the corporate office and not up to speed yet."

"That doesn't sound like Stanhope."

"Agreed. And he should have kept his mouth shut because the plant manager was right there running the meeting. It turns out that the plant manager was also the mayor."

"Oh, this is good," Arne said.

"Isn't it, just?" Sarah said. "At that point, the town meeting got out of hand, and try as he might the Stanhope lawyer couldn't bottle up the testimony without being run out of town. The townsfolk got the mayor to admit that he was the one who made the deal and, furthermore, that he shot the pigs and buried them on company property in the middle of the night. Some of the citizens wanted the EPA to dig up the pigs, but it was too late. They'd been in the ground too long under a layer of lime."

"Lime?" asked Bucky. "Or slime?"

"So, where do things stand right now?" Peter asked.

"Stanhope got it bumped up to the state level. They worked out a deal with the Alabama Water Improvement Commission, in which anything they admitted to the commission could not be publicly released without the express written consent of Stanhope."

"Which the company hasn't given," Peter suggested.

"Surprise!" cried Arne.

"Has any other newspaper reported this?" Peter asked.

"Some brief, local stuff about town meetings is all I've seen. Oh, and I hear Stanhope has been buying up half the homes and businesses in Annabella, including a church."

"Write it up and bring it to me." Peter turned to Tom. "Your turn."

"The *C8* contamination of the Ohio River has been going on for forty years or more," Tom said, "but it's not just Parkers Ferry. I've been looking at a second Stanhope plant in the town of Mount Washington, which is a fifteen-minute drive from Parkers Ferry. They're both dumping *C8* and who knows what else into the Ohio River and have been all along."

Tricia looked like she was going to launch herself across the table and throttle her colleague. Mount Washington must have been that other plant she referenced.

Peter interrupted. "Does anyone here know why so many of these plants are located in small towns?"

Lenny Kellerman, our economics guru, raised his hand. "It's a deliberate policy by many manufacturers. The idea is to be the dominant industry or employer in the community.

That way, you control the politicians and the regulators in your own back yard."

"So, it's not just Stanhope?"

"Not at all. It's in the printing industry and a whole bunch of others."

We all nodded sagely.

"What I'm looking at goes back to 1969," Tom continued.

I caught my breath. 1969 was the year the Cuyahoga caught fire. I forced myself to pay attention to Tom.

"There were all kinds of individual lawsuits being filed by people who claimed to have gotten cancer or had other health problems. Stanhope won every case. But then some lawyers began collecting individual plaintiffs into a class action lawsuit. It dragged on for years. Finally, the EPA got pulled in and did a survey of water pollution in various water treatment districts along the Ohio River. They found high levels of C8 in six of them: three in Ohio and three in West Virginia. A couple of years ago, a federal judge certified that residents in these six water districts could join a class action suit. All they had to do was prove that they drank the local water for at least one year since 1969. Even if residents moved away in the '70s or '80s, they could still file."

"Why 1969?" I asked. "I mean, there wasn't even an Environmental Protection Agency until 1970."

Peter shook his head in disbelief. "Talk about big stories lying out there in plain sight! Tell me again: when was this suit filed?"

"The class action was filed in 2001."

"That's thirty-two years."

"Credit Stanhope for that. The judge didn't even certify who could be included as a plaintiff until 2004."

"So, what's the current status?"

Tom took a couple of melodramatic breaths, which fooled nobody. "It's a huge spiderweb of suits and counter-suits and spinoffs and settlements. I'm making charts and diagrams, and I have to confess I'm overwhelmed. There must be a hundred Stanhope lawyers all objecting to or delaying things. I talked to one attorney who said that there were literally thousands of lawsuits. Thousands! And here's another little statistic I ran across. An outside expert reported that between 1951..."

Peter cut him off. "I thought this went back to 1969. Now you're saying it goes back to 1951?"

Tom shook his head. "See what I mean? You start asking questions, and the picture gets bigger and bigger."

"Go on, then."

"According to this expert, up to two million pounds of C8 were dumped into the river or sent up the smokestacks in Parkers Ferry and Mount Washington between 1951 and 2003."

Right about that time, we became a different newsroom. The jokes fell away, and the condescension we habitually displayed for our media competitors to the south suddenly felt cruel and inappropriate. These were fellow citizens, as much a part of America as anyone in the newsroom. We all knew that Stanhope was an enormous creature, swimming around in international waters where tax laws and environmental regulations weren't enforced. Now that bloated creature had migrated up the waterways, gobbling up anyone trying to limit its intake of nutrients or its regurgitation of poison.

"What's the safe level for humans again?" asked Jane, the scientist.

Tom glanced at his notes. "It depends on who you ask.

Stanhope says it's unknown, but uses a threshold of 100 parts per trillion as the maximum for their operations. The latest EPA number is 70 parts per trillion. But get this: another outside expert did a medical study of people living near Mount Washington and said that a more realistic threshold should be five parts per trillion—not seventy. If you drink water that has more than five parts per trillion of C8, you are may experience adverse health effects."

"When was the new estimate made?" Jane asked.

"Last year."

"Alright, let's bring this back home," Peter said to the now silent room. "We've got Stanhope plants poisoning the Ohio River for fifty years, if not more. But what about the Stanhope plant right here in Cleveland? Has anybody heard anything about it?"

I watched Arne looking off in the distance, searching for a memory. Miraculously, he found it. "Wasn't there an accident a couple of years ago that killed some workers there?"

Tom and Sarah nodded. "Yeah," said Tom. "Summer of 1999."

"Did we end up finding anything?"

"Nope," Tom said. "Not a thing."

"Let's hope there's nothing similar going on here," Peter said. He made a show of looking around the room. "Mouse, you stumble over anything?"

"Not yet," I told him, trying to make myself sound mysterious. Instead, I just looked irrelevant.

"You talk to that friend of yours?"

"I reached his nurse. He's recovering from some sort of medical issue. She wouldn't say what."

"Is he going to meet with you?"

"I'm waiting for the phone call." How lame was that?

What had been a raucous, exciting meeting slumped to the floor like a sweatshirt tossed in the corner.

CHAPTER 8:

Agent Orange

We drove separately to the Buckeye Bar, our regular watering hole. Stan was on duty.

"Mouse; Arne," he greeted us, pulling a couple of Burning River Pale Ale from the tap. Instead of staying at the bar to chat with him, we walked over to one of the tables.

"I'm not going to talk about what I did in Viet Nam, and I don't want you asking," Arne announced. "You got that?"

"It's entirely up to you."

He looked around. "Shit. Why do we keep coming in here? This place is a dump."

"Because it's close."

He looked at me with disgust. "That was supposed to be a rhetorical question."

I didn't respond. Arne wanted to talk, and he'd get there on his own time.

"After I got back, I started hearing stories from veterans about health problems. I had a few, but they weren't worth mentioning: a little joint pain, some weakness in my legs. Some of my buddies, though, were really messed up. They were convinced that it was because of Agent Orange, and eventually, enough stories came to light that a large group of veterans filed a class-action lawsuit against Stanhope that got lodged in 1977. It worked its way through the court system until it ended up at the Supreme Court in '88."

"Eleven years?"

"Yeah, that's how long Stanhope fought it off, with the federal government fighting right alongside them for obvious reasons. And here's something you don't know about me. My name is in that Supreme Court case, buried in the back with all the other plaintiffs. Me, Arne Price, taking my court right up the ladder. And we won. Dammit, we finally won. That was a big deal. Still, it was far from a complete victory. It left too many people out, and one of the classes of people left out were the offspring of servicemen. Note that I said 'men.' It gets complicated, but the bottom line is that the defense department realized early on that women in the armed services who were exposed to Agent Orange might be in danger of giving birth to deformed babies. So they kept a close eye on them. Nobody figured that men might be able to pass on damaged genes to their children. I mean, it's one little sperm cell. It's not like the entire body of the mother. But guess what? Men could pass along damaged genes, just like women. And they did. And if you think about the math and the number of men exposed compared to the number of women, you can imagine that the government was not eager to admit there was any linkage. And it's hard to prove, because there are genetically damaged kids born to people who've never been remotely near any Agent Orange, and there are thousands of years of examples that occur before Agent Orange was even invented. So how do you prove it? And then there's the time lag. If symptoms show up years after you've been exposed, that's one thing; just imagine if they show up after you wait for the next generation to be born."

He trailed off, reached for his beer, and took a long swallow, never taking his eyes off me. "Go ahead," he said at last. "Ask your question. I can see you're dying to ask it."

Even with his permission, it was hard to ask, but as his friend, I knew I had to. "Arne, why is your name on the Supreme Court case?"

47

"I had a daughter who was born with a defective heart valve."

"Oh, god."

"She died before her eighth birthday."

"I'm so sorry." I tried to do the math in my head to figure out whether this happened before or after I met him, but I couldn't figure it out. "Do you want me to ask any more about it?"

His answer was as quick and sharp as a slap to the face. "No." He took a long, steadying breath. "You know what I'm hearing now? It's affecting grandchildren."

I caught Stan's eye and gestured for another round. We stayed quiet until he brought it over and took our empties away. A good guy, Stan. He didn't say a word.

"Enough about me. Let's talk about the fucking government."

Just the way Arne said 'fucking government' made me put him in a whole new category, one I'd never considered: my friend was a Viet Nam vet. Funny thing about categories; you find one or two, and you think you've got somebody defined. It's a dangerous habit, especially for a reporter. Without even knowing it, I had him in three boxes, if you will: African American, fellow reporter, and best friend. Now I had to put him in another. And one of the implications of doing that was it put me in a contrasting box called post-Viet Nam. It suggested that I would never fully understand Arne and vice versa. We were of different generations. This insight took no time at all, but the full impact of it was going to bother me for months.

"Because of that court case and some others," Arne was saying, "I know a lot of history most people are unaware of. Lots of stuff about Stanhope and the Pentagon."

"Does Peter know this?"

"Fuck Peter."

I regretted interrupting him. "Agreed," I said quickly.

"You know, Viet Nam was not the first time the US fought in the Pacific theater. Before that, we were fighting the Japanese, and many of those places were full of jungle. So the Army turned to their close buddies at Stanhope and asked them to develop herbicides and defoliants to kill off those jungle plants that got in the way of building air bases and allow our troops to maneuver through the jungle more easily."

"I hate to interrupt," I said, "but what's the difference?"

"Between what?"

"Herbicides and defoliants."

He smiled briefly. "Yeah. Another of those things most people don't know, not unless they've been there. An herbicide kills a plant; a defoliant just kills the leaves. If you want to move through the jungle without a machete, say, you'd want a defoliant. On the other hand, if you wanted to completely clear an area for a landing strip, you'd want an herbicide." He shrugged. "A lot of overlap between the two."

"So, what did they use?" I asked. "It wasn't Agent Orange."

"There were a bunch of them, none of which I can name," he replied. "Just think of them as precursors of Agent Orange. I do know that the Defense Department tested over one-thousand chemicals during World War II and continuing up to Viet Nam and the invention of Agent Orange. We were spraying some of those precursors on Viet Nam for several years before Stanhope came up with the ultimate poison. They wanted something that would act as a defoliant but also kill off the underbrush. Ideally, it should be safe for humans to handle, since we'd be handling a lot of it. So the war planners started considering how to use these chemicals to starve the enemy. The way it worked was this: you'd find a trail or an area controlled by the Viet Cong and bomb the shit out of it. First bomb it, then drop Napalm on it, and then after that, you'd spray it with what they called 'trail dust.' You know the old Smokey the Bear signs that said 'Only YOU can prevent forest fires?' What we said in 'Nam was, 'Only you can prevent a forest.' Nice, eh? Most of us at the time thought we were doing the right thing, and that there weren't any major health concerns for people. Just plants."

He took a sip of beer. "Where was I? Oh, yes, back to World War Two for a second. We actually had plans to poison the rice fields in Japan. We'd have done it, too, except that they surrendered after we dropped the bomb on them."

"I never knew any of that," I said.

"Yeah. They don't teach it much in schools around here. If you grow up in Vietnam, I bet you'd hear about it. It was actually the Brits who first used herbicides as a weapon of war. This was in Malaysia. Technically, it should have been a war crime, based on the Geneva Conventions after the First World War. The Brits got around that by saying what they were doing in Malaysia wasn't a war; it was an emergency. Anyway, the US and the other allies weren't about to get in their way, and so they went ahead."

"Once again," I said, "nothing I've ever heard about."

"Most vets haven't heard about it," Arne conceded. "But here's the follow-up to that. You know who Dean Rusk was, don't you?"

"Vaguely." Once again, I felt the generational gap between us.

"Kennedy was the President who got us into Vietnam. You do know that, at least."

"Yeah."

"Well, Dean Rusk was his Secretary of State. Kennedy asked him if spraying the enemy's crops would be a war crime, and Rusk pointed out that the Brits had done it and gotten away with it, so now there's a legal precedent for us to do it."

"Help me out, here, Arne. Why exactly would that be a war crime?"

"Honestly?"

"Honestly. I really want to know. This is all stuff I've never read about or talked about, and it's coming at me so fast I'm having a hard time processing it."

"Yeah, and everyone knows you're not exactly the quickest thinker on the block," he replied, and for a moment, we were back to just being Arne and Mouse. Then he got serious again. "It's a war crime because it doesn't discriminate between combatants and civilians. If you bomb a convoy of trucks carrying food to the front lines, that's totally legal. It's what war is all about. But if you starve an entire population: women, children, old folks, the sick and the lame who can't fight, that's a war crime. It's a kind of genocide. And if it's done with chemicals, then it's even worse, based again on those Geneva Conventions."

I felt stupid having to have it explained.

"So, anyway, after the Brits used chemicals in Malaysia, we went ahead and did the same in Vietnam."

"To starve the enemy?"

"Officially, it was all about clearing out the foliage so we could see the Viet Cong moving through the jungle. But, as Henry Kissinger said, 'Food is a weapon.'"

I was feeling sick just thinking about it.

"You've got to remember that this was a different kind of war we were waging. Guerrilla warfare. You didn't have front lines, and the enemy didn't have uniforms, and when we came after them, they simply blended into the rest of the rural population. We'd come to a village, and everyone was our friend. We'd leave, and later that night, the villagers would give food and information to the Viet Cong hiding just outside. So, starve everyone, and the villagers would simply have less food to share, even if they were threatened, which happened a lot."

"Did it work?"

"Oh, yeah, especially when you consider the third reason we were doing it. We had better control over the cities than the countryside, so part of the strategy was to drive rural people into the cities. Hundreds of thousands of them did just that because we brought famine to their land."

"God, I hate this!" I said.

51

"Wait; there's more. Somewhere in the Pentagon, some soulless war planner was fully aware that there were real health concerns over Agent Orange, that it might harm people. And the calculation was this: once we drove the civilians off their farms and little villages, then if we keep dropping Agent Orange on the countryside, if there are any health effects, it will just be among the enemy, and who the fuck cares about them? We're trying to kill them, anyway." He stopped and leaned in toward me. "Tell me what's wrong with that thinking."

"It's cruel."

"Very, very true. But that's war, my friend. Here, I'll help you out. There are two problems with that approach. The first is that it's not just the enemy walking around in all that chemical shit. It's us poor grunts. We're getting exposed to it, just like they are. Hence, all the health problems of returning vets."

All I could do was sit there and take it in.

"And the other problem is that one of the ingredients of Agent Orange is *dioxin*, which is a very stable chemical, which means it doesn't degrade very fast in the environment. It stays around for years and years, toxic as hell. So, what happens when the war ends? You've got a unified country that can't feed itself."

"Yikes."

"And it builds up in fatty tissue. It can be in the water, say, and a fish eats it. Then a larger fish eats that one, and many others, so the *dioxin* gets more and more concentrated in the big fish. Then a human catches the big fish and eats it. Now, all that *dioxin* accumulates in the human. Day after day, month after month, year after year, never breaking down. Meanwhile, our troops come home and stop absorbing more *dioxin*. But what about the enemy we exposed? Not just enemy troops, but all those farmers we drove off the land? There's a disgusting bit of testimony before a Senate panel, where a Pentagon planner admitted under oath that they knew there might be long term health problems caused by the *dioxin* in Agent

Orange. They just didn't give it much thought because it was mainly going to fall on the enemy. It's right there in the record."

"That's cold," I said.

"It's racist," he insisted.

That set me back on my heels. Was he implying that I was a racist?

He let me squirm for a moment. "Hey, we all are racists to one extent or another. When I got back from 'Nam, I hated the Vietnamese people, every last one of them. It took me years to let go of that. There are still plenty of individuals I will never stop hating. Some fought on our side and some against us. Evil fuckers. But that's because of their behavior, not their race. As I said, it took me years, but in the end, I couldn't escape the reality that we're all human. A birth defect in a Vietnamese child is just as devastating as one to an American child, whether that child is black, brown, white, or yellow. It's easy to say that and not mean it. I couldn't even say it when I first returned home."

He had taken the sting out of calling me a racist, but the truth of it was still there, a kind of heaviness in the lungs. "How many Vietnamese did we expose to Agent Orange?" I asked.

"According to them, at least three million were damaged by the spraying. I hear that the Red Cross estimates it was more like one million. I don't care. If it's one person, it's one too many. And now we know that those original million or two million or three million people are giving birth to deformed babies, and even grandbabies. And that *dioxin* is still in the soil and the water."

He trailed off, looking exhausted. As for me, all this information was circulating through my brain, toxic in its own way. I honestly didn't think I could handle one more piece of damning information. It was all I could do to keep from breaking down right then and there.

Arne set his glass down hard enough to make Stan look

up from the crossword he'd been working on. Once he saw that nothing had broken, he shrugged and went back to it. Arne stood up without another word and walked out, leaving me sitting there across from a lingering shadow of rage and despair. I felt about as bad as when the twins died, and Duncan and I went our separate ways. I turned a thousand memories over in my mind like I was raking up leaves into a big pile.

I thought about Duncan, and how he ended up working for Stanhope Chemicals.

I thought about Dr. Tennyson, the guy fighting Stanhope, and now retiring from the battle.

I thought about the twins.

I thought about Arne, the guy who got poisoned by Stanhope, the guy who lost a daughter.

And I thought about myself, the guy who's been closing his eyes to anything outside of Cleveland. Even then, I was only registering the best parts of Cleveland, the people who didn't contribute to the war in Vietnam or die over there or return injured in mind, body, and spirit.

An inner voice, terrifying because it was so soft, whispered at the back of my mind. "Time to wake up, Mouse. You have work to do."

CHAPTER 9:

The Day Nurse

The first thing I did the next morning was call Dr. Tennyson. I expected to reach his answering machine, but to my surprise, a woman picked up on the third ring. "Dr. Tennyson's residence."

"Is he available?" I asked, trying to hide my surprise.

"Not at the moment, I'm afraid. May I ask who's calling?"

"This is Mouse."

There was a long pause. "Is this a joke?"

"No. I'm a friend of his since he first moved here."

"And you say your name is Mouse."

"That's just what everybody calls me. I write for the Plain Speaker."

A sharp intake of breath. "Oh! You're that Mouse?"

"At your service."

"Oh, Mouse, I just love your column. Love it, love it, love it."

"Feel free to keep going, but first, tell me your name."

"It's Debbie."

"Hi, Debbie."

"Hi, Mouse."

"Ah, see, we're friends already."

She blew out a breath. "I can hardly wait to tell my friends you said that. Wow. Wow."

This sort of star-struck rambling rarely happens around me, but it does happen. I've learned to take charge, just to keep the surface from fracturing like thin ice on a lake. "So, Debbie, who are you, and why are you answering Dr. Tennyson's phone?"

I heard her take another steadying breath. "I'm his day nurse. I spend six hours with him, Monday through Friday."

"Is he alright?"

"It's best if he tells you himself. I mean, I can tell you he's basically fine and is up and about most of the day. You don't have to be worried."

"It's too late for that," I told her.

"No, really."

"Did something happen? Did he have a heart attack or a stroke or something?"

Her tone changed to nurse mode. "Take a deep breath, Mouse."

I did as she said.

"That's good. Now, another."

It helped. "So, is he home?"

"Oh, yes."

"Just unavailable."

"I think he's in the shower." I heard the smile in her voice.

"Can you ask him to call me when he's up?"

"I'll be glad to ask. I've got to warn you, though; he's not returning most calls these days."

"Oh?"

"Ever since he retired, you know."

I hadn't known, and that shocked me. "But people aren't respecting that, I assume."

"Not at first."

"I'm pretty sure he'll want to talk to me."

"How long did you say you've known him?"

"Ever since I was eight years old."

"That's a long time, I imagine."

I was beginning to seriously like this woman. She had that blend of Midwestern, aw-shucks friendliness and East Coast who-the-hell-are-you edginess that so many Clevelanders exhibit until they get to know you face to face. "It might even be longer than you've been alive," I countered.

She giggled at that. "You know, you sound just the way you write."

"Why, thank you, Debbie."

She giggled again. "I'll let him know. I'm sure he'll call you back."

"Thanks again."

"Just one thing? Don't freak out if he doesn't get back to you today or even tomorrow. It doesn't mean there's anything wrong, and it doesn't mean you're not important to him. It's just the way he is, these days. I don't know what he was like before, but he's involved with a major project he's been putting off for years, and he doesn't like to break his attention with a lot of phone calls."

"Can you tell me what it's about?"

"Not a clue. It's something to do with fossils and microscopes."

"Debbie, that's the most reassuring thing you've said

so far."

"I don't understand."

"You know what kind of scientist he is, right?"

"He's an ecologist."

"Well, yes, but he didn't start out that way. His PhD was in paleontology."

"What's that?" she asked without a trace of embarrassment.

"Fossils."

"And dinosaurs?"

"You bet," I said. "And that's why I said it was reassuring. He's going back to his roots, now that he has time on his hands."

"I'm so glad you told me that."

"You should ask him about it."

"I will. But I better get going. I'll tell him you called."

"Thanks, Debbie."

"Bye, Mouse."

I got off the phone, not sure how I felt. It worried me that he needed a day nurse. It worried me a lot. Debbie seemed calm about his condition, though, and the fact that he was busy working was great. Still, a nurse!

I wondered when he retired. I should have known about that, been invited to a reception at the very least. I know I'm trying to cover too much, but Dr. T is my surrogate father. Am I really that out of touch with my life?

CHAPTER 10:

How Coffee Hour Saved
a Beloved Bakery

While I was berating myself for not knowing about Dr. Tennyson's retirement and waiting for him to get back to me, I still had a column to write. I was supposed to be out and about, keeping my ears open on behalf of the journalists. I just wasn't in the mood. Still, my twice a week deadline wasn't going to go away. I had to write something. I did what everyone else does; I consulted my tickler file. It's chock full of reminders to follow up on stories I covered in the past.

That's where I found some notes about the charming, old world Svoboda sisters, Elishka and Katerina. They had emigrated from Czechoslovakia shortly after it split up into the Czech Republic and Slovakia in the late '80s. The only relatives they had in the United States were living on the West Side of Cleveland, so that's where they put down roots and founded the Dvorak Bakery. Almost immediately, they gained a large cohort of fanatical fans. It didn't take long before I heard about them and stopped by to sample their baked goods. Wow! They were the best I'd ever had, and the sisters were gracious and fun to talk to as well. I mentioned them briefly in a column, which they proudly displayed on their back wall for years. Had I wanted to, I could have gotten free pastries for the rest of my life. Well, I did want to, but Peter had rules about such things, and so I declined their repeated offers and simply became one of their regulars.

Through them, I gained an awareness of the whole Czech community, including some of the priests from the famous St. Theodosius Russian Orthodox Cathedral, who frequented the bakery even more than I did. One of them, Father Vladimir, gave me a tour, which blew me away. I had no idea we had such an architectural wonder hidden right here in Cleveland. It turned out that it wasn't so hidden, after all. People who are interested in Orthodox churches regard this as one of the finest in the country, and many travel here specifically to see it. Over the years, I have written about the cathedral and some of its members many times. They keep inviting me to attend some of their Easter celebrations, but I never have gotten around to it.

But I digress.

About a year ago, Elishka Svoboda called me up in a panic. "Mouse, we don't know what to do or who to talk to. Can you come see us?"

"I'm on my way," I said.

"You know we moved, right?"

I did know, but I'd forgotten. They gave me the new address. "You sure didn't move very far," I remarked.

"We'll tell you all about it when you get here."

I got there in twenty minutes. The new place was quite a bit larger but decorated like the old one. The same pastries were displayed under the counters, except that there were even more counters now, which displayed offerings I'd never seen before. But that wasn't what caught my attention. Where were all the customers? I was literally the only one. Katerina was standing behind the counters looking lost. She quickly summoned her sister from the back, and we sat down together at one of the little tables, which were another new feature of the larger space.

The only reason they moved to their new location was that their old landlord wanted to up their rent by 30%. This amounted to nothing short of extortion in their eyes, and they weren't about to put up with it. So they cast around, found a realtor, and discovered a slightly larger space only a quarter-mile away that they could rent for less than the current one. They jumped on the opportunity, told their old landlord to stuff a kielbasa up his *prdel*, and moved. What their realtor hadn't mentioned was that this short move put them into the turf of a different street gang, and their old customers found themselves hassled or even robbed when they visited the bakery. Meanwhile, their new neighbors weren't aware of them enough to make up for lost business. Besides, Katerina said, they missed their old customers.

The subject of West Side gangs had never come up before, so I had to ask a lot of questions to get an idea of what they were up against. The West Side of Cleveland is a hodgepodge of ethnic groups and neighborhoods, a kind of miniature Balkans. So it wasn't Black gangs against White gangs or Puerto Rican gangs against Italian gangs like we have on the East Side. This was Czech versus Croat versus Lithuanian versus Serbian versus Russian gangs, who had turfs that stayed pretty much static over the years, but also a fluid set of alliances and rivalries that changed almost daily.

"Where's the cathedral stand in all this?" I asked her.

"The cathedral is neutral ground."

"Even though it's officially a Russian Orthodox cathedral?"

"If we were bigger, we'd probably have five or six cathedrals serving five or six nationalities."

"But you say St. Theodosius is neutral ground."

"Not only that, but Sunday morning is understood to be a kind of truce," Katerina said.

"At least until noon," Elishka added.

"Definitely until noon, but pretty much all day, really," said her sister.

"Maybe we should call the cathedral and see if they can help you out," I suggested. "Are you members?"

They nodded.

"Call them."

The idea frightened them more than the gangs. "Oh, the priests are very busy men. This is our problem, not theirs."

"Nonsense," I said. "If you won't, I will. I mean, if you agree. I know Father Vladimir pretty well. Let me go talk to him on your behalf."

The two sisters fussed at me a bit but gave in. I called the good Father immediately and reached him right away. When I briefly described the problem, he said he would walk right over. "I could use a good apricot kuchen if any are still available."

He was in luck. They had a whole counter full of them, made fresh that morning.

"Mouse, you are a miracle worker," Katerina told me.

Father Vladimir came strolling in a couple minutes later. He looked – to be honest – like he'd been eating his fair share of kuchen over the years. In the spirit of diplomacy, I allowed the sisters to serve me one at the same time as Vladimir as a free-will offering. I don't think Peter would have minded, even if I told him.

The ensuing conversation was one of the most unexpected and fascinating ones I've ever been part of. Vladimir talked about the various gangs and their territories with the casual expertise of someone who deals with gang issues all the time and very directly. He knew some of the members personally, but if he didn't know one directly, chances were pretty good that he knew their parents or some close relative. "You should have come to me right away," he told the sisters sternly as if by not doing so they had committed a serious sin.

They apologized profusely.

He turned to me. "Mouse, you're the one who called this meeting. What would you suggest?"

"I have no idea," I replied. Then I did. "How about having the Dvorak Bakery supply the bread you use for your services? And then publicly thank them in the bulletin. Get people used to the name in connection with the cathedral?"

Oh boy! What a tangled mess that suggestion created. Suddenly, all three of them wanted to educate me at the same time. It turns out that bread is a big deal among the Orthodox. It's not the nuns or the priests who bake it, and it certainly isn't some neighborhood bakery. The parishioners (and here he used some Greek sounding word I can't remember) are to bake it at home according to set recipes and accompanied by prayers. These loaves of bread are gifts from the people of God, not the priests of the church. Once they bring this bread into the church ahead of the service, the priest "prepares" it during the first part of the mass, out of sight behind the altar and all the icons. If I got it right, this preparation involves blessing it and breaking it into bite-sized pieces. At this stage, it's called *prosphora*. Later on, during the service, the priest then consecrates it – which is different from blessing it. Consecrated bread is now called *antidora*. But not all of it gets consecrated. Some of this blessed bread (the *prosphora*) is set aside for those who approach the altar and are not in full communion for one reason or another. I, for example, could approach the altar and be given a piece of *prosphora* but not *antidora*.

"And what would that mean?" I asked.

Father Vladimir was not insulted by the question in the least. "It would mean something like me saying, 'I'm glad you're here and here's a piece of bread that carries the best wishes of the community.'"

I'm just summarizing here. The actual back and forth went on for quite a while and involved all three of them taking delight in educating me. I remember saying it sounded like a cycle. The church members bake the bread, it goes to the cathedral, it gets blessed, some gets sanctified and is offered to the members, the rest gets handed out to the broader community. Then the bread that the community members eat becomes part of their bodies, with which they can bake a new batch, and so it goes, over and over again.

"We could make an Orthodox out of you in no time," Father Vladimir told me.

This statement triggered a response from both sisters as quick and instinctive as a fish hitting a crank bait. "I'll sponsor you!"

I'm not sure when I've felt more welcomed, not that I had any desire to accept the offer.

We got back to the business of helping the bakery.

"You know," Father Vladimir said, "we have a coffee hour after mass. It's very crowded, and we offer coffee and all kinds of cookies and baked goods. There's nothing sacred about what we put out. It's just treats. How would you two like to provide the baked goods for coffee hour next week? We could make a special announcement, and I'd have no problem if you wanted to put a small sign on the table with your name on it."

That seemed like a good start, but would it be enough? I asked them.

"Then I'll have a word with some of the parents," Vladimir said. "Privately. Let's see what happens."

Elishka asked if they could provide goodies for every coffee hour as an offering to the church. Vladimir was not in favor. They went back and forth and agreed that the Dvorak Bakery would supply coffee hour pastries one week per month for the next six months. Then they could re-evaluate the plan and decide what to do next.

That was eight months ago. I couldn't write about it at the time because nobody knew how it was going to turn out. I sure could now, though – again, depending on how it turned out. It shocked me to see that I hadn't been back there since then. I hoped that no news was good news. I picked up the phone and gave them a call.

They were delighted to hear from me, but also cross because it had been so long. "Come over," they implored me. "You need to see this for yourself."

I drove over and found the place full of customers. Some I recognized and some I didn't. They also had a young girl helping out behind the counter. Elishka came out and filled me in with all the details. The bakery was now unofficially neutral territory for all civilians. If you were a gang member, don't cross the line, but everyone else was welcome and not to be hassled. Business was booming. They were still providing pastries once a month to the cathedral, and many members of the church community were now loyal customers, as well.

I asked her if I could write about their experience, and she was more than happy to give me permission as long as Father Vladimir agreed. I got him on the phone, and, just like that, I had my column for the day. All I had to do was write it up and have Peter piss on it to remind me who was running the show. A few corrections, and it would be off my desk and into page layout.

A good day's work, and, for a time, it took my mind off of fretting over Dr. Tennyson.

CHAPTER 11:

Persistent Organic Chemicals

Peter sent a memo around announcing another emergency staff meeting, and this time there was no screwing around with Mouse. I was on the list of those who were required to attend. The agenda was to learn the basics about PCBs and C8 from Jane Smillens. It was scheduled to last an hour, and that made a number of us wonder if she was up to the task. Jane is smart as a whip but very shy. Those who have worked with her directly (i.e., not me) speak highly of her but say that she prefers to listen, go away for a while to research an answer, and then deliver a written response. Bucky Spencer started an informal betting pool on how many minutes she would talk before asking for questions. It sounds cruel, I suppose, but it's part of the culture. I have been the subject of more betting pools than anyone else, I'm told. How long before Peter blows up at Mouse? How late will Mouse be this week? That sort of thing. I tossed a dollar in the pot and wrote down 59 minutes. I sure hoped I was wrong: the idea of listening to an hour-long lecture on chemicals reminded me too much of my worst high school classes.

Peter's memo did one thing, though. It emphasized how seriously he was taking this lawsuit.

I made sure to get there on time. The atmosphere was decidedly more solemn than Tuesday's meeting, but Peter seemed more relaxed, which was a surprise. "Okay, guys, you all know what the topic is, and there's no need to introduce our speaker. The only thing I want to say is that I have spent three or four hours doing nothing but reading up on what PCBs are, and the more I read, the more confused I got. There are a thousand technical names, and every time I looked up what they meant, I found myself running into another thousand terms I was supposed to know about. I assume the same thing is happening to you, as well. So I asked Jane to give us an overview of what we're looking at and define at least a few of the terms we're going to bump into. I don't know what she is going to say or how she's going to approach this topic. It's really an impossible assignment, so I'm going to take off my editor's hat and simply join the audience, wishing her well and hoping I can absorb at least the basics. I did ask for a handout so we could follow along. I haven't even seen it because Jane was still revising it an hour ago. Let's give her a hand and our full attention." With that, he swapped chairs with Jane.

Jane's handout was a stapled collection of five pages. The first one was an outline of her talk; the rest were definitions of technical terms. We all flipped through them and promptly fell asleep. Well, not everyone. Just me, and just for a second. Arne elbowed me, and I perked back up before my head hit the table.

"Good morning," she said in a quiet voice. "What Peter said is true, even for me. You try to find a definition for one term – PCBs is a perfect example – and you end up running into all these others. You try to understand these new terms, and it gets more and more technical. My first thought was to start with a definition of PCBs, but that's what happened. So, the way I want to approach this is to back away from that term and go several layers up to see where PCBs fit into the larger topic of chemicals that are dangerous to the environment— especially us as human beings—and global politics."

Peter's head jerked back. He hadn't seen that coming.

She saw his reaction. "I know: you're wondering why I want to go there. The truth is, it's the last thing I want to talk about, but I can't avoid it. Stanhope is a global business, serving markets in every continent except Antarctica. The products they make are hurting everyone on Earth, and the kinds of chemical spills and illegal dumping that we're talking about in the Cincinati case are happening all over the world. If you think about it this way, you will understand just how much Stanhope stands to lose if the lawsuit goes against them. It's not just a billion dollars to clean up a few hundred miles of the Ohio River and compensate a few thousand people directly affected. If they lose this one, it will set a precedent for court battles from Buenos Aires, Argentina to Sydney, Australia, and from Moscow to the tip of India."

"Let me give you one example to show how this is unavoidable. Did you ever wonder where Buenos Aires got its name? It means good air, which distinguishes it from all the foul-smelling swamplands to the north. Smell is one way to talk about good air, but not the only one. You see, those swamplands were swarming with Anopheles mosquitos, the kind that carries malaria, which meant that Buenos Aires – let's call it healthy air – was the only port for ships from around the world to dock at in a thousand miles of coast without fear of getting malaria. This remained true until Stanhope began manufacturing stupendous amounts of a wonderful new pesticide called *DDT*."

Even I knew about *DDT*. Or so I thought.

"I'm starting with *DDT* for several reasons. First of all, if you turn to the definitions I have in the handout, you'll see that it stands for 'dichloro-diphenyl-trichloroethane.' Do you see why most people don't call it that? Only a chemist is going to remember that long a name, and the only reason a chemist can is that each of those syllables stands for a term they understand already. *DDT* is so much easier to remember. Now flip to the definition of PCBs. You'll see that it is shorthand for 'polychlorinated biphenyls.' So that's one thing they have in common. But notice one difference: (with an apostrophe) or *PCBs* (without the apostrophe) is plural, which means that there is more than one specific formula. In fact, there are 209 different *PCBs* out there as of right now. Only thirteen of them are toxic. If you want to think of an analogy, think of cake mixes. You could lump them together under a term called CMs – short for cake mixes. And let's say some were contaminated with a poison like arsenic, but that involved only thirteen flavors of cake out of 209. You could say that CMs are toxic, which is a lot shorter than listing thirteen of them in one column and 206 in another, but you pay a price for doing that. The price you pay is you are over-generalizing. And that is one of the challenges we are all going to have when we try to cover this lawsuit. NOT ALL *PCBs* ARE TOXIC."

We all wrote down, not all *PCBs* are toxic. I added the apostrophe.

"Here's something else I want you to notice: these are not brand names. As patents expire, new brands come onto the marketplace all the time. Also, a company like Stanhope might develop a new chemical like Glyphosate – which is also in the handout -- and use that chemical in dozens of specifically branded products. In the case of *Glyphosate,* there are several dozen brands manufactured by Stanhope under the familiar term of MowDown™. But there are other brands using slightly different versions of *Glyphosate* being manufactured and sold around the world by competitors of Stanhope. Put all of them together, and you'll find that there may be literally hundreds of products incorporating that chemical. So, be glad that those chemical names, often shortened to terms like *PCBs,* are used."

"To return to the cake mix analogy, imagine there are 209 flavors of cake mixes. Thirteen of them are contaminated with arsenic. Now imagine that one of those is chocolate cake, and imagine that yellow cake is not toxic. This is complicated enough but then go to the grocery store. You'll find that there are chocolate cake mixes sold by Pillsbury, General Mills, Duncan Hines, and a dozen others. Within the category of chocolate cakes, one is called Pillsbury's German Chocolate Cake. Another is called Betty Crocker Black Forest Cake, and another is Duncan Hines Moist Chocolate Fudge Cake. And of course, these brands keep evolving and changing."

Peter raised his hand. "I think you've made your point, Jane. Can we move along?"

She froze, and for a moment, it was like she didn't know how to speak.

"Sorry," Peter said. "I didn't mean to interrupt your flow of thought."

We saw her take a deep breath. Her face was red and getting redder all the time, but she managed to carry on. "One way to tie everything I've been talking about together is to use the term POP, which stands for Persistent Organic Pollutants. It's a relatively new term that came out of a convention put on by the United Nations held in Stockholm, Sweden, in 2001 – five years ago. The Stockholm Convention – as it's universally called -- was ratified in 2001, but it didn't take effect until May 2004, which means we are only a few weeks from its second anniversary as a law or set of standards agreed to by every country on Earth."

"The Stockholm Convention did several things. One was to organize our thinking about toxic materials like *PCBs* and *DDT*. Another was to eliminate or at least drastically limit their manufacture and use worldwide. And again, I want you to remember that Stanhope is a multinational corporation that has been manufacturing and selling hundreds of brands of these POPs globally, and making a fortune doing so."

We all wrote down *Stockholm Convention* and *POP* = *Persistent Organic Pollutants* or some variation of that.

"POPs are a group of chemicals that share the following

properties: they linger in the environment for a long time, they become widely distributed geographically, they accumulate in the fatty tissue of humans and wildlife, and they have harmful impacts on human health or the environment. The Stockholm Convention listed twelve such chemicals, often called the 'dirty dozen.' Another term you'll come across is 'forever chemicals.' Most of them are pesticides. That would include DDT, for example. Some are chemicals used in industry, like certain PCBs. And some are byproducts produced in the manufacturing process or come about when certain chemicals break down in the soil or are incinerated. Certain PCBs – remember that there are 206 kinds – are included in this category."

"I'm not going to talk about the twelve forever chemicals, just the ones that are involved in the Cincinnati lawsuit. To start out, picture the Ohio River as it flows through Pennsylvania past Pittsburgh and then defines the border between West Virginia, Kentucky, Ohio, Indiana, and Illinois, where it merges with the Mississippi. Right there, you have a miniature version of the United Nations, with each state having its own environmental laws, some very much more relaxed than others. Into the Ohio River comes this flow of Persistent Organic Pollutants, including PCBs, but not just them. I bet every one of the dirty dozen forever chemicals listed in the Stockholm Convention have been accidentally or deliberately dumped into the river at some point. The major culprits are the big chemical companies like Stanhope, but once again, not limited to Stanhope. And it's not just chemical companies. You also have the steel industry and the automotive industry and on and on and on. In addition to manufacturing plants, you have agricultural runoff, which contributes its own share of POPs that were applied to cropland as pesticides and fertilizers and got washed down to the river. You add all of that together, and you end up with one of the most polluted rivers on Earth. So, how are you going to sue one manufacturer like

Stanhope for harming human health? This is not an easy task, and we don't know the details of how this lawyer in Cincinnati is proceeding--not yet, anyway. But we can make an intelligent guess about the terms and the reasoning behind them. And all of them relate to the Stockholm Convention and its list of twelve POPs."

"Start with Stanhope's Parkers Ferry Plant, which produces all kinds of products and byproducts. Some of them include specific *PCBs* that are listed as Persistent Organic Pollutants. Let me list the most likely. You will be listening for brand names, but we've been through that, and you know why we don't hear them. The first POP we're likely to hear about is *PCBs*. Some of them are end products in terms of the manufacturing plant. Let's say a barrel of a chemical used to make automotive paint or a barrel of a chemical that is part of fertilizer or pesticide. As long as it stays in the plant, it's not a problem, because it hasn't entered the environment. Right? Well, that's right as long as you aren't one of the workers at that plant who gets exposed to those chemicals. Let's say you are in the shipping department, and one of the barrels gets tipped over and leaks on the floor. You might inhale fumes, or maybe you are the one who has to clean it up. Now you are directly exposed to that chemical. It enters your body either through your nose or your skin. What do we know about that chemical, given that it is listed as a POP? We know that once it gets into your body, it is harmful. We also know that it gets absorbed into your fatty tissues, and once there, it lasts a long time. So it's not like getting drunk and sobering up the next day as your body gets rid of the alcohol. If it's a POP, once it enters your body, it's going to stay there for a long time."

"Here's another way that those *PCBs* can enter the environment. They can be dumped into the Ohio River, either legally or illegally. What happens then? POPs are not soluble in water, so they sink to the bottom and stay there for a long time. Plants absorb them, insects absorb them, fish eat them, larger fish eat smaller fish, etc. Along the way, a process called bioaccumulation takes place. You start off with 1 part POP to a million parts water. Then some tiny organism absorbs some that stays in it until a larger organism eats it. By that time, instead of one part per million, it's now ten parts per million. And that larger organism – let's say it's a minnow – eats thousands and thousands of these little creatures. They absorb the POP into their fatty tissues, so now they have 100 parts per million stored in them. On and on it goes, and at each stage, the amount of POP goes up and up. And guess who sits at the top of the entire food chain? Humans. By the time we eat a catfish sandwich, the concentration of that POP can be as much as 70,000 times more than what is in the Ohio River, all because it persists in fatty tissues."

"How else can those *PCBs* enter the environment and ultimately into human beings? Let's say a barrel of some specific PCB is used in the manufacture of a pesticide. The pesticide is sprayed on a field of corn. Some of it enters the soil, and some of that soil enters the Ohio River in a rainstorm. Some enter the actual corn kernels. You eat that corn, and the PCB enters your body and stays there for a long time, poisoning you. Or let's say you feed that corn to a pig. The pig eats a lot of corn before it gets slaughtered, so that whole process of bioaccumulation takes place in it, as well. You eat the pig, you take on another load of concentrated PCB."

"One more way to get *PCBs* into your body. Let's say the Parkers Ferry plant makes a barrel of some PCB that gets shipped to a company in Oklahoma, where it will be combined with other chemicals to make fertilizer. On the way there, the train derails. Now you have a chemical spill seeping into the ground or drifting off into the air as a cloud of toxic chemicals all mixed together. So dangerous is that cloud that you have to evacuate everyone living within five miles of the spill, depending on which way the wind is blowing. The wind doesn't care what state you are living in or if it's blowing across the border between one nation and another. Maybe that wind picks up some of that toxic cloud and blows it all the way to Mexico. Now you have one of those criteria for POPs established by the Stockholm Convention: wide geographic distribution."

Some of my colleagues were taking notes frantically on the back of the handouts. Some were zoned out, unable to process any further material. I listened without taking many notes at all. For whatever reason, I have an incredible memory for spoken words, even if I didn't fully understand them. Because I was maintaining eye contact with Jane, I found her talking more and more directly to me, even though she must have known that I had the least use for her presentation and probably the least understanding.

"If you remember," she continued, "I said that *PCBs* were listed under two categories on POPs. One was as a manufactured product in and of itself. That's what we've been talking about. The other is as a by-product produced as part of the manufacturing process. Here's where it gets thorny, I'm afraid, and here's where it is most likely to confuse you. I know I've been talking for a long time ..."

Yes! I thought. My one dollar wager was going to pay off.

"... but bear with me. This is where the real action is, and these are going to be the terms you're going to run into time after time when it comes to the lawsuit. The product you are going to hear about all the time is Teflon™. That's a brand name. Forget about its chemical name. The point is, certain kinds of *PCBs* are produced during the manufacturing process when various chemicals are combined under conditions of high heat and pressure. These are byproducts, and they are impossible to eliminate entirely. Some of them end up contaminating the final product; some of them collect in the bottom of the tanks where they are produced, and when those tanks have to be cleaned out, they can spill; and some of them end up in the atmosphere from dirty smokestacks or – God help us – an explosion. We had one here in Cleveland two years ago. Anybody remember it?"

Tom raised his hand. "At the Stanhope plant, right? A couple of workers got killed, and there was a discharge of toxic chemicals into the air. I think."

Peter growled at him. "You were the one who covered it for us, so I hope you remember."

Tom looked down.

To her credit, Jane stood up for him. "I was part of that story behind the scenes. To be honest, I didn't understand the bigger picture at the time or how to untangle all the BS that Stanhope was putting out."

There was an uncomfortable moment while she waited for Peter to respond. When he kept himself in check, she went on. "Okay, here we go. This is where it all comes home. There are two of these byproducts that are listed in the Stockholm Convention as POPs. They both start with the same three initials: *PCD*. That stands for *Polychlorinated dibenzo*. The last letter can either be a *D* or an *F*. If it's a D, it stands for *dioxin*; if it's an F, it's a *furan*."

We watched in wonder as Jane Smillens – our own, timid, self-effacing Jane Smillens – became visibly excited. I don't mean cheerful excited; I mean angry. In part, I think she was mad at herself for not understanding the implications of that explosion in our own backyard. Most of her anger was at Stanhope, though. That was clear as a bell.

"Forget *PCDFs* (*Polychlorinated dibenzofurans*). No doubt they are in the Ohio River, and they are bad news. Forget about them. The ones you need to pay attention to are the PCDDs (*Polychlorinated dibenzo-p-dioxins*), and it's that last part that matters: *dioxin*. Remember how I harped on the fact that there are 206 different *PCBs* and that only 13 are toxic? Well, there are 75 different *dioxins* we know about, and only 7 of them are

POPs. Those seven, though, are the worst chemicals in terms of human health with the possible exception of *DDT*. They linger, and they are nasty. One type can linger in the soil for up to twelve years. Think of all the opportunities for it to enter the food chain for over twelve years. For obvious reasons, only scientists talk about *PCDDs* or *Polychlorinated dibenzo-p-dioxins*. Most people just talk about *dioxins* (plural), or even worse, *dioxin* (singular, as if it was one chemical).

"What do these dangerous forms of *dioxin* do? They harm our immune systems, they cause enzyme disorders, they may cause cancer. They kill fish and accumulate in the bodies of anything that eats fish or drinks out of polluted rivers. There are dioxins in breast milk. There are dioxins in virtually every kind of meat, whether it is farm-raised or wildlife like a duck or a deer. Dioxins are in the atmosphere. We – along with every other animal – absorb them into our lungs. Plants absorb them from the soil or through their leaves, so you're still vulnerable if you are a vegetarian. Some scientists suspect that dioxins cause birth defects or even genetic mutations that can be passed on to your children and possibly even your children's children."

At that, this super-Jane personality collapsed back into plain-Jane, our timid, familiar science reporter. It was like watching one of those cake mixes collapse if you take it out of the oven too soon. What did we do? We applauded like hell; that's what we did, Peter included. We meant well, but she took it poorly. You could see it in her eyes. All she wanted was run out of the room and hide under a bush for a week.

Peter spoke for all of us. "Thank you, Jane. That was far more than I expected, especially given one day's notice. I can see you're tired. Go take a break. You have certainly earned it."

"Can I just ask one question?" said Arne.

"About what?"

"It's about Agent Orange."

"Ancient history," Peter said,

He turned to the rest of us. "Thank you for coming in early. I'm sure there will be all kinds of questions for Jane, but give her a day, alright? Read over her notes – several times. I know I'm going to. And I'm going to keep them on my desk for ready reference as this story plays out."

As we filed out, I turned to my best buddy. "What the hell, Arne?"

He shrugged. "Yeah, I know: bad timing. I'll apologize to Jane."

"Not today, you won't."

CHAPTER 12:

Mouse Dives into Research

F eeling stung by the staff meeting, I decided to do some honest to god research, the kind real journalists do. I was glad now that I hadn't talked with Dr. Tennyson. I needed to know at least a little about Stanhope before trying to interview him. I made my way down to the archives, thinking of how proud Peter would be.

Once I got there, I realized I had absolutely no idea what I was looking for or how to go about it even if I did. I wandered around so people would see me, then pretended I just remembered something urgent and left in a hurry. I went to the lunchroom and looked around for someone I could talk to. Ah! There was Lenny Kellerman, our business reporter. He looked tired and irritable.

"Hey, Lenny, what's up?"

"Just grinding away like everyone else."

"Whew. Tell me about it."

He looked at me dubiously. "When I said *everyone else*, Mouse, I wasn't referring to you. You don't do that."

"And I never will," I promised, earnestly. "What I do is cheer people up, and from the look of you…"

"Yeah."

"Let me guess: Peter has been putting pressure on you."

"Like I've never seen him before."

"In that case, welcome to my world."

He gave me another dubious look.

"Here, let me cheer you up. Let me ask you some questions about Stanhope, and you can show me how much you actually know. It might not impress Peter, but I'll stomp and holler and sing your praises."

"Go away, Mouse."

"I knew you'd say yes. So, let me start with something straightforward and close to home. How many people work for the Plain Speaker?"

He wasn't expecting that. "Roughly 700."

"Wow. That's big."

"Compared to what?" he asked.

"Well, Stanhope, for instance. I bet you don't know how many people work for them."

"That depends on what you mean about working for them. In terms of full-time employees, the latest number hovers around 72,000."

"That's bigger."

"Yes, Mouse."

I decided not to ask what that meant. "How many scientists and engineers, do you think?"

He had an answer at the ready. "Thirteen thousand, according to them," he said. Sure enough, he was cheering up.

"Compared to one for The Plain Speaker."

"You mean Jane?"

"Yes."

The look on his face said he wasn't sure whether he thought of her that way. I began to take offense on her behalf, but he left it at that. If he had started talking about the difference between scientists and science reporters, I would have started talking about the difference between business reporters and businessmen. Better to move on. "How about lawyers?" I asked. "We've got lawyers, right?"

"Once again, it depends on how you define your terms. We have a fulltime staff of five lawyers, but then we have several law firms on retainer."

"How many, do you think?"

"You know, I can't tell you. When Media IV bought us, we came under the umbrella of their corporate law department and its many outside defenders."

That's the problem with interviewing specialists: they never give you a straight answer. "Well, do you have any idea how we compare to Stanhope?"

The very idea of comparing our legal team to theirs struck him so ludicrous that it made him crack a smile so big you could see it on the outside. "Tell you what, Mouse, if you're really interested, I know exactly where you can look it up. I came across those numbers in an article I skimmed just the other day."

"Uh, sure, Lenny."

He got up and rapped his knuckles on the tabletop. "I'll drop it on your desk later today."

He was gone before I had a chance to thank him. I wasn't sure I'd gotten that much out of him, but I had learned a few things, and better yet, he had given me some much-needed perspective. I spent a few minutes writing down some notes before I forgot what he'd told me.

I was still at it when Jane Smillens walked in, poured herself a cup of coffee, and sat down as far from me as possible. She stared off into middle-distance for a long time before taking her first sip, then went right back to staring. The intensity of that stare and the tension she was holding in her body told me she wasn't giving her mind a break. She was thinking hard, and whatever it was, she seemed to be stuck.

Maybe I could help her, I thought.

I ambled over and asked if I could sit down. Jane was too tangled up in thought to say no. As it was, she nodded absently.

"You look stuck," I said.

"I do?"

"Yeah."

That seemed to upset her. "I wasn't drooling or anything like that?"

"No. Just looking intense."

She took a shallow breath and let it out emphatically. "This Parkers Ferry spill is bad news, and I feel like I ought to be able to write something that matters, you know?"

I didn't know, so I asked. "Matters how?"

She took her glasses off. "Well, you know, the way what you about write matters."

That came as a shock. "Now wait a minute, Jane. The whole point of what I write about is that it doesn't matter. It's just about regular people going about their business as best they can."

"But they're the ones getting poisoned, don't you see? It's not the rich folk or the company owners who are drinking all that polluted water. They know better. It's your people who need to understand this crime."

Again, she surprised me. "Crime," I said. "That's a pretty strong word."

"If you ask me, it's not strong enough."

I'd never seen her this agitated. I was impressed enough to take her seriously and not just try to reassure her on the spot. "I was just talking to Lenny," I said, "and he got me thinking about lawyers, so let me ask you this: if you have a crime, presumably you have a perpetrator, an action, and a victim."

"And a law," she added.

"I guess so. Okay. So, let's say the victims are the kind of people I write about, and the crime is dumping C8 into the Ohio River – and presumably, there's at least one law against that – so, the question is, who is the perpetrator?"

"I thought that was obvious," she said. "Stanhope."

"Yeah, but Stanhope does a lot of things that have nothing to do with C8. So, within this huge beast of a corporation, who is the real perpetrator – or perpetrators, plural? I mean, who is directly responsible?"

She frowned for a moment. "That's kind of a difficult question when you get down to it because it probably involves many different levels. At the lowest one, it might be one workman making minimum wage, who turns the wrong knob or opens the wrong valve. But then you have to ask about who trained him, and who supervised him, and who checked to make sure that the valve stayed shut?"

"So, you have two levels: the worker and his supervisor."

She flinched. "It doesn't have to be a man, you know."

"If the valve was left open, I'm betting it was."

That calmed her down. "You can't stop there," she said. "You've got to remember that this has been going on for years. It sounds like it involves more than one plant. That means it's a policy issue. I'm not sure you can prove it, but it almost has to be intentional."

"Which means that you've got senior management and the legal department involved."

"You have to, right?"

"Let's say it goes all the way to the CEO of Stanhope," I said, realizing that I didn't know the name of that individual. "And let's say the Plain Speaker lays it all out, and let's say that leads to a huge penalty and the stockholders are furious, and they vote the CEO out. And the new CEO digs into it and fires everyone in the chain of responsibility. Would you call that a total victory?"

"Well..."

"Well, what?"

"I'm thinking about your audience. The victims. It's not helping them."

I saw her point. "Let's say the settlement includes a billion-dollar payout to the victims."

"That's better."

"I agree," I said. "But Jane, this raises a question, and I don't want you to take it the wrong way. Where does science fit into this? Why should you even be involved in the story?"

She stiffened and then began to look like a fish swimming to the surface for a nugget of food. "We're missing something, then," she said. "Science and engineering are all over this crime. Without them, *C8* wouldn't exist in the first place."

"So, it wouldn't matter if the wrong valve was left open."

"There wouldn't even be a valve."

This was more fun than I anticipated, and I think it was enjoyable for her as well.

"Say, before we go further, could you explain something you just said?" I asked her. "When I said *science*, you said *science and engineering*. How come? And what's the difference between them?"

She answered my question with one of her own. "Is that the sort of thing your readers don't know?"

"I sure don't," I admitted, "and I assume a lot of my readers are the same way."

She gathered her thoughts. "A scientist tries to figure out how the natural world works."

"Got it," I said, "but doesn't everybody, at least to some degree?"

"I'm not so sure about that!" she snapped.

I think she didn't like being lumped in with my readers. "Well, what's the difference between a scientist and an engineer, then?"

"Ah! Now we're getting there. With science, you have a set of tools and assumptions that you use, and you use them carefully, and you allow other scientists to review and question your results."

"Okay," I said. I wanted to write it down, but I didn't want to interrupt the flow of her thoughts.

"An engineer uses scientific knowledge and a lot of the same methods, but the goal is to build something new, something practical, something you can hold in your hand."

I gave her a look.

"When a scientist is done, you generally have an article or a new theorem. Something abstract. When an engineer is done, you have an object designed for a specific application —

like Teflon™.. Sometimes, you also get a byproduct like *C8*."

"What's that stand for?"

"Trust me, you don't want to know. It's one of those chemical words with ten syllables or more."

"But it's a product of engineering, right?"

"A byproduct."

"What's the difference?"

That made her laugh. "Depends on whether you can sell it or not."

I could hardly believe it: Jane was making a joke. Good for her.

"There's also the difference between an intended result and an accidental or unintended consequence."

There went the joke.

"I assume nobody intended to make *C8*. They intended to make Teflon™.. The *C8* chemical was an unintended byproduct." She took a sip of coffee while she thought about how to further explain the joke, just in case it had any life left. "Of course, sometimes those unintended results turn into valuable new products in their own right."

"Like what?"

"Ever hear of Post-It™ Notes?"

"Sure."

"They were the result of a failed attempt to engineer a new adhesive. A whole team of engineers ended up with an adhesive that barely held at all. So, failure, right? But then some product manager saw the benefits of such an adhesive, and 3M made a fortune."

"That's really interesting," I said. "Can you give me an example that involves Stanhope?"

"Oh, can I ever," she said. "How much time have you got?"

"For you, all the time in the world."

She gave me a look that was part frightened and part flirtatious. "Mouse, are you hitting on me?"

Terror seized me. There was no right answer to that

one. Or maybe the look on my face was the right answer.

"Never mind," she said. "I was just teasing."

"Seriously, though," I said quickly, "if you've got the time, I'd love to hear whatever you've got."

"Ever hear of a chemical called Glyphosate?"

"You talked about it in your presentation."

"You want the biggest story in Ohio? Forget about C8. Look into Glyphosate."

CHAPTER 13:

The Invitation

By the time Friday rolled around, and I still hadn't heard from Dr. Tennyson, I began to panic. Was he really alright? Or had he decided I was no longer a special friend, given that I hadn't been in touch in so long, or even reached out when he retired?

Debbie called me mid-morning, just as I was about to call her.

"Is this Mouse?" she asked.

I thought I recognized her voice but wasn't sure. I get a lot of calls.

"It is."

"This is Debbie?" she said, making it a question. "From Dr. Tennyson's?"

I suppressed a sigh of relief. "Hi, there, Debbie. What time should I come?"

"Would ten o'clock Monday work?"

Damn. That might be a problem. "I've got a staff meeting that sometimes goes a little long," I told her. "I'd hate to keep him waiting. How about eleven or eleven-thirty?"

"Maybe we should shoot for Tuesday, then. He usually takes a nap right after lunch. I'd hate to have him run out of steam while you're catching up."

"I hate to wait another day, but that probably makes more sense. I'm really eager to see him."

"And he is to see you," she said. "Me, too, for that matter."

"But of course," I told her. "Do you like donuts? There's a great shop that's right on the way."

"Is it the one you just wrote about?"

"You bet: the Dvorak Bakery."

"You don't have to..."

"But I'm going to."

"Chocolate glazed for me. I don't suppose you know what Dr. Tennyson likes?"

"He's always been a sucker for bismarcks."

"Then do that. We'll be waiting."

"What time?"

"Ten o'clock — no — nine-thirty, since you're bringing donuts."

"I'll bring lots," I promised.

CHAPTER 14:

Glyphosate

"We've been talking about *PCBs* and *C8*," Jane began, "but now we need to switch gears and talk about *Glyphosate*. It's an herbicide, developed by Stanhope." She stopped herself in mid-sentence. "Actually, the story begins ten years earlier in a different company altogether. The original use of it was to clean out pipes in hot water systems. So it was patented as a chelating agent."

"I won't even pretend to know what chelating means," I said. "Is it important?"

"Not really," she admitted, "but let me just explain."

"Ah, Jane? Stanhope?"

She gave me a dirty look but then moved on. "Along comes Stanhope," she declared with a flourish. "Stanhope is looking around for chemicals that kill plants, and one of their scientists checks out as a potential herbicide."

"What's an herbicide?" I asked.

The depth of my ignorance threw her off her stride. "Are you really asking me that?"

"I'm afraid so."

"An herbicide is a substance that kills plants."

"Which is a bad thing."

"Not when they're weeds."

I made a sound like a balloon deflating. "What's the difference between a plant and a weed?"

"You tell me, Mouse. Go on, give it your best shot."

"A weed is a bad plant."

"That's an interesting answer," she said. "It's not the kind of answer a scientist would give."

"Am I supposed to feel bad about that?"

She sighed. "Ah, there it is, again; that word bad. Scientists don't use words like good and bad."

"Oh, I hardly think that's the case. I mean, how would you get through the day if you didn't use words like that?"

She looked pensive. "It can be lonely. But maybe you can help me here. When you said a weed is a bad plant, what makes it bad?"

I thought about my conversation with Lenny. "You can sell a plant, but you can't sell a weed."

She leaned forward as if I was some exotic creature. "Let's switch terms before I lose my mind. Weeds are plants, okay?"

"Yeah, what I said; bad plants."

"The terms we want are crops and weeds."

"If you say so."

"And they are both plants."

"Okay."

"And plants aren't good or bad. They're just plants."

"Tell that to a farmer," I said.

"It's all about location," she said. "Do you realize that some farmers raise dandelions as a crop?"

"What on earth for?"

"Dandelion greens are used in salads."

"Not where I eat."

"Probably not. But it's true. So let's say you have a

pristine front yard, and one day you see that dandelions are sprouting up in it. You call them a weed. Your next-door neighbor raises them as a food crop. To him, any grass that starts popping up in his field is a weed."

I admitted that I had never thought about it that way.

"And, you know, this actually is quite relevant to Stanhope and *Glyphosate*. You remember how I said some scientist realized that Glyphosate was an herbicide? Well, I'm going to have to retract what I said about using terms like good and bad because we don't have all day. So, from Stanhope's point of view, what qualities would make one kind of herbicide better than another?"

"It's more powerful?"

"Possibly, but not always. Let me list three things Stanhope was interested in. The first is whether it was harmful to people. The second is whether it harmed all plants or just weeds. And of course, its cost was the third. If it was cheaper to produce Glyphosate than what was on the market already, then Stanhope could charge less and still make a large profit."

She waited for me to respond, and a moment later, I got it. "But then you have the problem of whether dandelions or grass is a weed. How does that work?"

"In the case of *Glyphosate*, it is much more likely to kill a dandelion than a blade of grass. The general category is whether a plant is broad-leafed or not. So, let's say you have a lawn that has a combination of Kentucky Bluegrass, dandelions, crabgrass, and creeping Charley. If you spray the whole lawn with *Glyphosate*, everything is going to absorb it, but the difference is that the bluegrass will absorb much less of it than the others, which are all broadleaf. So, as long as you don't put too much on, only the weeds will die."

"But if you put too much on, it would eventually kill the bluegrass," I said.

"Absolutely. It's a poison, and like all poisons, it's all about how much you absorb."

"So, what does the dandelion farmer put on his field?"

She chuckled. "I have no idea, but I'm sure it's not *Glyphosate*."

"It's not just for lawns, though, right?"

"Even if it was, that could be a nice profit center for Stanhope, but you're right. It's the most widely used herbicide on the planet."

"Whoa! How come I've never heard of it."

"That's because Stanhope markets it under the brand name of MowDown™ ™."

"You mean they're one and the same?"

"Not exactly, but if you look at the ingredients, you'll find that *Glyphosate* makes up 95% of MowDown™ ™."

"So far, you are making it sound like *Glyphosate* is a big success story and that we should be grateful that Stanhope discovered it," I said. "That's not where I thought we were headed."

"Indeed," she replied. "There are a couple of issues with Glyphosate that Stanhope doesn't want you to know. The first is that it might cause cancer in humans."

"But I thought you said it wasn't harmful to people."

"That's what Stanhope says, but there have been a lot of scientists who don't agree."

"Well, doesn't the EPA have to certify it?"

"Absolutely, but that doesn't mean they're always right."

"Lobbyists?"

"Lawyers, lobbyists, and politicians. And I hate to say it, but some crooked scientists might be involved, as well."

"Then why isn't there a huge hue and cry?" I asked. I was afraid I knew the answer.

"Too much money is involved."

"Yeah, but if it really does cause cancer..."

"Tobacco causes cancer, and it's still legal."

My mind was spinning with the implications of what Jane was telling me. "You think this is a bigger story than *PCBs*?"

"Mouse, this is worldwide. A few countries are banning it, but overall, the use of MowDown™ is increasing. It's one of the most profitable chemicals in the world."

"Let me play devil's advocate, here," I said. "If it's being used worldwide and if it does cause cancer, then you'd think there would be farmers dying of cancer right and left. Unless I'm missing something, that's not happening."

"Oh, it's happening, alright. Hundreds of thousands of farmers are dying of cancer every year. The problem is, it's hard to say exactly what is causing those cancers. One of the real challenges is separating out all the possible causes and trying to figure out which ones are the most probable. There's another challenge; *Glyphosate* hasn't been used that long, and some cancers are caused by a gradual buildup over time. Something as toxic as *PCBs*, bam, you're dead or dying in no time; something like tar in cigarettes, you might not see any problem for twenty or thirty years."

"How long have we been using MowDown™?"

"It was patented in 1970 but they didn't start selling it until 1974. And then, of course, it didn't go from zero usage to worldwide dominance overnight. I mean, it was pretty quick, but not instantaneous."

"So, we don't know."

"Let's say there are a lot of suspicions raised by a lot of reputable scientists."

"Based on what?"

"Lab tests, for starters."

"How does that work?"

"One thing you do is to compare *Glyphosate* with similar chemicals that you know to be cancer producing. Then there's animal testing."

"Oh, yuck. Like dogs and chimpanzees?"

"Well, mice, usually."

"Hey, those are my relatives!"

I could see that she wasn't sure if I was joking or not. To tell you the truth, I wasn't sure, myself. I forced myself to ask. "Is this like where they inject huge doses of a chemical and wait to see if the mouse gets cancer?"

"It's one of the best ways to find out, short of testing on humans directly, which we obviously can't do." She looked away for a moment. A lot of people were squeamish about live animal experiments. It was possible that she might be one of them. "There are rumors about doctored lab tests, missing data, expert testimony from pathologists who were funded by Stanhope. If I had the time, that's where I'd be putting my attention. Let others deal with *PCBs*."

"Have you mentioned this to Peter?"

"Several times."

"And what does he say?"

"He says we don't have the resources to pursue it."

"You mean, the resources to pursue it and *PCBs* at the same time."

"No. Even if we dropped the whole *PCB* thing, it would take a whole team of scientists and investigators working together, perhaps for years. Not one lowly science reporter."

"So, if not us, who?"

"That's a job for the government."

"But if they're being bribed by the lobbyists..."

"The other option is the NGOs like the Sierra Club or the Natural Defense Fund or maybe Audubon Society. I know they're looking at it."

I jerked back.

"Mouse, what is it? What did I just say?"

"Jane," I said, "can you keep a secret?"

"Sure."

"What would you say if I told you I have a childhood friend who was one of the founders of the Natural Defense Fund, and I am going to be talking to him tomorrow?"

"I'd say you should ask him about *Glyphosate* as well as *PCBs*."

"Anything in particular?"

"Yeah. Ask him about that mouse test."

I wrinkled my lip.

"Anything else?"

She blew out a long breath. "Where to begin? There's so much you and I haven't talked about. You might make a note to ask him about herbicide resistance. And, while you're at it, ask him about how long it takes *Glyphosate* to break down in the soil. I think I read something about that being an issue. It might be nothing, but I'd like to get his take on it."

"Even though we don't have the resources to pursue it."

"I'd really like to know."

"Sure. Anything else?" I asked.

"Just one thing. It's a big one. Would you take me with you?"

"I'm afraid that would be awkward. It's been a while, and he's not in good health."

She waved the request away. "Peter wouldn't let me, in any case."

"Sorry, Jane."

"Hey, it's not your fault. And Mouse, I'm glad you came over. We should talk more, especially after you meet this friend of yours. What's his name?"

"Dr. Tennyson."

"Is that what you call him?"

"Usually."

"Seems kind of formal if he's a childhood friend."

That was an area I was not going to get into with Jane. "It's a long story," I said. "If you met him, you'd understand."

"Formal kind of guy?"

"Formidable is the better word."

"Well, good luck, then. And promise you'll debrief me after you talk with him."

CHAPTER 15:

Lawn Care

The Dvorak Bakery wasn't exactly on the way to Dr. Tennyson's house, but this was a special occasion. I remembered that Debbie liked chocolate glazed and Dr. T liked bismarks, so I had Elishka get four of each along with a couple of cinnamon rolls. She kidded around with me about trying to make my new girlfriend fat. "That comes after you get married," she said, laughing as gaily as a Disney cartoon. Just stopping by for a few moments brightened my entire day.

Over the years, Dr. Tennyson has begun looking more and more like Abe Lincoln. Perhaps I see him that way because that's how I think about him. Except not a President. Oh, dear. Strike that last sentence. To see him now, looking even gaunter than that, his clothes hanging off him, his shoulders slumped, his neck looking like a vulture's, filled me with sorrow.

I was surprised he came to the door rather than nurse Debbie. He explained that she was in the kitchen, making coffee. I handed him the donuts and he shuffled back to give them to Debbie. Letting her make coffee was a startling change to a ritual the professor and I had followed for years, and even though it had been some time since I last visited, I expected him to follow it. He would greet me at the door, usher me into his living room and almost immediately leave me there while he went to the kitchen and brewed fresh coffee. He could have had it ready and waiting, but he never did. There was something about giving me sole possession of the front half of the house – the part where the twins and I used to hang out – that was important to him, I think. Once I got used to it, it became precious to me, as well. It said: you belong here; I trust you; this is your house. I asked him once why he waited to make coffee. Didn't he believe that I'd show up on time? He said coffee had to be freshly brewed to taste right. That was fine with me. Dr. T was never one to talk about feelings.

We sat in our usual chairs in front of the fireplace. It was a relatively small one, flanked by marble slabs and crowned with a wide ledge, which still held a collection of artifacts Dr. Tennyson's wife Lysandra had collected in her anthropological work. We were awkward with each other.

"How's retirement?" I asked, breaking the silence.

He groaned. "Tiring."

"I thought work was tiring, not retirement."

"Worst mistake I ever made," he replied, "except that I had no real option. Too worn down to continue, and I knew it. But just sitting around is worse."

"I hate to hear that, but maybe I've got something you can do that will cheer you up."

He gave me a look.

"I've got a secret to tell you, but you have to promise me you'll keep it to yourself."

He gave me the slightest of nods.

"The Plain Speaker is working on a huge expose of Stanhope dumping *C8* into the Ohio River."

"Old news, I'm afraid."

"But do you know about the lawsuit that's finally

reached a courtroom in Cincinnati? They're talking millions of dollars. Maybe billions."

His eyes came alive.

"Not only that – and this is the real secret – my editor says the Cuyahoga plant might be involved in some way."

"Are you sure about that, Mouse? As far as I know, they've never made Teflon™ there or anything else that would involve *C8*."

"Nobody's sure of anything. There are rumors about political payoffs and secret deals, some of them involving Cleveland banks and politicians. Again, nothing is proven. But he's ordered the whole news division to look into it."

"So, you came to me."

"Who better?"

He put his hands on his knees as if preparing to get up. "Tell me, is this a formal interview?"

It was a tricky moment. "I know the rules. This isn't an interview."

"But, your editor sent you."

"Well, sent is a strong word for it. I guess it's more like he gave me permission to see you."

"What's that even mean?" he demanded.

"Technically, he doesn't want me actively chasing after this story. He just wants me to keep my ears open. If I do hear anything by accident, I'm supposed to pass it along to him so he can assign it to the investigative reporters to follow up on, depending on the material."

He frowned. "I still don't get it."

"Let's say you and I get talking, and you mention some lawyer you've gone up against who might be crooked. I'd tell Peter, and he'd assign it to one of our legal reporters."

"Ah-hah."

"If it involved science, he'd hand it over to our science reporter Jane Smillens."

He dismissed her with a shake of the head as if dodging a snowball.

"Hey, don't dismiss her like that," I said. "She's pretty damned smart."

"And so are you, Mouse. When are you going to start taking yourself seriously? Demand some respect?"

"I am respected," I declared. "Just not as a scientist; that would be ridiculous."

"There, I have to agree with you."

I waited in vain for a follow-up compliment.

"Before I forget," I said, "I'm supposed to ask you about *Glyphosate* degradation."

"Oh! Pretty big words for a nonscientist."

"Stop it. I already said I wasn't a scientist."

"Neither is she."

We glared at each other.

"She's a reporter."

"Who happens to know a lot more about science than I do."

"Humph."

It was the perfect moment for the caregiver to walk in, which she did, bearing three mugs of coffee on a tray. Three mugs. Dr. Tennyson and I exchanged glances.

"Mouse, this is Debbie; Debbie, Mouse."

She looked to be about my own age, pleasant and comfortable in her skin. "I'm a great fan of yours," she said, handing me a mug. She gave one to Dr. T and pulled up a third chair, casual as can be. "So, what are we talking about?"

I was shocked. My time with Dr. Tennyson was sacred.

It was his house, though, so I let him decide how he wanted to handle it.

He didn't blink an eye.

"Mouse was just talking about degradation."

"Oh, I just hate it when people start saying degrading things about others," she said to me.

Dr. T couldn't help smiling. "I don't think that's the kind of degradation he is talking about."

She looked confused.

"Go ahead, Mouse, give her the context," he said sadistically, playing with me like he a cat with a, well, with a mouse.

Debbie must have seen my panic, or maybe she was startled by this sudden aggressive streak in her client. "Did I say something wrong?"

"No, no, no," he assured her. I think he was a little startled himself. Certainly, his tone was gentler when he asked me to continue.

I gathered my wits together and framed an answer. "I was talking with a friend about *Glyphosate*. It's the scientific name for MowDown™ herbicide."

She perked up. "The stuff I spray on my lawn?"

"Exactly." I began to preen. She was, after all, my audience, a perfect representative of the people who read my column. I wasn't writing for scientists; I was writing for her. Let Dr. Tennyson try to do that.

He might have been thinking that this was an opportunity to observe me in action, which was something he never got to see. He dropped the sarcasm and encouraged me to continue.

"This friend wanted to know what happens to Mow-Down™ after the plant absorbs it."

"Well, I don't see that that's any big mystery," Debbie said. "The plant dies."

"I think there's more to it than that."

"Like what?"

I tried to deflect her question to Dr. T, but he wouldn't accept it. "Go ahead, Mouse, see if you can't figure it out on your own. I'll fill in any blanks if you need help."

This was embarrassing, but it was also an opportunity to tap into his knowledge in a different way. Instead of my interrogator, he would be my coach. I needed to put my stupid pride away and be humble enough to learn in front of one of my readers. I thought about the dead plant. Ah! "So, now you have a dead plant – let's say a dandelion – in your yard. And let's say you don't pull it up. You just leave it in the ground."

"Until I mow it. Then it's gone."

"But the root is still there."

"I didn't think about that," she said. "I mean, since I poisoned it, it's not going to grow back. It's like it's gone. But you're right; the root is still there."

"And most of the MowDown™ is still in the root, and when the root degrades – which is just a fancy word for rots – the MowDown™ enters the soil."

Dr. T. burst out laughing. "Mouse! The root doesn't degrade; it's the MowDown™ ™ that degrades."

Debbie looked from one of us to the other. "So degrading is not the same thing as rotting?"

The professor part of Dr. T took over before I could further bungle the answer. "The word you're looking for is 'decomposing,'" he said. "But think about what a lawn really is. To you, it's a carpet that sits on top of some dirt and has the annoying habit of adding flowers when you're not looking."

"That's hardly fair."

"Let me describe the way I see it, and then you can tell me which definition is closer to your own. To me, a lawn is a crop you throw away before it matures."

"That's just stupid," she blurted out, forgetting for a moment that he was her client. To cover her embarrassment, she turned to me. "Is he always like this?"

"Just with me."

He jumped back in. "You don't think of yourself as a farmer, but in a way you are. Some farmers raise grass. Other farmers raise dandelions. So, one farmer sees a dandelion and calls it a weed; the other farmer sees it as a crop, and if there is any grass coming up, he sees the grass as a weed."

She nodded reluctantly.

"But a lawn owner raises a crop of grass and then mows it down when it's a couple of inches high and throws it away to rot in some landfill."

"How about composting?" I asked.

"Rotting close by," he said dismissively.

Debbie wasn't used to this kind of banter, so I spoke up on her behalf. "That doesn't mean she thinks of her lawn like a carpet lying on top of some dirt. At least she knows that there are roots in there."

"You might think you know about roots, but I rather doubt it. A lot is going on down there that you are completely oblivious to. Roots aren't just a carpet pad to keep your lawn from sliding around, you know."

The famous sarcasm of Dr. Tennyson used to frighten me, but I'd gotten used to it. In fact, if it did anything, it energized me. "You're the one who's sliding around. We were talking about *Glyphosate*, remember?"

"I haven't forgotten," he said with a smile. "You can't talk about *Glyphosate* without talking about roots, but if you'd prefer, we can start with the leaves and work our way down."

"What fun."

"Do you ever think about the air that surrounds the leaves of plants?"

"Nope."

"How about you, Debbie?"

"I can't say I have."

"See, that's the difficulty we are all up against; we think we can take a plant out of its environment and study it as if we'd ordered it from a catalog. Plants need air, just like animals do. In the case of plants, they absorb a lot of carbon dioxide and release a lot of oxygen, but they're just as dependent on air as we are. Now, where are they going to get that air? Well, through their leaves, mostly. So, what do you think is going to happen if you clog up that air with soot or volcanic ash? The plants are going to die. So, one way to poison a plant is to interfere with its ability to absorb air through its leaves. Another is to take away its water. If you have a drought, the soil dries out, but you also have to consider the fact that the air is probably going to be extremely dry, as well. If you don't have a drought, you can do the same thing with poisons. So, really, talking about leaves isn't all that different from talking about roots, except that you see them."

"I still haven't heard you talk about *Glyphosate*," I pointed out.

"*Glyphosate* is a poison, which is fine, but it doesn't tell us much. There are thousands, if not millions, of poisons in the world. Let's say most of them would kill dandelions. The question is, why choose Glyphosate over all those alternatives? There are actually several questions you might consider. Care to suggest any?"

Debbie flinched but came up with an answer. "Cost."

He groaned. "I was so hoping that wouldn't be the first one that came to mind."

He turned to me.

"Whether I can buy it at my local hardware store," I said.

He shook his head in wonder. "I can't believe you came up with an answer even worse than Debby's."

I gave her a reassuring wink.

"Besides price and convenience," Dr. T went on, "here are some of the issues any farmer or lawn owner should be asking. First, what does the poison kill besides the weeds? Second, how toxic is it? Third, how do you apply it? Fourth, how does it work? Fifth, when do you apply it, and do you have to apply it more than once? And finally, question number six, how long does it last in the ground as a poison?"

I didn't know about Debbie, but I hadn't considered a single one. I took out my reporter's notebook and asked him to repeat the list.

Since I was showing him due respect, he patiently repeated them.

I looked them over. "I don't see the word degradation. Where does that come in?"

"Number six," he said, "but let's hit the others first."

I began to complain about it taking too long.

"Oh, grow up," he said. "Now, wouldn't it be great if we could develop a poison that only kills one species? That way, you could spray as much as you wanted, as casually as you wanted, and the only thing to die would be the weed you were targeting. The problem is that all life is based on DNA, and that means there are deep similarities in the structures of every living thing. That means that poisons seldom kill just one organism; what's toxic to one will be toxic to many other, similar organisms. I'm not saying equally toxic, but harmful, none the less. So let's say you find a substance that kills crabgrass very effectively, but it also is toxic to dandelions, grass, house plants, and geraniums. You might still be able to use it if it only harms them a little bit. You apply a low dose; everything gets sick, but the crabgrass dies, and the other plants recover in a day or two. You can even apply this concept to specific parts of an organism. Think about someone with cancer. You inject poison into them that is more toxic to the tumors than it is to the other parts of the body. The poison takes a terrible toll on the patient, but it theoretically kills the tumors before it kills the whole person."

"Got it," I said.

"MowDown™ up works that way. It's more harmful to dandelions and other broadleaf plants than it is to most grasses, but if you put enough on your lawn, it'll kill everything.

"Really?" Debbie asked.

"Try it. Find a dandelion that is in the middle of some healthy-looking grass and spray the hell out of it, making sure you spray the grass around it at the same time. See what happens."

"You're saying the dandelion will die before the grass does?"

"Before, yes, but both will die."

"Then, I'd have a bald spot in my lawn."

"And you will have learned something."

"I think I'll pass."

He turned back to me. "The next thing we ask is how toxic the poison is. That's where your C8 comes in. It's so toxic that even a small spill becomes an emergency. And, let's face it, accidents do happen. Chemical spills are bad enough but think about viruses like smallpox, that can multiply and spread. Now you've got an epidemic. Or think of a fungus that kills unwanted shrubs and undergrowth, but you find out too late that it also kills chestnut trees. Suddenly, four billion American Chestnut trees are gone. Those are extremes, of course, but the general rule is that you want to use the least toxic poison that gets the job done, all other things being equal."

"That makes sense."

"We also want to know exactly how poison works, if that's possible."

"Why?" Debbie asked. "I mean, if it works, it works."

"Sure," he replied, "and for thousands of years, that's what we did. We stumbled upon something that works, and we used it without understanding how it worked. If you can figure that out, though, you can find ways to make it stronger or make it cheaper, or we might find ways to defend against it. There might be an antidote, for example, like we now have for snake bites. IF we know exactly how it works, we might be able to purify it or alter it just a little bit so that we don't have as many side effects. Tell me, Debbie, do you grow marijuana in your back yard?"

She drew back in alarm.

"Even just a little for recreational purposes?"

She began to sputter.

"Yeah, probably not," he said. "But if you did, and you didn't want your neighbors to know it, wouldn't you prefer to grow the strongest, purest strain?"

"I swear, I don't grow it."

"Bad example, in any case," he conceded.

"You mean because it isn't a poison?" I asked, just to needle him.

"Tell that to your lungs," he snarled. "Let's move on. What's next on our list?"

I consulted my notes. "When to apply it and whether you need to apply it more than once."

"So, Debbie," he said, "do you spray weed killer on your lawn in the Spring?"

"Actually, I use weed and feed. That way, I kill the weeds and help the grass at the same time."

"Did you know that Canada recently banned all forms of weed and feed? That's because too much of it gets sprayed on healthy parts of the lawn that don't need it. The excess drains into the groundwater, rather than being absorbed into the roots of the grass. What you end up with are algae blooms like we see around Toledo. That's just the fertilizer part. The pesticide part – which is not necessarily Glyphosate – takes several days to be absorbed by the broad leaves of the dandelions. If it rains during that time, the poison gets washed off and also enters the groundwater. Even if it doesn't rain, it's like a coating of dust, and if you have kids or pets, they're going to pick up that dust on their feet or shoes and carry it into the house. You might think this doesn't matter, but the various poisons accumulate over time, and we can see and measure the buildup in blood and urine samples from little kids and pets who have been exposed to weed and feed. Once it gets concentrated in the blood and tissues, it can have serious effects in adults; in kids, it's much worse."

Debbie was aghast. "I have grandchildren who play in my backyard."

"Then stop using weed and feed, immediately."

"What if they're already contaminated?"

"Nothing to be done about that, I'm afraid."

I couldn't stand seeing her so distraught. "If it were as bad as all that, there'd be all kinds of warnings. They'd be screening kids at school."

"There are warnings on the bags," Dr. T said, "but how many homeowners follow them to the letter? And as for screenings, the problem is that a blood test might show the presence of certain toxins, but it wouldn't tell you how they got into the body. Who's to say it was your own back yard? Let's say you are one of the conscientious ones who use an organic herbicide, but your next-door neighbor sprays his yard like crazy, and all that dust gets blown onto your yard. Try taking that to court. That's why I like the Canadian law that simply prohibits weed and feed altogether."

Debbie got up. "Well, that was most enlightening. I'll leave the two of you alone and get some work done."

When she was out of earshot, I told Dr. T that he didn't need to scare her like that.

"I was mainly talking to you."

"It doesn't matter. You scared her. Besides, it doesn't really apply to me. I don't have kids, and I live in an apartment complex. I have no say in how they maintain the grounds."

"But, your readers have yards."

"True." *Not that they would want to hear about it,* I thought. *Too many articles along those lines and they'd start looking at me like some kind of crank.*

"If it was just back yards, I wouldn't harp on it," he went on. "The thing is, Mouse, yards are just a microcosm of farming. Take a car trip across the middle of Ohio. Take note of all those acres – mile after mile – acres upon acres of corn, and imagine all that land being sprayed two or three times a year by some version of weed and feed or MowDown™. And think about all those chemicals entering the soil. The advantage of having farmers apply it is that they have to weigh the costs of the herbicides against the gain in crop yields, so they do their best to apply the least amount possible to do the job. And, trust me, they do read labels. The average homeowner puts down twenty to thirty times more poison than required. That's a fact, by the way. But what the heck, it's only twenty bucks a year, and who worries about saving twenty bucks if your lawn greens up nice and fast?"

"I bet a lot of it gets thrown out, too," I said.

"I'm sure you're right." He looked lost. "You know the image I have that really haunts me? It's of a panicked house-wife seeing a wasp in the kitchen and spraying half a bottle of wasp killer at it. That's a powerful neurotoxin, and I can't think of a better way to screw up the neural system of a young child." He shook his head, looking exhausted. "How did we got onto lawncare, anyway?"

"I was asking you about degradation."

He looked confused.

"Which you said was not the same thing as rotting or decomposing."

"I'm sorry I laughed at you."

"I'm used to it," I said.

"But this was in public," he added as if it didn't matter when we were alone. "I'll try not to do that anymore."

Rather than make a big deal about it, I said, "I do like it when it's just the two of us."

"Me, too." He didn't pause but went right on. "So, let's talk about soil."

Oh, God! I thought. Not soil. If I had to list the things I don't care about, soil would be right down there at the top. "Do we have to?"

"What would you rather talk about?"

"Hemorrhoids. Prostate cancer. The heartbreak of psoriasis."

He got that look that told me he was going to spend even longer talking about soil than he'd planned.

"Actually, though, Doctor T, I do have something I don't much want to talk about, but need to."

"Oh?"

"Agent Orange."

He leaned back and closed his eyes. When he spoke, it was to the ceiling. "That's got to be a topic for another day."

It worried me to hear the heaviness and sheer exhaustion in his voice. "Maybe I should leave you alone for now."

"If you wouldn't mind, Mouse."

"You go take a nap or whatever you need to do."

"Call me tomorrow, would you?"

"Sure."

On the way out, I beckoned to Debbie to go check on him. "I think I wore him out," I whispered.

"Could be," she said, not unkindly. "But he'll be fine after a nap. You really got him going there. I haven't seen him this animated since I started."

"Are you okay?"

She made a shushing sound. "Water off a duck's back."

PART THREE:

TARGETING CASTILIA

[2004 – about a year and a half before the raid]

CHAPTER 16:

Media Strategy

The surveillance of Dr. Tennyson that started in 2004 was fruitful beyond expectation; the man was directly connected to half a dozen employees and connected by one degree of separation from ten more. Using the new contact mapping program from DARPA, Duncan documented that these employees were scattered across the organization, working at seven different manufacturing plants in jobs that ranged from a plant manager down to a machine shop operator. None of them seemed to be connected to each other. It was as if Jeremiah Tennyson had personally recruited them to rat out their own company. This was impossible, Duncan argued; Dr. Tennyson was a private man, almost a recluse. The idea of him traveling around the country, hanging out in bars near Stanhope plants, and casually striking up conversations with workers until he found the right malcontent was ludicrous.

The implications were alarming. Stanhope was riddled with disgruntled, angry employees who were actively seeking out people on the outside to talk to. Dr. Tennyson was highly visible as a foe of the corporation, but he was hardly the only person privy to some of their most sensitive information. Who knew how many other leakers were still on the corporate payroll?

In one way, the isolation of the various informants made the job of shutting them down easier. Ronnie Haskins set up a small working team consisting of Duncan, the head of Human Resources, and one of Shira's legal staff to make a list of leakers and fire them all within a three-month window. The official reason for terminating them was never that they leaked information to the press. The last thing Stanhope wanted was for one of them to file a whistle-blower complaint against them. There are always reasons to fire somebody if you really want to, and the human resource department at Stanhope was as ruthless as their legal department.

As the leakers got fired, the messages to and from Dr. Tennyson dried up. After six months, the risk of keeping a tap on his phone and computer began to outweigh the benefits. They cut him loose.

Duncan was sorry to do so but assuaged his disappointment by reveling in how isolated Dr. Tennyson was. "You're irrelevant now," he muttered to himself. "And look! Look who's thriving, expanding operations around the world: Stanhope. Chew on that, asshole."

While Duncan was shutting down the Tennyson network, Shira and Robert built up a many-layered defensive stockade around the class action lawsuit in Cincinnati. They couldn't just fire people the way Duncan and his team could, but they could try to keep the case from actually coming before a jury. Still, it just wouldn't go away. That Cincinnati lawyer Maeve Waldock was relentless, and the more they stalled, the more plaintiffs she added, and the larger the settlement she wanted.

Ronnie had a private conversation with Ginny Powell, VP of media relations. He asked her to do some background reading about the newspaper industry and how it was currently structured. He knew there had been a lot of changes, but lacked the details he would need to make any decisions.

Ginny knew her boss was a student of history and that one of his passions was the Civil War. She wondered if she should check out what the newspapers were like back then and contrast that to today's media world. Once she got started, a whole new panorama opened up to her, giving her a better perspective of the large changes taking place in their world today. The more she thought about it, the more confident she felt that he would appreciate this longer view, even if there were others in the room who would be rolling their eyes.

Sure enough, when Ronnie summoned her back to review her findings, she found Duncan Gabardine, Shira Beck, and Scott Radinsky, their chief acquisitions guy already sitting there in the conference room. Ronnie explained that he wanted everyone to hear what Ginny had turned up.

"The whole industry is restructuring," she began, but was immediately interrupted by Shira.

"Which industry?"

"Excellent question," Ginny replied. "That's part of the whole restructuring going on today. Right now, I'm focused on newspapers, especially ones in smaller markets like Toledo and Sandusky. Let me ask you a question. Does anyone know how long those smaller papers have been around?"

Nobody hazarded a guess.

"We're talking pre-Civil War. The Sandusky Daily News and the Toledo Vindicator have been in continuous operation as family owned businesses since the 1820's."

"Well, that's impressive," said Ronnie.

"Did you say Vindicator?" asked Shira. "That's quite a name."

"A lot of interesting names back then," Ginny acknowledged.

Shira gave a little laugh. "It would make a great brand name," she said, "though for what, I'm not sure."

"How about one of your legal teams?" Duncan suggested, just to piss her off. Which it did.

Ginny hurried ahead, ignoring Duncan. "Back then, they didn't have electricity to power printing presses – or any of the communications that used electricity like telegraph, telephone or radio. Just think about that for a second. News arrived by stagecoach or ocean liners and got printed by hand-cranked presses, one sheet at a time."

"Sounds like what Guttenberg invented," said Ronnie.

"It wasn't all that different," Ginny replied, appreciating his interest, "but that's what it was like when these local newspapers got started. There's something else that you have to take into account, as well. Back then, there was no such thing as a photograph, let alone any way to print one on a printing press. All you had were hand-made lithographs."

She sensed she was losing her audience. "Along comes the Industrial Revolution and in the span of two generations you've got railroads crossing the entire country, telegraph lines, telephones, cameras, big printing presses powered by electrical motors, and all the rest. A whole new kind of journalist came into being. They were called 'reporters' as opposed to simply 'writers' or 'journalists.' Things speeded up and became national rather than local. One of these new 're-porters' could telegraph a story about a fire or a battle in some war, have it printed overnight on high-speed presses, loaded onto trains, and distributed across a whole region the next day. The public became obsessed with this rapid-fire news, so this was when the special editions started coming out."

"Extra! Extra! Read all about it! Is that what you mean?" Shira asked.

"That's exactly what I mean. Not only would you have your daily or weekly paper, but if a big enough story came along, you could get this extra edition."

"Okay," said Ronnie, getting a little impatient. "So is

this when these conglomerates started up?"

"No. Not quite yet. What you had was the beginning of the big independent newspapers like the New York Herald extending their reach but not necessarily buying smaller papers. These were fierce competitors led by editors and publishers with strong connections to individual politicians or political parties. It was an insider's game."

"The kind we like to play," Shira said.

Ronnie gave her sharp look. "True enough. The question is whether it's still working for us." With a glance, he redirected their focus back to Ginny.

"So you've got tons of local papers like the Vindicator or the Straight Shooter covering the local news, and selling their papers in newsstands right beside these larger papers out of New York or Chicago. That lasts pretty much up to the end of World War Two. Over the next decade the big newspaper chains began gobbling up the smaller local rags. By 1960, guess how many papers like the Daily Journal were owned by a chain?"

"Over half?" Duncan said.

"Ninety percent of them," Shira said, delighted to put Duncan know-it-all in his place.

"That's quite a change," said Scott Radinsky.

"The thing about the big chains is that they were headed by newspaper people. The big ones like the New York Times or the Chicago Tribune or McClatchy and Gannett started out as family newspapers that gobbled up other, smaller newspapers."

"So that takes us to 1960," said Ronnie. "Then what?"

"Well, the chains are still there, but there's been a major transition in terms of who owns them. Now the hedge fund managers and other financial guys are in charge. They don't have backgrounds in newspapers or any other kind of media.

They are money people, pure and simple. And all they care about is the bottom line. Thousands of smaller papers are out of business altogether, and in those who are still around, staff has been drastically cut. In Sandusky, they are down to seven reporters. That's it. As you can imagine, the local editors and reporters don't like their corporate owners very much."

"I can imagine," said Shira.

"The good news for us is that true investigative journalism is almost a thing of the past, especially among the newspapers. Our whole strategy of building in smaller communities fits this nicely. These guys are struggling to stay alive from day to day. They don't have the budgets or staff to do anything in-depth."

She held up a finger. "However, news wants to get out. If it can't get out through the local newspaper, it finds some other channel. Television and the big cable networks are all moment by moment. Taking the time to dig into larger stories or events that move slowly is just not their thing. So, when it comes to things like dumping C8 into the Ohio River for forty years, well, that's just too slow a story. If a plant blows up, like what happened in Cleveland, then, yes, that gets covered, but just until the fire goes out or a different plant explodes somewhere else."

"You're confusing me," Ronnie said. "Where's all this going?"

Ginny was glad she'd given this serious thought and that she'd had a long conversation with Scott Radinsky a week earlier. "Think about our current situation when it comes to media. It works basically on two scales. At one end, we have connections with local politicians and newspapers like Congressman Wicker and Warren Davis at the Cincinnati Blade. So we've got our ears to the ground and a lot of control over what gets covered in places where our plants are located. That's great. At the opposite end of the scale, we have all our connections in Washington and strong relationships with the big newspapers like the New York Times, the Chicago Tribune, The Washington Post, etc., etc. What we don't have is much of a relationship with this middle-ground of these conglomerates like McClatchy or Media IV. If we want to control what gets covered by the Cincinnati paper, we can't rely on the local editor. A lot of what he ends up covering is dictated by these conglomerates."

"Much as he resents it," Ronnie ventured.

"Boy, does he. They all do."

"But now you're saying we need to get in bed with them."

Ginny took a big gulp. This was the moment all this was leading up to. "That's what I'm saying."

"Sounds expensive."

"That's why I took the liberty of talking to Scott."

Ronnie raised his eyebrows, unsure of what he thought about that. On the one hand, Ginny had been working outside her remit, but on the other, she was taking independent, thoughtful action, possibly saving them all a lot of time. He turned to his head of finance. "What are we up against?"

"It's maybe not as bad as you think," Scott replied. "As Ginny was saying, these new conglomerates could care less about journalism. If this was ten, fifteen years ago, the old newspaper guys would resist a move by us. What business do we have trying to pretend we're concerned with journalism? Today, that's not an issue. And here's the nice thing when it comes to a new plant. The Toledo paper, the Sandusky paper, the Cleveland paper, the Cincinnati paper, and the Columbus paper are all part of Media IV."

"How about Detroit?'

"They're still independent."

"I suppose you can't get them all," Ronnie said with a

sigh. "So, what's the play with Media IV? I assume you have one."

"They're not in great shape," Scott said. "I think we could get on their board of directors with a purchase of 15% of their stock."

"And make money from it?"

"Nothing spectacular, but a reasonable return on equity."

"The real value would be in having influence over what they cover?"

"That's the ultimate goal," said Scott.

"There's something else," Ginny said, breaking in. "Controlling a story after the fact is all well and good, but if we have a seat at the table, we could find out about what their reporters are digging into before the news even breaks."

"Like the lawsuit over Parkers Ferry," said Ronnie.

Ginny noticed that Shira was nodding along. She looked over at Duncan.

He caught her gaze and joined in. "We might sniff out leakers we haven't found yet."

"Indeed," said Shira. "And I'm also thinking about a possible move to Sandusky or Toledo. If some local reporter is hearing rumors, I'd much rather get in front of them before his editor encourages him."

Ronnie thought it over. "God knows, we're flush with cash. Look into it and give me some firm numbers. In the meantime, Ginny, why don't you sit down with the editor in Sandusky and sound him out about what's it like to be part of Media IV, and while you're at it, get a sense of the local politics there."

"Can I hint about us building a plant in his back yard?"

"Hell no. Not a peep." He drummed his fingers on the

conference table. "Ginny, draw me a complete org chart of every facet of Media IV. I want to know what papers they own, what radio stations, tv, anything else. Satellite broadcast? Whatever. And I want a list of their management team and every writer they use, whether full-time or on assignment, with phone numbers. Once you've got that, give it to Duncan. I want him to build us a program to look for patterns, kind of like what we did with Tennyson."

He turned to Duncan. "I want to know whenever one of our employees talks to a reporter, and I want it in as close to real time as possible."

"That's a lot of data and a lot of noise," Duncan said.

"I'm sure you're right, but let's take a poke at this, all the same. We'll start with Sandusky and see what shakes out. If it looks worth our while, we can expand our focus to include all of Media IV, and if that seems worth it, we can keep going."

He turned to Scott. "Go ahead and buy us a seat on the board of directors at Media IV. Do it as fast as you can, but be discrete about it."

"You do realize that we don't know shit about running a newspaper," said Scott.

"I'm not talking about running it. I just want to control it."

"It's your nickel."

"Yes, it is, Scott. Go spend it."

CHAPTER 17:

The Sandusky Option

Six months later, Stanhope owned a 15% share of Media IV and a seat on their board of directors. The Parkers Ferry lawsuit was inching its way to a trial date despite every obstacle they threw in its path.

Ronnie called a meeting of his executive team. It was time to pull the trigger: begin a very public shutdown of the Parkers Ferry plant and a very covert purchase of land for a new Sandusky plant.

Robert Harris went over their options at a private lunch with Senator Courtney, who had suggested that Sandusky would be a better choice than Toledo. The Maumee River that ran through Toledo was already one of the most polluted rivers in the country, and the mayor and city council were under enormous pressure to clean it up. The Sandusky River was pretty much taken for granted. Furthermore, Sandusky's population had been shrinking, and the mayor and city council were desperate for new business. They would welcome a new manufacturing facility with open arms.

Senator Courtney's recommendation came with one caution; for some reason, the area around Sandusky was a hotbed of organic farmers opposed to Stanhope and everything they manufactured and promoted.

Scott Radinsky argued that the organic farmers

couldn't be much of a threat, given that Sandusky lay comfortably inside the highest sales region in the country for MowDown™ herbicide and the whole panoply of MowDown Resistant™ seeds that formed the most profitable sector of Stanhope. "If sales mean anything, I'd say they love us in Sandusky."

"Still, if the Senator saw fit to mention them, we should check them out," Ronnie said. He turned to Duncan. "Why don't you take a day trip up to Sandusky and nose around? Tell us what you find."

Ronnie brought in a new face, a site planner named Lindsay Dow. He introduced her and explained that she and Scott Radinsky would do a joint presentation on their plans.

Lindsay projected a large topographical map of the lower half of the Sandusky River on the screen at the front of the room. "I'm going to start with geography and some existing structures," she said. "Scott is going to follow that by talking about the economics of choosing a site, and then I'll take over again and show you the plan we're proposing."

She began pointing out the critical features of the local geography. "The Sandusky River is 133 miles long, but for our purposes, we can forget about everything south of the Ballville Dam, which is 37 miles upstream from Lake Erie. Anyone ever hear of Ballville?"

Apparently not. "For all intents and purposes, it's part of Fremont," she added. "Anyone hear of that?"

Nobody seemed to.

She gave up to concentrate on the river. "Let's follow the wiggly line that represents the Sandusky River north from Ballville up to Sandusky. As you can see, it's basically nothing but farmland all around, and the curvy shape is a clue about how very flat the land is. The deepest the river gets is right there by the dam, a whole foot and a half deep. So, very shallow, very flat, very twisty river. If you love catching walleye, you'll love this because it's a wonderful breeding ground for them. If you want to build a manufacturing plant, it's a challenge. Any toxic release is going to affect the breeding grounds for walleye, and that means fewer fish entering Lake Erie, and that means that the local fishermen and tourists are going to raise a ruckus a lot quicker than the EPA."

"And a lot louder," Shira Beck added.

"Yep," said Ronnie.

Lindsay brought them back to the map. "Let's look at the other end, where the river flows into Sandusky. As you can see, the whole area is very complex. You've got this kind of dumbbell shape that represents Sandusky Bay. The city of Sandusky lies at the southeast corner. Then there's this peninsula that juts out protecting Sandusky from the rest of Lake Erie. This is Cedar Point, where the amusement park is. They say you can see all the way to Cleveland from the highest rollercoaster, but you'd better look fast because you're only there for 1.4 seconds."

She paused for a polite laugh.

"You can certainly see Sandusky and the whole bay area. This means that any new construction of a large manufacturing facility will be noticed by literally millions of tourists, which is not what we want. So, simply based on that fact alone, I recommended to Scott that we look in this area of the river that stretches from the back of the large bay to Ballville. That brings us down to a stretch of about fifteen to twenty miles: far enough from Cedar Point to be invisible and downstream from the dam."

Scott took over. "That's the geography," he began, moving to the next slide. "Here are the economics of the area. The big tradeoff is between land values, specific opportunities, and proximity to the harbor. The closer to the harbor, the better in terms of shipping, but conversely, the higher the cost of land. We also have issues with where the existing roads are. I won't bother you with you a stack of spreadsheets and scenarios, but here's where we see our best option. It's pretty close to Ballville. There used to be a YMCA camp – Camp Wamblee -- right on the river there, but it burned down in 1982. There was a second camp for girls just outside the village of Castilia. It's much smaller. The only reason to bring it up is that both parcels reverted back to the First Bank of Castilia when the YMCA defaulted on the lease agreement. For the past twenty-two years, the bank has been wanting to get it off their books and sell them outright. In the meantime, they have broken it up into some sub-parcels and are leasing it to local farmers, none of whom have the resources to purchase the whole thing. We held some very discreet conversations with the bank president, Elliott Washburn. Bottom line, we can buy it for five and a half million bucks, give or take. Washburn also raised the possibility that we make an offer to buy out Montrose's development in Castilia. Apparently, they want out.

"What have they got going on there?"

"A bunch of hippies and artists living there, farming some of the land and selling stuff to tourists on the way to Cedar Point."

"They still have communes?" asked Robert, breaking in.

"They still have hippies?" asked Shira, almost simultaneously.

"Surprised the hell out of me," Scott admitted. "It's actually a little more complicated than that. The commune runs it, but the parcel itself is leased from the bank by a real estate developer out east called Montrose Development. It's basically a land bank. As soon as the land around there becomes valuable enough, they'll exercise their options and sell it off to the highest bidder."

"Why would they expect land values to improve?"

"I don't know," Scott said. "There are rumors of a new road branching off the Ohio Turnpike leading to Sandusky. I haven't confirmed that though."

"Okay," said Ronnie. "A topic for another day. What's the scoop on the main part where you think we should build?"

Scott turned things back to the site planner. Lindsay spent the next half hour going through a detailed plan showing the various structures within the plant, access roads, parking lots, intake and discharge pipes from the Sandusky River, existing powerlines, and a host of other critical details. From time to time, she turned things back to Scott, who filled in a timeline and estimated construction costs as they moved from one stage to another. When they concluded, they passed out binders filled with supporting documents.

Ronnie congratulated them on a fine presentation. "Now," he said, "let's poke holes in it; see if it leaks. Anybody?"

Shira was the first to jump in. "There are going to be a lot of legal issues, no matter where we locate. Sometimes it's easier to work with a big city than a local township, where everybody knows everybody else's business and any decision they make will affect their own friends and relatives. In your proposal, we have this blip of a town called Ballpoint Pen..."

"Ballview," said Scott.

She grinned at him. "Ballville. That's small enough, but then we have this bank in Castilia, so now we have two communities, no doubt with their own zoning restrictions, and who knows what else that we're going to have to deal with."

"Any suggestions?" Ronne asked.

"Top of my head? Buy both parcels, sell off the hippie commune at a fire sale price, and move our holdings to a bank in Toledo or Cleveland. The sooner we get out of that incestuous place..."

"Now, Shira, be nice."

"Localized economy, then, the better."

"Okay. Any other thoughts?"

"Again, this is just top of my head, but could we approach the Castilia bank with a proposal to buy that land to build a distribution center?"

"You mean, rather than a manufacturing plant?"

"Just to get started. It's going to take three years to build the plant. Can we fiddle with the plan to begin with a functioning distribution center for a year or two before turning it into a plant? I mean, once we're there and our finances are in Cleveland, we will have a lot more leverage and a lot better understanding of the politics involved."

Ronnie turned to Scott and Lindsay. "How long would it take for you to work up that scenario?"

"A month, I suppose."

"I want it in two weeks."

They nodded reluctantly.

"Okay, anything else?"

"Does the name Fred Williams ring any bells?"

"The guy who tried to sue us for ruining his organic certification?" Shira asked.

"That's the guy, alright."

She explained the case to the others in the meeting. "You know how we always have to go after farmers who steal our patented seeds? Well, this Williams guy flipped that on its head. He claimed that his neighbor used MowDown™ on his fields. Some of it got carried by the wind onto his organic fields – enough that it showed up in an inspection by the organic farming association that recertifies farms every four years. Because our herbicides were found in his soil, he lost his certification, which cost him half of his business. So he sued his neighbor, and while he was at it, he sued us."

"So, what happened?" Ronnie asked. "Did we settle out of court?"

"We tried. He's a stubborn old man who'd rather go bankrupt than back down over a point of honor. Well, he got his wish. He refused to back down, we countersued, and he ended up losing his farm."

"So, he has no love for us."

"It was one of those unfortunate cases where we had to take a hard line to make sure it didn't turn into a precedent for future cases."

The only reaction Ronnie showed was a slight twitch of his shoulder. He knew it was necessary, but he didn't like it. It made Stanhope look like a bully.

Ronnie decided to bring things to a close and began issuing orders. "Scott and Lindsay, work up a plan for building a distribution center like Shira suggested. Let's say it gets built in six months. Trucks start using it while work continues around the main building, turning it into our new plant. We go public with our intentions as late as possible. Maybe a year later. By then, the locals will be used to trucks coming and going on the highways. The difference will be that the trucks arriving there will be hauling raw ingredients, and the trucks leaving will be loaded with finished products. The whole manufacturing process will be behind walls and out of sight."

Scott looked dubious. "I'm not sure that's going to work. Word will get out."

"By then, we'll have all the permits and zoning issues cleared up. People will protest, but it will be too late to do anything."

"Okay."

"How long do you need to sketch out a plan?"

"A couple of months."

Ronnie scowled. "You've got three weeks. Get it done."

"Yes, sir."

He turned to Robert Harris. "As soon as you chance to read over the plan from Scott and Lindsay, schedule another lunch with Senator Courtney. Don't show him the details; just give him an executive summary. See if he can assist or if he thinks it's unworkable. I want to know before we commit."

"Yes, sir."

Now it was Duncan's turn. "See what you can find out about that bank in Castilia and those real estate developers from New Jersey."

"Okay."

"And then take a day trip out there and see if you can tour that hippie commune. Find out all you can about this organic farmers group. Are they for real or just some fringe element?"

"Yes, sir."

Finally, he turned to Ginny. "We're on the board of Media IV now. Use that to get an appointment to sit down with the editor of the newspaper there."

"The Daily Journal."

"See what you can find out about the local scene. If Castilia comes up, ask about those hippies. If it doesn't, ask about the environmentalists in general."

"Yes, sir."

"Oh, and one other thing. See if you can get him to talk about being swallowed up by Media IV. Say we can help him, but keep it vague. We want him on our side, letting us know what's about to happen before it does, and telling our story to the locals. Charm him. You know how to do that."

She raised her eyebrows at him.

"You charm me every day, sir."

CHAPTER 18:

Targeting Castilia

Ronnie began the first meeting of Stanhope's executive committee in 2006 by asking each person to list their biggest hope and worst fear for the coming year. The hopes varied widely, but universally the biggest worry was the lawsuit in Parkers Ferry and the urgency of shutting that plant down and building a replacement.

"How did your lunch with Senator Courtney go?" he asked his lobbyist.

"It was long and very liquid," Robert replied.

"Old school Washington."

"At least it didn't involve coke or party drugs. That's still confined to the staff level, thank God. I'm getting too old for this racket."

Ronnie wondered if this might be Robert's last year. He hoped not.

"Anyway, he thought Shira's plan was a good one. Ease our way into the situation and build as much goodwill as we can. He'll help grease the wheels for us. It's going to be a high-touch, in-person process. He suggested we install a full-time person until the new plant opens."

"What did he have in mind?"

"He gave me a couple of suggestions. We could put a

media person in place or set up a charitable foundation head-quartered in Sandusky. We could also build a research facility there to help farmers in the region with whatever challenges they are facing."

"The senator may be crass, but he's not stupid," Ronnie said.

Robert nodded.

"Did you ask him about this bank in Castilia?"

Robert puffed out his chest. "The First Bank of Castilia," he announced grandly. Then he drooped his shoulders in fine dramatic form. "He said he'd never heard of it."

"Oh, well." Ronnie turned to Ginny. "You met with the editor of the Daily Journal?"

She smiled wryly. "It helps to be on the board of Media IV. The editor is a guy named Mark Malandry, and he's a pure newspaper editor from head to toe. Grew up in the business and can't imagine a better job than being a small-town news guy. Kind of surprised me. Wouldn't he prefer to work for a bigger paper like the Plain Speaker? Nope. He likes to know his readers and be part of making Sandusky and its surrounding area a better place to live."

"An idealist, in other words?"

"Kind of singed around the edges, but yes. I told him we were new to the board of Media IV and wanted his unvarnished opinion on what their takeover of his paper was like. Let's just say he didn't hold back. 'Mean fuckers. They'd stab their own mothers in the back if it got them a better return on their investments.' That's a direct quote. He told me the only con-versations he's had with his new owners are about money and trimming staff. He had to let one of his reporters go, so now he's down to four, counting himself. I dangled the possibility of reversing that, and his eyes lit up. We treat him right, and he could be a real ally."

Ronnie asked what her approach would be.

"Something along the lines of what Senator Courtney was saying, I guess. I wonder if we could set up a local charity or outreach office and hire somebody who would work half time for us and half time for Malandry. We could pay our guy well enough so that what he made at the newspaper wouldn't put him in poverty."

"Intriguing," said Ronnie.

"And dangerous," said Shira. "We don't want to imbed another leaker in our company."

"Something to talk about later, then," he told her. "Back to you, Ginny."

"I asked him about the Fred Williams case and whether it was part of the past or still resonating. 'Festering' is the word he used. Among a certain core group of farmers and environmentalists, our name is mud."

"That's on his head," Shira declared. "We gave him every chance."

"Well, nobody's forgotten. That's for sure. The majority of the farmers think he's a stubborn old coot with old fashioned ideas of how to make money off the land, but even they didn't like the way it turned out. I asked him about the group that supported Williams, and I got the impression that he was one of them. He told me about that commune in Castilia and how it's sort of the center of the whole organic farming network. I asked him how long they've been around, and he said twenty years. I guess they've turned into entrepreneurs or something. They started with basically nothing, and now they have a thriving community that is a mixture of organic farmers and sculptors with a few high-end artisans thrown in for good measure. One of them makes saddles that sell all across the country. He's got a waiting list a mile long, including some Hollywood studios, but he refuses to hire anyone to help him. Another is a guy who customizes motorcycles for rich techies in Seattle and San Francisco. He, too, has a waiting list. Does one custom job at a time. But at the same time, while he's doing that, he also runs a small garage that takes care of the commune's tractors and is always available to the wider community in a pinch. You can walk into his space and see a new Harley sitting next to a 1950 Ford tractor. It's that kind of place."

"Strange," said Ronnie.

"Unique. I guess they're famous all across the country among a certain set of people, but you wouldn't know they exist unless you are part of that scene. They've got this annual festival at the Spring Equinox that's been going for ten years. It keeps getting bigger and bigger."

"What's it called?"

"The Flaming Trout Festival."

The group looked around the table in a kind of wonderment. This was not the kind of conversation they were used to having.

"I can tell you a lot about that if you want," Duncan interjected. "I went out there and got a quick tour of the place."

Ginny gave him a dirty look. She had never liked Duncan, and she didn't appreciate him upstaging her little presentation. Unfortunately, the little worm was one of Ronnie's favorites. So it was to Duncan that he addressed his follow up question, not her.

"Did they explain why they call it Flaming Trout?"

"They've got this organic trout farm in a little pond there."

"What the hell is an organic trout farm?" asked Shira.

"According to them, it boils down to two things: they only feed their trout organic food, and they keep them isolated in this pond so they never get any of the parasites or diseases that trout can pick up in Lake Erie."

"And that's what started the festival?"

"Actually, no. Not directly. What kicked it off was when a couple of their artists got together and built this huge glass sculpture of a trout. The thing must be three stories tall. It's beautiful to tell you the truth. And they've got all these lights on the inside which turn different colors. That's what started it. But then they built a tall windmill out in the parking lot to generate a lot of their own power and moved the trout sculpture in front of it, kind of incorporating it into the base. For the festival, they light up the trout and then, at the dot of midnight at the equinox when winter officially turns into spring, they set the windmill blades on fire."

"What?"

Duncan nodded happily. "I guess one of the hippies was an engineer in his previous life, and he rigged up a whole system to pump kerosene to the blades, so they keep burning for hours. Each year, they have to replace them."

"What happens to the trout?"

"Oh, it's well protected. It's just the blades that get destroyed."

Robert Harris liked the whole idea. "Maybe we should go," he said. "When is it coming up? Anybody know?"

"Equinox is March 21st this year," Duncan replied quickly, making Ginny grit her teeth. "But I don't think we'd fit in. It's mainly bikers and weirdos. Lots of drugs, from what I hear. It's modeled on the Burning Man Festival out west if you know about that."

Shrugs all around the table.

"There's something very strange going on in Castilia," Duncan continued.

"Stranger than a flaming trout?" Ronnie asked.

"Maybe not stranger, but relevant to us, and maybe a real opportunity."

The room got serious.

"You asked me to look into the bank and this development company that leases the land where the commune is – Montrose Development, headquartered in Trenton, New Jersey. I was wondering why a New Jersey developer would be involved in a weird little project in Castilia, Ohio. It turns out there is a family connection. One of the Montrose brothers is the proverbial black sheep of the family. He's a biker and a drug addict. The rest of the family wants to keep him out of the way and out of sight. A few years after the YMCA camp burned down, this guy met the head of the commune and they became friends. Then, when he had a bad accident..."

"Hold on," said Shira. "I'm getting lost. Do these characters have names we can use?"

Duncan grimaced. "I was afraid you'd ask. Okay. The CEO of Montrose Development is Kyle Montrose. His druggie younger brother is known as Skullman. The head of the hippies is known as Froggie."

"Christ!" exclaimed Shira. "What are we dealing with?"

"As I said, I was afraid you'd ask."

Ronnie was getting impatient. "Can we just get on with this?"

"We're back in the late 1980s here," said Duncan. "Skullman has a nasty accident and needs a long time in the hospital to deal with his injuries and then an even longer time in some sort of drug rehab program. The family wanted to get him as far out of the Anaheim biker community as possible. One thing leads to another, and they end up talking to this Froggie guy and make him an offer he can't resist. Montrose will take over the lease on the land, give them some funds to build it up a bit, and charge them next to nothing to live there. In exchange, the commune will take care of Skullman. Give him a new family, as it were, even build a new house for him after he's completely out of rehab. The hippies go for it. Skullman moves in. He's still there, and the family has one less thing to worry about."

Ronnie began drumming his fingers on the conference table.

"So, that explains how Montrose got involved. The question I had to ask myself was, why have they stayed so long? Why not get out? Flip the property, make a bundle, and trust that the status quo will continue regarding Skullman. It turns out that Montrose is dirty as hell. They've got connections to the Mafia and have been under surveillance by the Department of Revenue for years. A lot of money laundering going on. From what I can sniff out, they're using this little commune as a front to hide dirty assets from overseas, relying on the naivete of the hippies and their local bank to shuffle funds back and forth without raising suspicion. It worked for years and years, and no one was the wiser. But here's the thing. The feds have gotten worried about all the drugs getting passed around at the festival, and I guess they had a couple of undercover agents take pictures last year. Identified a couple of major players from the cartels meeting up there. And that got them linked up with this ongoing investigation of the Montrose group."

"Hold on," said Shira. "Who's cooperating with who, exactly?"

"FBI, ATF, and Revenue."

"Jesus! All this attention on little Castilia?" she cried.

"I won't ask how you know all this," Ronnie said diplomatically, "but please, do continue."

"You know how the Castilia bank wanted to unload both properties?"

"The one on the river and the one in Castilia?"

"Exactly. What I'm thinking is that with all this pressure and attention on Montrose, they may be open to selling the Castilia property for a song before they get dragged into some drug bust and suddenly having all their financial misdeeds come to light."

Scott gave it a moment's thought. "Could be. What about the brother?"

"They'd probably get him out of there and let us deal with the hippies however we wanted."

"Let's say you're right," Scott replied. "I still don't know why we'd want to own that property."

"We don't," said Duncan. "But what we want is leverage on the bank. What I'm thinking is that we find a way to leak a little information to them about the FBI and Department of Revenue suspicions."

"Leak?" said Ginny. "Isn't your job to stop leaks?"

Duncan was not fazed. "Turnabout's fair play."

Nobody contradicted him.

"You've obviously got a plan here," said Ronnie. "Go ahead and lay it all out."

"Well, this would be Scott's deal, not mine. All I would do is lay the groundwork. Have Scott make a lowball offer on the river location in Ballview – assuming we really want to go ahead with it. Let them reject it. Then I'll tip them off about the dangers of associating with Montrose. See if we can get a sit-down with the bank and Montrose and negotiate a fire sale deal that saves us a bundle and makes all their problems go away."

"But leaving us owning the Castilia property?"

"Yeah, until we sell it off."

"And move all our banking out of there at the same

time," said Shira.

Ronnie took over. "A lot of moving parts here, but we're as much under the gun as any of them. Time is not on our side with this damned lawsuit in Parkers Ferry. So, let's do this. Scott, make an offer to the bank to buy the riverfront property for a distribution center. And make sure it's a low-ball offer, just like Duncan suggested. Ginny, stay in touch with that editor and explore ways to get him his reporter back or whatever else might put him in our debt. Nobody says a word about Montrose or Castilia. Got that? Not a word until I give the okay. Duncan, keep doing whatever it is you do and keep me informed. Maybe we can just buy the property we want and be done with it. That would be the cleanest option. I'm more interested in speed than in the sales price. But if this gets sticky, we may want to follow up on Duncan's plan. Okay, then, everyone on board?"

Nods all around until he got to Robert.

"You've got an issue?"

"Just a question. Should I give a heads up to Senator Courtney?"

"Not on any of this. The only thing we share with him is our interest in building a distribution center. I don't want some other lobbyist getting him drunk and finding out our larger plans."

"Got it," said Robert.

The meeting was over.

PART IV:
The Assignment

[2006 – two weeks after the raid]

CHAPTER 19:

A Collusion of Editors

Peter Zenger was surprised when his secretary informed him that Mark Malandry, his counterpart at the Sandusky Daily Journal, was on the line. They had run into each other a few times but never really made any kind of connection. He was even more surprised when Malandry asked if they could meet in private somewhere outside of Cleveland. He suggested they meet halfway in the lovely town of Vermilion. He wanted to share some concerns he had and didn't want them to be seen talking together.

"Can you give me a hint?" Peter asked.

"It rhymes with Media Whore."

"Now I'm interested. How soon were you thinking?"

"Tomorrow."

They had lunch in a lovely restaurant overlooking the harbor, where the Vermilion River runs into Lake Erie. It was a beautiful spot, and they had no problem getting a seat by the windows since it was still March. In six weeks, the place would be crowded.

They chatted aimlessly for a bit, forming a quick rapport. It was Mark's initiative, so Peter let him bring up the reason for the slightly clandestine lunch when he felt ready. They ordered, and he got right to it. "You know Leonard Donnelley? VP of something or other at Media IV?"

"I might have shaken hands with him at some point."

"He came to see me yesterday with an ultimatum."

"Which is why you called?"

"Yeah," said Mark, "the minute I saw him drive out of the parking lot." He looked around for eavesdroppers. The closest patrons looked like they were in their eighties and were talking loudly so they could hear each other. "Are you old school enough to have a pocket notebook on you?"

Peter reached into his breast pocket and pulled one out.

Mark asked him to write down six dates:

Friday, February 24

Tuesday, March 14

Tuesday, March 21

Thursday, March 23

Friday, March 24

Wednesday, March 29

Tuesday, April 4

"Any of them strike you as significant?"

Peter shook his head. "Other than yesterday the 29th, no. I assume that's significant because of Donnelly's visit. Right?"

"Yep."

The waitress came to take their order. Peter discreetly turned his pocket notebook over.

"Let's start at the top," Mark said. "Early February, Stanhope Chemicals buys a 15% share in Media IV and gets a seat on their board of directors."

Peter kept himself from showing his shock. He hadn't

heard about that.

Mark saw right through him. "Don't worry, I didn't know about it at the time, either. Kind of interesting, wouldn't you say? You'd think our bosses would trumpet the fact to the whole world. I only put it together later. So, now we're at the top of our list. February 24 is when the big Cincinnati lawsuit against Stanhope gets announced."

"Oh, that's right," Peter said. He was not about to disclose that he'd called his special meeting two days earlier to tell his team to get on it.

"A week and a half later, this media rep from Stanhope comes waltzing into town wanting to talk to me. You know, Stanhope does a lot of business in Sandusky, but this is the first time anyone from there has bothered to stop in and say hello. So, it gets my attention. She's the one who tells me they own a piece of Media IV, and that really gets my attention. She spins this bullshit story that she's just making the rounds of the different outlets, checking in to get a feel for what's happening on the ground and how we're being treated by the conglomerate. I say all the usual stuff about times being tight and having to cut back, but, you know, we all understand the situation, and we're totally loyal to our new masters in Cincinnati. She lets me jabber on a bit, but then she tells me she's been hearing otherwise from some of the other papers. Talks a good story about improving the newspapers rather than just sitting on the board and pulling in a modest profit. I'd have dismissed her out of hand, except that she'd clearly done her homework. She knew exactly how many people were on our staff and the fact that I had to cut one of our four reporters last year."

"How are you coping with that?" she asked.

"I told her I was taking up as much of the slack as I could, myself, and that we were picking up more and more news stories from other papers owned by Media IV."

"Like the Plain Speaker?" Peter asked.

"I don't know if you've noticed."

Peter hadn't, but he did recognize the pattern since they'd been doing the same thing. It seemed like half the stories the PS ran were picked up from sister papers like Mark's Daily Journal as well as NYTimes and Washington Post.

"Ginny goes on to tell me how she's been telling her bosses at Stanhope that they need to pay more attention to the farming communities they serve and that one way to make them strong is to invest in their local newspapers. Her intent was to find small, independent ones like us, but then she realized she was late to the game because we were all getting gobbled up by these conglomerates like the Sinclair Group and Media IV. They did some analysis and decided to get involved with one conglomerate to see if it helped them better understand how the newspaper business worked in general. At the same time, they hoped to learn more about what the local communities were really saying about Stanhope. They narrowed it down to three, and Media IV was the cheapest opportunity, so they started there. And now she wanted to know what we needed to do right by our community."

"What did you tell her?" Peter asked.

"I told her to send money so I could hire my reporter back."

Peter scoffed. "How'd that go over?"

"Better than you might guess," Mark replied. He cut himself off while the waitress brought their food. "We floated a couple of ideas about how Stanhope could hire somebody halftime to work for them in educational outreach so we could pick up the rest as a part-time reporter. We both saw it as a tricky move, but it was interesting to see how seriously she was considering the idea. I told her if she was interested in seeing the town in a whole different light, she should come to the Flaming Trout Festival."

"The one that just got busted!"

"Hold on. I'm getting to that. I told her when it was, and she said she couldn't make it but asked me to send her any clippings from our coverage."

"Oh. So she wasn't there."

"No. Off she went, and I didn't hear another word from her, not even a thank you. I put it out of mind. And then came the whole fiasco of the feds storming in and arresting some hippies and a couple of tourists after everyone they were looking for had already left town. If I gave Ginny a thought, it was only to wish I'd had that extra reporter on hand. Well, and how glad I was she hadn't been there. It didn't exactly show us off in our best light."

"We enjoyed your coverage in Cleveland," Peter said.

"I bet you did."

Peter snorted.

"Now, look at that list of dates. You see the 21st? That's when the raid took place. One day later, Ginny shows up to ask me all about it. Doesn't wait for the clippings. Wants to know everything. We're right in the middle of writing the damned stories, and she's on me, trying to look over my shoulder. And it's not like she's some twenty-year-old rookie; she's got to be in her fifties. I fob her off on my photographer, who shows her a couple of hundred photos. She asked if she could have copies of them, but he's not dumb. Says she has to ask me. Meanwhile, I'm running around trying to get the story out. The best she can do is tell me she wants to be sure we keep covering the story and keep her in the loop. I told her yes just to get her out of our hair."

"Sure got her attention, I guess."

"Raised a few questions, once I calmed down enough to think about it," Mark replied.

"You think it was more than a coincidence?"

"I want to, but I can't see how. From the little I've been

able to pick up, the festival has been in the feds' crosshairs for a couple of years, plus it's got nothing to do with Stanhope. They're passing drugs around, not trading insider information."

Peter looked at his timeline. "So what's this on Friday the 24th?"

"That's when they released all the hippies except their leader, a guy named Froggie."

"Interesting name. You know him?"

"Everybody knows him personally or at one remove. Totally harmless, but a real character. Runs a small trout farm in one of the natural ponds we have around here on the land the commune rents. They call it the Bite This Commune, and the trout operation is called Bite This Trout."

All Peter could do was shake his head. Local stories! They did have their charms.

"Oh, and while we're at it, they had some disgruntled engineer from out east join, and he and Froggie created a sub-business called Froggie and Tadpole's Smokin' Fish. Now you buy a fresh, dressed trout at their gift store, or catch one yourself from the pond and either take it home or have them fry it up on the spot, or buy some smoked trout or salmon or whitefish from the grocery store. It's all organic and very high quality. You can even buy some in a few of the upscale Cleveland grocery stores, and I hear they serve a few restaurants, too."

"So these are the kind of extreme public dangers the feds were after?"

"That's who they caught, anyway."

Peter had to laugh. "I don't know where any of this is going, but you've got me enjoying the story."

"I'm glad you're amused," Mark replied. "Back to Friday the 24th. As I said, that's when they let the hippies go – all but Froggie."

"How about this Tadpole guy?"

"He'd already left town."

"Okay. So, Froggie. What happened to him?"

"They charged him with child endangerment, illicit drug dealing, obstructing justice, tax fraud, and urinating in public."

"Really?"

"Basically, anything they could conjure up. They needed a scapegoat, and he was the most prominent guy still in town."

"And you covered it."

"Of course."

Peter checked his notebook. "That was last Friday."

"Yeah."

"I assume you sent Ginny her clippings."

"I made sure of it," said Mark. "I imagine she got them today."

"And then this guy from Media IV shows up?"

"Leonard Donnelly, the guy you say you've met."

"Just in passing."

"Right. And even when he shows up, I'm still thinking this is just a strange coincidence, but then he starts to directly contradict what Ginny was saying. He wants me to drop the coverage. His exact words were: 'Our surveys say the public has moved on.' Can you believe that bullshit? 'Our surveys.' Are they really asking readers in Albuquerque if they skipped over a story about Castilia? And even if they did have that kind of surveillance, why bother bringing it up? We were pretty much done with the story ourselves. I told him he was micromanaging. He told me if I didn't like it, I could always retire."

"That blunt, eh?"

"That blunt."

"He said we'd had our fun with the feds, but it was time to let it go."

Peter frowned. "And you caved?"

"Let's say I finessed the answer. I got on the horn with Sam Dylann in Toledo to see if he'd be willing to send one of his reporters to cover the bail hearing set for the next Tuesday."

"The last date you had me write down."

"Yeah. He turned me down, saying that this Donnelly jackass called him up right after talking to me and warned him to stay away from the story, too."

Peter performed a strange little visual excursion looking down at his food, then up at Mark, then at the notebook, then back to the food. He did this two times. "Donnelly shows up, tells you to do the exact opposite of what Ginny wants you to do, then, while you're calling me to set up today's lunch, he's busy browbeating your buddy in Toledo."

Mark nodded vigorously.

"Seems like a lot of activity over a local story."

"Doesn't it, though."

"So, what's your take on all this?"

"I've stopped believing it's all a bunch of coincidences, even if I can't see any pattern. And I have a request for you."

"I was beginning to see that coming," said Peter.

"Would you be willing to send one of your reporters to cover the bail hearing?"

"Officially?"

"No, for both our sakes. If it comes out, I don't want you getting in trouble. And if it comes out at my end, I want plausible deniability."

"Did you ask your friend in Toledo?"

"I did, to be frank, but he turned me down. Said his guys are too well known in Sandusky, and he'd be officially asked to stay out of it. He's the one who suggested you."

Peter rolled his eyes. "Sure. I'll be happy. The problem is finding someone to send. You know I'm pushing everyone on my staff as hard as I can to pursue this Cincinnati lawsuit case."

"It would just take half a day. Drive out in the morning, back mid-afternoon."

"I just don't know."

"Doesn't have to be your star reporter."

Peter suddenly perked up. "Now, that does give me an idea. Sure, why not? Have you got the details about this court hearing?"

Mark Malandry reached into his coat pocket and took out a typed report with all the details. "Let me know what he finds out. It may be nothing; in fact, it probably will be nothing. But I'll owe you one, either way."

"We might have to make this a regular little get-together, you and me."

"I'd like that," Mark said. "Next time, if you don't mind, I'll invite Sam Dylann along. You two would like each other."

Peter agreed, then posed a question. "What's the proper term for a gathering of editors? You know, like a group of sheep is a flock and a bunch of goats is a herd?"

Mark was happy to play the straight man. "I don't know."

"A collusion," he said. "A collusion of editors."

CHAPTER 20:

The Assignment

F riday afternoon, Dorothy called to say Peter wanted to see me.

"What have I done this time?"

"Just go see him."

When I entered his office, he looked distracted. He gestured for me to close the door and take a seat.

"What have you been up to this week? Hear anything we can use?"

"Not really."

"How about your friend Dr. Tennyson? Is he up to seeing you yet?"

"Next week, Tuesday. I have an appointment to see him."

"You'll have to reschedule. I'm sending you to follow up on that botched FBI raid in Castilia a couple of weeks ago."

"The one with the burning trout."

"Flaming trout," he corrected me.

"Well, excuuuse me."

"I don't know if you've followed it since the story broke."

I admitted that I hadn't.

"I'm not surprised," said Peter. "It was a big deal for a few days, but then we all moved on to more pressing stories."

"Like the Chewbacca Wookie roar contest?"

Peter looked over at the corner, where he keeps hoping an antidote for me will appear.

"A guy in Akron is getting divorced, and I guess things got a little strained. So he prints up flyers and posts them all over his neighborhood, offering a $100 prize to the best impersonation of Chewbacca doing his roar thing and listing his wife's phone number."

"Just when I thought you were sitting around wasting time, you come up with a story like that," he said. If I didn't know better, I'd imagine there was a touch of mockery in his voice.

"I really wanted to follow up on that, but, you know. Akron."

"I'd rather you followed this other thing up."

"Blazing catfish."

"Flaming Trout."

I settled back. Might as well hear him out.

"This Flaming Trout festival has been getting bigger and rowdier over the past few years. There's a whole contingent of bikers who show up from around the country."

"In the middle of March? To set a trout on fire?"

"I guess certain people are really into these pagan rituals."

"Can't they just get drunk and go to a Browns' game like the rest of us?"

He looked disgruntled by the vagaries of the human race. "Different strokes for different folks."

Too bad we weren't at a bar; I'd have drunk to that.

"Regardless, the FBI and ATF got wind of drug dealing and maybe even weapons being sold at these festivals. Last year, they sent some observers to check things out. Got pictures of some heavy hitters on the watch list, but they weren't prepared to do anything at the time. Too many people, not enough agents. This year, they were ready. They waited for the last night of the festival when the sponsors burn the trout."

I held up my hand. "I'm sorry, Peter, but you've got to give me a second here. All I can picture is a bunch of boy scouts roasting trout over an open fire."

It was nice to see him crack a smile. He hadn't been doing that much over the past couple of weeks. "I guess there's this windmill that looks like a giant trout at the entrance to the commune. It's made of glass and has all these lights inside it. At the festival, they pump kerosene into the blades and light them on fire. The trout itself doesn't burn, just the blades."

"Like one of those old 4th of July sparkler toys?"

"Something like that."

"Okay," I said, still wondering where this was headed.

"So, this year, the feds were ready."

I knew better, but I couldn't help myself. "That's the FBI for you. Bust that trout right in front of everybody, just for the glory of it."

I had stopped him in mid-paragraph, which always pisses him off. He made a soft noise like Chewbacca being strangled in the next room. "The trout is not the point," he said through gritted teeth. "It's the dope dealers, the bikers, the felons, the fugitives they were after."

"Oh, I know all about that," I assured him. "I read it in the Sandusky Daily Journal. You can't get more authoritative than that."

I was pushing him too hard. "You leave the Daily Journal out of this, Mouse. If you're not careful, you may end up asking them for a job."

I said nothing.

"Getting back to the FBI. This was a huge embarrassment. Everyone else was treating it as a big joke, but not them. After all that fuss and expense, exactly one defendant is still in jail. He's the head of the commune, and he only goes by the name of Froggie. They're holding him on some minor possession charge while they try to pin some serious stuff like drug dealing and child endangerment – even human trafficking – on him."

"So, Froggie is the story."

"No, not really. From what I hear, it's all bullshit. They'll never make it stick. The real story is the botched raid. What the hell happened? How did word get out? It's a major black eye for the feds. That's the story I want you to cover."

"Me?"

"Yeah, you."

"It sounds like something the Daily Journal should cover."

"You're going to be their reporter on the ground."

"You're lending me out?"

"Just to cover the bail hearing."

"Why?"

"They need someone nobody knows or might recognize."

"And the reason for that is ... ?"

"The FBI is determined to figure out who gave them the photos that got them interested in the first place and then who tipped off the bad guys before the raid. They suspect it might be the same person, and they definitely suspect it might be someone working for the Daily Journal."

"So, they want me to go undercover."

"No, you go as yourself. You are just following up on a story to see if there might be any Cleveland connections. There are rumors to that effect, by the way. Some of these bikers are hiding out in Cleveland. It could even be true."

That made sense, but what didn't make sense was assigning a significant crime story to me. "Deep down inside, you don't think there's anything to those rumors, do you?"

"I feel like I have to check it out. I've got the others chasing Stanhope, and our dear friends at Media IV are getting impatient for results. I can't spare any of them. We're running out of time, and I'm scared they're going to tell me to let the big story go."

"Can they do that?"

"Of course not. There's still such a thing as freedom of the press. But they can always find some reason to fire me."

He wasn't kidding, I thought. Nor was he telling me everything that was going on behind the scenes. *Lord, spare me from corporate politics!*

I was determined to ignore the implication that he was only sending me because I was superfluous. "You know, I haven't been outside of Cleveland in forever."

"It's only an hour and a half away."

"Do they speak English?"

He tried to look stern. "It's a form of English called Small Town American."

"I'll stick out like a sore thumb."

"Just use your normal Mouse charm."

"I'm not sure charm is what's needed to infiltrate a violent, drug cartel biker gang running sex slaves."

"All I want is for you to come back with a goddamned

story I can run. If you can tie it to Cleveland, great. If not, find somebody interesting to talk to. Manipulate them into talking about Cleveland. Even one sentence will do. Make sure to quote that. Focus on the feds, but if they won't talk to you, drive over to Castilia and do your man on the street routine. I'm sure you can get people to talk about the raid and how they botched it. Somebody tipped the bikers off. I bet half the people in that little community know who that person is and why they did it."

"You think they'd admit that to a total stranger?"

"Of course not. They'll all point to one of their neighbors. The problem will be that no two people will point to the same neighbor."

I found myself getting intrigued. "Am I supposed to co-ordinate with the Daily Journal?"

"You stay the hell away from them!"

That was interesting, I thought, startled at the sudden outburst. "When do you want me to go?"

"Monday morning," he said. "There's a court hearing on Tuesday. The hearing itself is no big deal; setting bail conditions is all. But what happens immediately before and after the hearing might be interesting."

I found myself feeling apprehensive about this little excursion. "I suppose I could go right after the staff meeting."

"Skip the meeting."

I'd be waiting years for him to say that. Now that he had, I didn't like it.

"I don't want you talking about this little foray," he explained. "The rest will wonder if it's got some hidden connection to Stanhope and want in. I don't need the distraction."

"You're the boss," I said. *And if you think I can't keep a secret, I guess I have to live with that.* "But I have one condition."

" And what, exactly, might that be?"

"If I'm going to be infiltrating international drug smugglers posing as hippies, I want to borrow the armored car you ride around in all the time."

He waved a magisterial hand toward the door. "Mouse, get out of my office."

CHAPTER 21:

Driving to Castilia

Y ou know, I've never been all that introspective. That's the way I say it to myself. Somebody else – Arne, for instance – might flip a couple of words and say I've never been introspective at all.

Funny how a slight change in word order can almost reverse one's meaning.

I remember seeing a comedian on a talk show a long time ago say that the most interesting sentence in the world is: "I didn't know that." Her point was that it meant something completely different, depending on which word you stressed when you said it aloud. *I* didn't know that means one thing; I *didn't* know that means a different thing; I didn't *know* that means something else, and I didn't know *that* means yet another thing. Interesting, eh? But we're not done yet (says the comedian). You can create even more meanings if you emphasize any two of the words. Try it out; it's true. It helps if you use a lot of gestures and facial expressions, but even if you heard someone in the next room trying out different ways to say it, you'd know something devious was coming your way.

Actors rely on this emphasis technique all the time. So do politicians, lawyers, and cheating spouses. Reporters like myself just have the printed word. That makes us more honest and trustworthy than others.

Feel free to laugh at that last statement.

I'm driving to Castilia, obsessing about Peter Zenger and trying my best to be introspective. It just doesn't come naturally to me. I'm one of those people who know that what they have going on in their minds is not unique or particularly interesting. Other people's thoughts are fascinating, however, especially those with the innate ability to control what others focus on. It's like that spiel about I didn't know that. I can walk into Peter's office with one thought in mind and leave with a different one without realizing it. For example:

Me: I want to cover a big story.

Peter: There's a really strange thing happening in Castilia (note – population 734). You could cover that.

Me: Thank you for this opportunity. I won't let you down.

And I won't, either. I won't let him down. Come hell or clean water, I will find a story today or tomorrow morning. I say this with complete confidence. Why? Because I'm not introspective, not caught up with my own desires and perceptions the way some of the others would be if Peter had sent them. Not to name names, but let's say he chose Tricia for this story. She would be thinking all the way out there about what this meant for herself and her career, and how much more impressive she was than the people she was about to meet. With a mindset like that, what is the likelihood she'd come back with an interesting story? Or a story at all?

So, that's my advantage: low self-esteem, coupled with high curiosity.

I have to admit that I'm a little apprehensive about this trip. I don't know a thing about Castilia other than it has a strange blue hole in the ground. That's my focus, heading into town. Once I get there, I'll have to start meeting people who live in a community I can't even imagine. Not compared to Cleveland, anyway. I'm not saying I know everything there is to know about Cleveland. Not at all; Cleveland is as unknowable as the Milky Way. As long as I stay in Cleveland, I'll never run out of stories to tell, and I know enough of her secrets and unwritten rules that I can sniff out stories without even trying. I'm like a bloodhound. I know what my surroundings smell like, and when I come across some new odor, some scent that doesn't fit, I can follow it wherever it leads.

That's not going to be true in Castilia. Every scene, every sound, every odor is going to be new to me. It's going to be like hearing that sentence, I didn't know that, spoken by a hundred robots, each putting a slightly different spin on it, but all sounding like robots. How am I supposed to know what stands out as not belonging to the natural order of things?

I know thousands of people in Cleveland, but I have no friends, no deep and intimate relationships that extend over many years – unless you count Dr. Tennyson. I can imagine that in Castilia, that's going to be unheard of. In a small town, you are going to know everybody in a much more intimate way than I do. I'm not talking about sex here. I'm talking about knowing the little quirks and preferences of others, their opinions on a wide range of topics. I guess sexual intimacy is in the mix there, too. Small towns are no strangers to infidelity. The point is, rather than being the bloodhound sniffing around for what doesn't belong, I'll be the fox surrounded by a hundred hounds who will know instantly that a stranger is among them. This frightens me, not in the sense that I'll be in any danger but rather in the expectation that people won't open up to me for the simple reason that they just don't come across that many people they don't already know. I will carry the odor of strangeness like a cheap cologne.

I'm taking the slow route to Castilia, following the Lake Erie Scenic Byway rather than taking the Ohio Turnpike. I hate to admit it, but I didn't even know this byway existed. It's going to double my travel time, but so what? I've had road repair more than double my commute in Cleveland. I'm realizing as I drive that I have a distorted sense of the lake. I think of it as an appendage to the city, as if Cleveland was built on one lot of ground, and it purchased the lot next door as a swimming pool and a barrier to keep the Canadians out. That's completely backward, I realize. Lake Erie is the boss here; Cleveland is just one lakeshore property and not a good one at that.

Well, here I am. The sign says, "Welcome to Castilia," so I guess this is it. Time to make some new friends. If I can.

CHAPTER 22:

Go Tell Aunt Hildy

I was a naughty boy. Before leaving for Castilia, I slept in, went to a coffee shop, and took my sweet time reading the PD, enjoying the fact that my fellow reporters were duking it out in the staff meeting at that very moment. I'm a long way from retirement, but this little taste was as sweet as the cinnamon roll I was nibbling at. I got back to my apartment at 11:00, stretched out on my bed, and took a half-hour snooze. All this was before I even packed. Here's to you, Peter!

If you're serious about getting to Castilia from Cleveland, you head down to the Turnpike, but if you have all the time in the world, you take Route 6, which parallels the shore of Lake Erie. On the way, I stopped at the little city of Vermilion and ate a civilized lunch at one of the hotels. It was 1:30 by the time I walked out, feeling like an executive. It would take me less than half an hour to get to Castilia. Why not explore my surroundings here a bit before leaving?

The Vermilion River is noted for its trout and smallmouth bass fishing. Taking the advice of my waitress, I headed to the Vermilion River Reservation and hiked along the limestone cliffs enjoying the scenery. It was a magnificent day, and I stayed by the river two hours before heading to my destination.

Castilia was quite a bit bigger back when I visited it as

a child. Half the buildings on the two-block main street were boarded up. It wasn't depressing for some reason. I got out of my car and looked around, trying to figure it out. Why did I feel this inner glow of peacefulness, even happiness? There were flowers everywhere, for one thing. And it was spotless. I might have been in Switzerland minus the mountains. The stores that were closed were – how do I put this? – tastefully closed. Respectfully closed. No graffiti. The windows at street level were washed, and none were boarded up with plywood. It looked like the owners had gone on vacation for a month, and fully intended to return with new inventory. I locked my car purely out of habit.

One of the significant advantages of a small town is that it is easy to find the people you want to interview. Let's say you are from out of town, and you want to meet the Mayor of Cleveland. How many people would stand in your way? A lot. There is a whole hierarchy of helpfulness at play. It starts at the bottom level, the people who are farthest away from the mayor. These are the helpful ones, the people who will stop long enough to find out what you need and follow up *on the spot*. Let's say 90% of the people at the bottom fall into that category. So, now you are talking to their supervisor. How likely are they to help you, *right then and there*? Let's say 75%, though that's probably a little high. But you are moving closer to your target. Let's say you're talking to a department manager. Your chances are around 50/50. Up the ladder you go, and at each rung, the odds of finding somebody helpful goes down. Oh, they'll say they will, but do they follow through? Nah. They're too busy, too important, and too afraid of their own boss. If you are persistent enough, you can, in fact, sit down with the mayor. It's just that by the time you do — a year later — your reason for doing so is long gone.

Being a reporter can help sometimes, but just as often, it proves to be another barrier. It's a two-edged sword, this news business. Over time, though, you can build your own network of people willing to help you *right now, right then and there*. If you treat them right, they're no longer scared of you. And if you stay in touch, even when you don't need anything from them, you find out that they have all these social connections that skip layer upon layer of bureaucracy. You discover, entirely by accident, that the janitor's son plays hockey with the grandson of the mayor's chief of staff. You casually mention wanting to meet the mayor. The janitor picks up the phone and calls the chief of staff, who serves on the committee that organizes the awards dinner for the hockey club, right alongside the janitor. "Hey, you got a second? I got a guy here, calls himself Mouse, wants to talk to you. Here, I'll hand him the phone." It's just like Chutes and Ladders. Suddenly, you feel like Superman, able to leap tall buildings in one bound.

It takes years to build up networks like that. It took me decades, but now, my network covers the entire metropolitan area of Cleveland. Which is great, but it doesn't do squat for me in Castilia.

On the other hand, this is a very small town, where everybody knows everybody. That means you can start anywhere and be pretty much assured that you are at most two people away from your target. You don't have to be strategic. All you do is talk to the first person you meet. Start literally anywhere.

Like where? Like that diner over there with five vehicles parked in front: two cars, three pickups. The Cardinal Café. Perfect.

It was 4 pm, early for the dinner crowd, and I was surprised to see the place was full of very animated people. Something was up. Was it the raid on the commune? If so, I was in precisely the right place at precisely the right time. Thank you, Peter Zenger!

The one over-worked waitress came over. As far as I could see, nobody was eating, just drinking coffee. Nonetheless, she was moving fast and looking frazzled. Ordinarily, I would have started with her, taking my time just chatting before asking about the commune, but time was something she didn't have at the moment.

"Help you?"

I glanced at the menu to get the words exactly right. "I would like a cup of your fresh-brewed, delicious, fire-roasted coffee."

That made her actually look at me. Was I mocking her? Or the restaurant? Was I some sort of lunatic? Or was I coming on to her? Was I smiling at her like some long lost cousin, waiting for her to recognize me?

"Um," she said, my smile narrowing the options down to lunatic or cousin.

"Sorry, I know you're busy." I pointed to the others. "Is this about the commune?"

"Well, Froggie, anyway."

What a delightful answer. She was already turning to leave. "Listen, I'm a reporter from Cleveland. Human interest stuff. Who can I talk to about Froggie?"

She pointed to a woman who was taping a flyer to the front window. "That woman there."

"What's her name?"

"Aunt Hildy," said the waitress and walked off to get the coffee pot.

First Froggie and now Aunt Hildy. I felt like I was on the Andy Griffith Show. *Go tell Aunt Rhody the old grey goose is dead.* I wished I hadn't thought of that, because now I had to fight the urge to call her Aunt Rhody. Hildy, Hildy, Hildy, I chanted to myself as I crossed the diner.

"Excuse me," I said, "but are you the one they call Aunt Rhody?" *Damn!* "I mean, Hildy, Aunt Hildy."

She cracked up. "Don't worry, chickpea, you're not the first. What can I do for you?"

Forthright and friendly. I decided to answer in kind. "I'm a reporter from the Plain Speaker," I said. "You may have heard of us. We're from Cleveland."

She began to grin. "Well, this is an honor. We don't get reporters around here, especially from the big city. What's your name, hon?"

"Mouse."

"You're Mouse?"

"Yeah. That's me."

"Oh, we love you around here."

I was honestly flabbergasted.

"You look surprised."

"I thought our total circulation in Erie County was one copy."

"We pass it around."

I let out a little laugh. Usually, I'm the one who gets others laughing. "Do you realize that you just gave me a compliment I will cherish for the rest of my life?"

She waved my expression of gratitude away. "Oh, now."

"What's that you're putting up?"

She glanced down at the stack of flyers in her hand. "This? I'm assuming this is why you're here." She handed me one.

The flyer was a simple, amateur effort. It featured a large headline, a photo, and a small amount of text. The headline screamed FREE FROGGIE! The photo showed a corpulent man in his fifties wearing a ruffled dress shirt and a Panama hat with a pheasant feather extending jauntily upward. He was smiling like he'd just overheard the Buddha exchanging dirty jokes with a fitness instructor.

163

"You're coming, right?"

I quickly scanned the text at the bottom. "Where's this St. Alban's Church?" I asked, "and how do I get there?"

"I'll show you. Where are you staying?"

"I don't know. I literally just got here.

She took out a cell phone and dialed a number. "Emma? It's Hildy. You got any vacancies? Good. I'm sending someone over. His name is Mouse. Yes, the reporter. Isn't that something?" She winked at me. "Oh, you'll like him. He's very good looking."

She put her phone away. "Okay. You'll be staying at the Crossroads Motel. Go ahead and check-in. We'll pick you up at 6:30 if you don't mind getting there a bit early."

"That would be wonderful. Where's the Crossroads?"

She gave me a puzzled look. "At the crossroads."

I gave her a blank look.

"There's only two roads that go through town, pea pod. It's where they cross."

I put on a poker face. "I suppose there's only one motel there."

She mirrored my expression. "Yes. It's called the Crossroads."

"So, it's the best one."

"Unless you want to stay in Sandusky."

"Not for the world," I said, honestly.

She soaked it in.

"You mean you'd rather stay in little old Castilia than in Sandusky?"

I shrugged. "Apparently, this is where my readership is."

Now she laughed, unable to help herself. "Get on with you. We'll pick you up at 6:30."

We? I thought.

She bustled off. I contented myself with observing the crowd, doing my best to see with the eyes of a painter rather than a reporter. It's a trick I taught myself. It keeps me alert but not judgmental. I see this, I see that, I see the next thing over. Nothing is more important than anything else. There's no attempt at cause and effect or back story or hidden agendas, just observing what's immediately in front of me. I started with the black and white photo of Froggie and imagined painting him if he were there in the flesh. Froggie's mouth was more full than the average, and his eyes were widely spaced. I wished he was there just so I could see those eyes in real life. In the photo, they were flat and uninteresting. I imagined they'd be quite different in reality.

I switched my attention to Aunt Hildy and fell in love. If I were an artist in real life, I could have rendered Froggie in crayons or chalk. With Hildy, I would go straight to oils. There is a depth of color and tone to her face that only oils could render. At the same time, I would need to be sparing in how I used the oils. She had the freshness of a high school cheerleader. Her hair is the color of wheat, her eyes the color of a rainbow trout diving into the water. I'm guessing that she hit her absolute pinnacle of attractiveness in early high school. Since then, a few extra pounds and some years of life have made her less of a yearbook photo and more of a painting you'd put on a wall. She stood 5'8" when she pulled out of a slight, comfortable slouch. Her mouth was full and succulent as if she had just swallowed every last bit of a perfectly ripe peach. Her gestures were broad and generous, tending toward gathering everyone in rather than excluding them. Was I in love with her? You might think so, the way I am going on about her, but you would be wrong. It wasn't sexual. I loved her as a character, an individual who existed in her own world and not in mine. She was – forgive me for the expression – a little too matronly for my taste, resembling one of my elementary school teachers too much to make her an object of desire. And yet, she was lovely. She was as delightful as a perfect birthday present, the one that you weren't expecting, the one you cherished the moment you unwrapped it.

She caught me staring at her and looked away. I did the same, embarrassed that she'd noticed. I returned to merely observing. My two short conversations had already produced a ripple on the surface of this little pond. Now the thing to do was persist by doing nothing. Somebody would swim up to check me out. It was just a matter of time.

CHAPTER 23:

The First Born

A tall young man walked in, greeted a few people with a casual nod, and sat down opposite me. He was dressed like a welder in heavy work shoes, blue jeans, a heavy long-sleeved shirt, and a leather apron that protected him from neck to knees. His grip was ferocious, but his manner was friendly. I don't think he wanted to intimidate me; he simply didn't know his own strength.

"I'm Elroy," he said as if we'd just clinched a deal.

"I'm Mouse," I said, feeling a little intimidated.

He nodded solemnly, as if I'd just confirmed his worst suspicions, and yet there was this underlying friendliness to him. I wondered if he'd been in the military. "Aunt Hildy said you wanted to learn more about Froggie."

"Do you know him?"

"I'm his son." He pointed to a cluster of people in a booth across the diner, singling out a thin, severe-looking woman with dark hair. "That's my mom, Janey."

Well, thank you, Aunt Hildy!

"Does that mean that all three of you were in jail together?"

"Just a couple of days, then they let us out."

"All but your father."

That amused him. "Oh, don't worry about Froggie. He's a bigger threat to the jail than it is to him. Give him another week, and the whole joint will be a commune."

I asked him how old he was.

"Twenty-three."

"And how old is the commune?"

He didn't know. "I think it was going for a couple of years before my birth. You'd have to ask Aunt Hildy or my mom."

"Or your dad?"

He looked amused at the very idea. "Froggie doesn't live in ordinary time."

This kid was beginning to intrigue me. "So, Elroy, what do you do? Are you a welder?"

"I am today. Tomorrow, I'll be something else. Whatever needs doing."

"You're not in school?"

"Actually, I am, but with all this confusion, I have to do a lot more than my share. We're not that large a commune, and we lost two members overnight. That's huge. I'm not complaining, mind you; everyone who's left is having to pitch in."

I tried putting myself in his shoes. "What's it like for you with them gone?"

"Pretty lonely," he confessed. "They were half of my family."

I waited.

"You know, when it first happened, it felt like they just left for a vacation or one of their sudden trips. But everybody keeps telling me that I'll never see them again, and it's beginning to sink in that they're probably right."

"Who tells you that?"

"My parents. Aunt Hildy. The cops."

"But you're not sure."

"I guess all I can do is hope."

I felt the ghostly finger of Peter Zengler tapping me on the shoulder, telling me to get on with it. "My editor called them a biker gang. Is that true?"

"It's complicated," he said. "There are some biker gangs at the festival, but they weren't members of the commune. Some of them had ties to one of our members, but that was long ago. They show up every year for Flaming Trout and hang out. Then they drift off and we don't see them until the next festival."

"This guy who's friends with them. He have a name?"

"Skullman."

I was careful not to react. *I'm just a painter, observing without judging.*

"Just to be clear, you're telling me that Skullman used to be part of one of the biker gangs, but isn't any more."

"Yeah. It's no secret."

"Is he one of the members who left?"

"Yeah."

"You look sad."

"He was like a second father to me."

"And you have no idea where Skullman is?"

"Not a clue."

"If you had to guess?"

I saw him pull inward. *Damn. I'd pushed him too hard.*

"If I had to guess," he said, slowly, "I imagine he's out west somewhere, probably on his own. That's how he met

Froggie. They were both just driving around out west and happened to bump into each other."

"How about the other one who left? Any idea why?"

"I don't want to talk about it. Hope you don't mind."

"Of course not," I lied. "Just tell me this: was this other one a biker?"

"No."

I sat there waiting him out. I was pretty sure he'd say more, just to break the silence.

"Skullman was one of the founding members. The other guy joined when I was nineteen. We all called him Tadpole."

"And now he's gone, this Tadpole guy."

"Well, let's say he hasn't come back and he hasn't gotten in touch. He usually avoids the festival. The last anyone recalls seeing him was the morning it started, so we didn't think anything of it. But it's not like him to stay away."

"Tadpole is kind of an unusual name."

"Says a guy who calls himself Mouse."

"Ha!" I said. "Point taken."

He liked hearing me say that. "Anything else you want to know?"

Oh, nothing much. Just a few hundred follow-up questions. This Tadpole character definitely interested me. For that very reason, I redirected my line of inquiry.

"Where did you say you were in school?"

"Bowling Green."

"That's supposed to be a good university," I said without thinking. I mean, could I have sounded any more condescending? Me, Mouse, the kid who barely made it through community college, telling him he was going to a good college.

"I could have graduated last semester, but I'm staying on an extra term to finish up my capstone project."

Another thing I knew nothing about. "What's that?"

Bless his heart, he didn't make me feel stupid for asking. "Not every program has one," he replied. "In my case, I'm hoping to become an architect, and they tell me having a capstone is really useful if you want to get into the program at Toledo."

"So, what is this capstone project all about?"

He misunderstood my question. "They call it a course, but it's really just one independent study."

I reworded the question. "Does it have anything to do with the commune?"

"You better believe it does!" he exclaimed, showing more animation than he had so far.

I felt like I just caught a glimpse of a younger, happier version of him the way he probably was before the raid. At the same time, I felt the ghostly foot of Peter Zenger kicking me in the ass. *You're not here to interview a college kid about becoming an architect. Get back to the bikers, Mouse. For God's sake.* I shoved the thought away. "Oh, Elroy, this is good! A commune with its own, in-house architect. Tell me more."

"I'm not the only one," he replied. "My mom's a sculptor who knows more about architecture than a lot of the professionals. She designed our house. We all did to some extent. We worked with some Mennonite builders and figured out the designs together. Have you visited the commune yet?"

"No, I just got here an hour ago."

He asked if he could borrow my notepad and a pen, and began sketching in the layout of the whole commune. His pen strokes were precise and confident; there was no erasing or contemplating how accurate it was. He may – or may not — have been able to draw a face, but he sure knew where buildings and roads and the pond were located relative to each other. Once he finished, he spun it around so I could see it right side up. He explained that it used to be a summer camp, and showed me the cabins and the big dining hall and another even larger structure where they used to have assemblies and do craft projects. He pointed to one end and explained that there used to be tennis courts there, but that now they had a large organic garden. There was a decent-sized parking lot with a little guard shack next to it, where they sold vegetables in season. Then he pointed out a large structure near the pond with a smaller structure next to it. "That's the trout farm," he said.

"Of course," I said.

He pointed to a group of closely-spaced little squares that could have been outhouses for all I knew and explained that these were smokehouses all connected to a large outdoor fireplace. "This is where *Froggie and Tadpole's Smokin' Fish* takes over from the trout farm."

"Tadpole again!" I exclaimed, unable to help myself.

He just stared at me, putting me in the same position I'd put him in earlier, having to break the silence. Just because I use the silent treatment all the time doesn't mean I'm not immune to it myself. "What if he doesn't come back?" I asked. "Will you change the name?"

Elroy shook his head. "We talked about it. If he doesn't return, I'll become the official Tadpole. I've done it before and I can do it again."

"What does being Tadpole involve?"

"Mainly leading tours when Froggie's busy."

"That's all?"

"That's all he did as Tadpole. The rest of the time, he was holed up in his cabin, being an inventor."

"Wow. What kinds of things does he invent?"

"Beats the hell out of me," Elroy replied "He's totally paranoid when it comes to that, afraid people are going to break in and steal his ideas."

"Even you guys?"

"That's just the way he is. I probably know him better than anyone and I've never been allowed upstairs in his cabin, not even once."

"So he's a total loner?"

"Not exactly. I mean, he's definitely shy and he definitely doesn't like crowds, but if you can get him involved in solving a problem, he's real helpful. He helped me a lot with designing the greenhouse and the smoking operations."

"Wait a minute," I said. I looked down at his map. "You designed all those buildings?"

"With his help," he said modestly.

"And that was part of your capstone?"

"That's one of the things that led up to it, but the capstone is a whole other part of developing the commune, even bigger than the smoking operation."

I wanted to take a break to process all this information, but we were running out of time. "So, what happens, now?" I asked him.

"You mean to me? Or to the commune?"

"Both."

"Who knows? The whole money thing is scary. Unless we can replace the ones who left, I don't know if we can survive. I don't even know if I can graduate if I can't pay all the fees and stuff I still owe."

At this point, I was ready to pull out my wallet and pay for them myself. Elroy was blowing my mind. Each sentence was like a chapter heading. I wanted to know everything about this kid and this commune. I asked myself what Peter would want to know. *The money.*

Unfortunately, we were out of time. The café was rapidly emptying, and we took our cue from the others. I shook the kid's hand as firmly as I could, which was pretty wimpy by his standards, I imagine. "Elroy, I hope things work out for you," I told him. "And I hope we can stay in touch as this whole mess gets straightened out. Do you think we could do that?"

"Do you think you'll be back?"

"Definitely," I said. It was a promise I wasn't sure I could keep. But what the hell, even if Peter didn't send me back, I could always drive out for a weekend. I wanted to see this commune. I wanted to meet every one of them. I had a feeling that these were my kind of people. The newsworthy ones were the FBI agents, and I suppose Froggie, but Elroy felt like a younger version of myself.

Bigger, of course, and stronger. More confident. Smarter.

Oh, hell, he was nothing like me. But I sure liked him. I genuinely wanted him to thrive, despite whatever nastiness was coming his way.

CHAPTER 24:

The Rally

Aunt Hildy rapped on my door at 6:20. I guess people were prompt in Castilia. When I emerged a minute later, hurriedly combing my hair, she led me to a brand new, black Chevy Suburban without a speck of dust on it. When I climbed in, she introduced me to her to the driver. "Mouse, this is Thomas, my husband."

"Pleased to meet you, Thomas-my-husband," I said, noting the formality. "I appreciate the ride."

"Not a problem," he said, making it sound like it wasn't exactly a pleasure, either. I met his eyes in the rearview mirror. They were reserved, observant, evaluating.

"Are you both friends of Froggie?" I asked. It was a stupid question unless what you were looking for was his reaction. His eyes dropped to the road. Ah. Maybe not so stupid, after all.

Hildy laughed. "Everybody in Castilia is a friend of Froggie," she said, "even Thomas, though he doesn't want to say it out loud, especially to a reporter." She gave him a chance to explain, which he declined with a subtle twitch of one shoulder. "You see, Thomas is President of the First Bank of Castilia, which is where Castilia Development does its banking, and where the commune has its accounts, too."

My head was spinning. It was too much information to process all at once. "Could you stop the car, please?" I asked. "I think I want to go back to Cleveland, where things are nice and simple."

Thomas was already slowing down before he realized I was joking. I saw his mouth twitch in the direction of a smile. "It is complicated," he told me. "There are two corporations involved here, and we are bankers to them both. One is Castilia Development Corporation, which owns the land and the buildings."

"But not the sculptures," Hildy said.

"Not the sculptures," he agreed. "Then, there is the commune's business." He lost a beat. "Which is itself a corporation."

Hildy laughed. "Oh, Thomas, just say it. They call themselves the Bite This Commune, and their business name is BTC Enterprises."

Thomas looked embarrassed. He was a serious businessman with a client called Bite This Commune. What could he do?

"Plus, there's the whole political side," Hildy continued. "When I said everybody's a friend of Froggie, that was kind of from Froggie's point of view. Not everyone in Castilia likes having a commune in town. It's mostly because of their politics; they are into organic farming in an area that's mainly into modern farming techniques that use lots of fertilizers and pesticides. We try to keep it lighthearted here in town, but underneath the surface, there are some pretty passionate people on both sides of the issue, and Thomas has to please all parties. The raid has split the community."

"Temporarily," her husband said fervently. "It'll die down."

"I'm sure it will, lovebird, but right now it's at a peak. I just wanted Mouse to be prepared."

I decided to change the subject. "Why is this rally being held at an Episcopal church?"

"It's Froggie's church. We all go there. Tom and I go every Sunday, and Froggie goes with us every couple of weeks or so. He rides right where you're sitting. Janey comes along a couple of times a year."

"So, is this rally going to be mainly church members?"

Again, a twitch of the shoulder.

"No, my sweet. I mean, sure, he'll have a bunch of support from St. Alban's, but mostly it will be the environmentalists."

"And your minister is okay with that?"

"Priest," she said, a bit firmly. Her tone returned instantly to pure sweetness. "Father Marcus is the one who suggested holding it there. He's as active in the organic farming community as he is in the Episcopal Church. He's the one man who will know everyone there."

"Let me guess," I said. "Everybody in the church loves Froggie, but not everyone loves his activism."

"Yeah, pumpkin, that's fair enough."

I was about to ask more, but suddenly we were pulling into a small parking lot next to a church that could have been featured in any of a hundred BBC movies. My goodness, I thought, this is going to be interesting. I haven't even walked through the door, and there are ten plot lines in play.

We got out of the car, and I followed them into the basement, where I immediately picked out the priest. He was dressed in farmer clothes, but he had a clerical collar around his neck. Kind of hard to miss. I studied him while various people came forward to greet Thomas and Aunt Hildy.

Father Marcus Elliott was a tall man, dignified, thin

almost to the point of emaciation, but radiating relaxed physical competence. His eyes were bright but not manic, committed, but not fanatical. A man of the soil, I thought, and a man of God. Even before Father Marcus uttered a word, I understood something Peter Zenger didn't. This little battle about a jailed hippie organic farmer from Castilia was rooted – the word *rooted* came to mind with a kind of glow – in the same conflicting forces about to clash in a Cincinnati courtroom. It was a miniature version of a billion-dollar lawsuit.

Hildy came up, took me by the elbow, and seated me beside her with Thomas on the other side in the front row of chairs arranged in two concentric circles. It was standing room only.

Hildy beckoned, and Father Marcus came over. "Marcus, this delightful young man is a reporter from the Plain Speaker. Maybe you've heard of him. Mouse? Writes the City Mouse column?"

The priest lost his reserve and turned into my favorite uncle. "My goodness! You are the only writer at the Plain Speaker I bother to read on a regular basis. I'm so glad you're here. I hope we can chat after the meeting."

He moved on, making the rounds before standing at the head of the circle. "Let us pray," he said, and there was an instant bowing of most heads, though not all. "God of all creation, who cherishes the earth and all its creatures, down to the simplest lichen, down even to the rock underneath that lichen, we your created people are gathered here in the basement, the literal foundation of one of your churches, to discuss and respond to the jailing of one of our own, Froggie Hartzler. Be with us here in this place and now in this moment. Be here equally among those who address you through liturgy and articulated belief and those who prefer to worship you through service to your creation or those who deny your existence. You have created us all, and your love for us is not withheld from any corner of creation. Be with us, and through your grace, hear and guide us, and may our collective wills align with your will for us. Amen."

A stillness permeated the room like incense. He let the silence dissipate into the atmosphere.

"Okay, folks, let's talk. Who wants to go first? Just stand, tell us your name, and say what you want to say."

Too many people spoke for me to keep track beyond making a list of names and a one or two-word description of salient points they made. I was fascinated by them as individuals, of course, but also intrigued by a new community that had suddenly sprouted from the soil around Froggie as if his name was a harbinger of Spring.

Everyone in the room, it seemed, knew that Froggie used drugs recreationally. Everyone knew that he didn't deal them. It was pretty much assumed that he knew the bikers were dealing on and off the commune and probably were Froggie's own suppliers. Most of this sort of community consensus wasn't stated in so many words. It was alluded to, hinted at, taken for granted. And it was clearly no big deal.

The raid was portrayed as if jackbooted Nazis had invaded their peaceful little community. It was all us against them. They were arrogant, cruel, zealous ideologues from Washington, DC who took for granted that they were smarter than a bunch of yokels on the outskirts of Sandusky.

As I listened, subtle differences emerged around how the speakers defined us and them. It became formulaic: Hi, my name is xxxx. I am a xxxx (farmer, neighbor, member of St. Alban's, car dealer, whatever), and it's clear to me that this whole thing is yet another example of xxxx (Washington politics, the heavy hand of government, evil corporations running the government, Stanhope, etc.).

Wait a minute. Stanhope? Did somebody just blame this on Stanhope?

I nudged Aunt Hildy. "Who is this guy?"

"Fred Williams," she whispered. "I'll explain later."

"It's not enough to blame this on the feds," Fred Williams was saying. "The FBI is just doing what their bosses are telling them to do. And that's the politicians. But the politicians aren't in charge, either. We know who's pulling strings here, and why Froggie is in jail while the bikers hide out. You've got to ask yourself if this is all about drugs, why did they let the bikers escape? No, this isn't about drugs. This is about Froggie and the rest of us who dare to make a living doing sustainable, organic farming. This is the work of Stanhope. I'm telling you this. Some of you are nodding, and some of you aren't. That's okay. But let's say we were living in coal country, and the feds came stomping in. We wouldn't be talking about Stanhope, but we would be talking about some other corporation who was similarly threatened by some guy like Froggie, who just wanted to live on land that wasn't poisoned. Stanhope has been spying on us for years. They've had their eyes on Froggie about as long as they had on me. They got to me a couple of years ago, and you all know how that turned out. Now it's Froggie's turn, and they want to destroy him, too. 'Oh, come on, Fred,' I can hear you saying, 'how can Froggie pose a threat to Stanhope?' Well, let me remind you, you said the same thing about me. Some of you chipped in to keep me afloat, and I'm forever in your debt. Now it's Froggie's turn. It doesn't matter that he's no threat; all that matters is that they think he is. Why else would they send a corporate spy into our midst?"

And with this, he threw out his arm and pointed directly at me. "Who are you, anyway?" he demanded. "None of us here has ever seen you before. Who do you work for?"

I froze. I'll admit it. Froze like the proverbial deer in the headlights.

Aunt Hildy stood up, putting a hand on my shoulder.

Her husband looked down at the floor. "Fred, love, if you'd only asked, I would have introduced you."

Fred deflated instantly and noticeably.

"Everyone," she continued, "this is Mouse from the Plain Speaker, the closest thing we have to a friend in the big city. He's got nothing to do with Stanhope. He heard about the bust at the commune and thought it was interesting enough to drive all the way out to see what was going on."

Fred regained a bit of his swagger. "Is this true?" he asked me. "You're a reporter from the Plain Speaker?"

"Yes, sir."

"Alright, then, mister fancy reporter, what do you think is going on?"

"About what, exactly?" I countered. "Do I think there are spies from Stanhope attending this meeting?"

"Well, yeah, for starters," he said, a bit hesitantly.

I made a show of looking around. "I have no idea. I don't know any of you, so I wouldn't know who looked out of place. On the other hand, if I was a spy for Stanhope, I'd make sure I didn't stand out. I'd probably have been recruited years ago."

My own words surprised the hell out of me.

"Are you saying you might know something we don't?"

Fred's query was eerily on the money. You bet there were things I knew about Stanhope that they didn't. They didn't have anything to do with Froggie or some obscure commune, but I couldn't tell them that. My hesitation was beginning to make the crowd uneasy. "Well, okay," I said. "The reason I'm slow to answer is that I don't want to insult you or patronize you, but honestly, I'm sure that Froggie and his commune and this group of friends are of no interest or importance to Stanhope at all. They are an elephant, and you are a fly buzzing around the next elephant over. When my editor suggested I drive over here, he never mentioned Stanhope or agribusiness or even farming. As far as he was concerned, it was about the war on drugs and federal versus local law enforcement, and what appeared to be an embarrassing blunder by the feds. It still strikes me that way, but if you have anything to tell me, I'm, uh, all ears. That's why they call me Mouse."

At last, a laugh. The tension drained out of the room. I sat down. When Hildy patted my shoulder, I was grateful for the touch.

Father Marcus raised a hand. "I think our reporter friend is right. We need to focus on the drug charge. Any involvement of Stanhope – if there is any – can wait for later. Right now, we have Froggie locked up in the city jail."

He looked around the room. "Ah, there are you, Franklin. You're a lawyer. What do you think?"

Franklin looked more like a hardware store manager than a lawyer, though he was wearing a suit. "Who's paying for my advice?" he asked, cheerfully.

That got a laugh, but not from the priest. "Nobody is paying you," he said sternly.

"Then I don't have any thoughts on the matter."

That brought a round of angry whispering.

"Look, folks," Franklin explained, "you are confusing me with a judge. I'm an advocate, and my job is to make the best case I can for my client. I'm like a soldier. You don't ask a soldier, 'Who do you want to fight?' You have to tell him who the enemy is and who he is fighting for."

"I think that should be obvious," a voice said. "Go fight for Froggie."

"Okay, but who am I supposed to be fighting against?"

"The FBI."

"Actually, you're wrong, but let's say you're right. You're

saying you want me, a small-town lawyer with no staff to take on the FBI? That's like asking Christine Nichols to invade Mexico with a rolling pin and a spatula."

The crowd laughed, but not for long. Father Marcus spoke for them. "Franklin, are you saying it's hopeless?"

"Not at all, and the reason I say that is because it isn't the FBI who's prosecuting Froggie. In this case, the enemy is the county attorney, Donald Phelps. He's a decent guy. He'll push the case against Froggie as hard as he can because that's his job, but he'll play by the rules. He's not going to manufacture some false charges based on faulty evidence.

"Well, that's good to hear," said Father Marcus. "Do you know the judge?"

"Pamela Gooding? I know of her. She's a straight shooter. She'll give Froggie a fair hearing."

"So that leaves you."

"Come again?"

"Well, somebody has to represent Froggie. We think it should be you."

"Oh, he doesn't need me, which is a good thing for him and all of us. He has the lead attorney for Castilia Development, a guy named Richard Lennox, on his side. That man's a killer, a cold-blooded killer, and he's got a staff he can call on if needs to."

"You think he'll be able to get Froggie out of jail?"

The lawyer looked uncomfortable. "Look," he said, "anything can happen in a court of law. I've been around too many cases to ever predict an outcome with one hundred percent assurance. I think it's more than likely Froggie will get out on bail. The real question is how high Judge Gooding puts it." He looked around the room. "That's where we come in."

"Us?" said Father Marcus. "Why not Castilia Development? You just said they were paying their own lawyer to represent him."

"Let's just say that posting bail can be a complicated issue. They may or may not. If they don't, then we may have to raise it ourselves."

Hildy raised her hand. "Should we do that tonight while we're all here?"

Franklin shook his head. "I think we should wait until tomorrow. Let's see what we're up against. Froggie needs our moral support. He may or may not need our financial support. I hope everyone here shows up tomorrow at the courthouse. It matters more than you think."

The meeting continued on for another hour, losing its focus now that the lawyer was done answering questions. As an outsider, I found myself tuning out the content and paying attention to the nonverbal signals being transmitted from one subgroup to another, like birds in the arctic sharing a crowded rock on the shoreline, fighting for space, and looking for a mate. It was frankly refreshing to be observing a group of complete strangers tussling over issues I knew nothing about.

On the way home, I asked about that lawyer, Franklin Bucher. Did either of my hosts know him personally? They seemed to find the question highly amusing.

"Honey blossom, we've known Franklin our whole lives."

"How about the others in the room? How many of them did you know?"

"Ninety percent. There were a few out of towners mixed in; I assume organic farmers who are part of Froggie's network." She turned to her husband. "How about you, hon? Recognize any of the strangers?"

"I'm sure my list is the same as yours," he replied.

There were so many questions tumbling around in my mind that I felt I was at a laundromat staring at the dryers. We were all tired, and I was tempted to settle into the backseat and close my eyes. I tried one last question. "Elroy told me that only two members of the commune left before the raid. One was named Skullman, and the other was named Tadpole. You know anything about them?"

Thomas spoke up. "Actually, there were three who left. A guy named McQueen disappeared just as things got completely chaotic."

"I wonder why Elroy didn't mention him."

"Probably because he returned a couple of days later, acting as if nothing had happened. They brought him in for questioning, but by then, the whole thing was a fiasco, and they let him go with a caution."

"Was he a biker?"

"In a way, I suppose," said Hildy. "He's really more of a sculptor and mechanic who mainly shows up to help plan the festival and work on the current version of the flaming trout. He's part of that Burning Man Festival out west. Froggie and Skullman met him there, and he's been helping out ever since."

I made a mental note to find out more about the Burning Man Festival. In the middle of doing that, I fell asleep. The next thing I knew, Hildy (who was already becoming my own Aunt Hildy in my overloaded mind) was gently shaking my shoulder, telling me we were at the Crossroads Motel, and they would see me in the morning down at the courthouse. I hoped I thanked them. I'm not sure I did. It was all I could do to find the right door and stumble onto my bed.

CHAPTER 25:

The Bail Hearing

The designated crime reporter for the Plain Speaker is a formidable woman named Terry Trowbridge, and I'm sure her account of the hearing would have been quite different from the one I have to offer. It would have been better, for starters, and it certainly would have been more about legal issues than personal ones. What can I say? She has expertise; I have opinions.

The courtroom was packed. I asked Hildy if this was unusual. "Very," she replied.

The judge, Pamela Gooding, called the next case, asking that the defendant named Ferdinand Hartzler appear before her. This simple request was greeted by guffaws of unrestrained laughter and merriment by the spectators. She looked up in irritation. "Did I say something funny?"

His lawyer, Richard Lennox, stood. "Excuse me, your honor. If I may?"

"Yes, Mr. Lennox?"

"I'm pretty sure that nobody in this courtroom has ever heard the defendant's legal name. He is known to one and all as Froggie."

She looked at the gallery. "So, now you know," she said, sarcastically. "Here's something else I want you to know.

There will be no further outbursts in this courtroom. If you are a friend of Ferdinand ..."

A few snickers escaped from the back of the room.

She glared at them. "... you will control yourself. If you cannot do so, I am instructing the bailiff to remove you from the courtroom."

The crowd hushed.

Two sheriff's deputies escorted Froggie in. It's hard to say what I noticed first: his size or his mode of dress. Froggie is not just fat; he is genuinely, gloriously, proudly obese -- and just as colorfully dressed as he is fat. He showed up in red pants, oversized suspenders, and a flaming orange shirt. He walked in slowly, using a hand-carved cane that showed a rainbow trout leaping out of the handle. His skin was as pale as the throat of a bullfrog. His eyes were a little too big and protruding. I immediately thought of Toad in "Wind in the Willows." His lips were full and fat and, frankly, a bit disgusting. I imagined them dripping with grease in the middle of a banquet. And yet, there was an aura of royalty about him. Do you know that famous portrait of Henry VIII? He had some of that about him. Here was a man set apart from the rest of us, a man used to establishing his own rules, living life on his own terms. Although he moved with evident pain and used his cane with every step, he gave the impression that he owned this courtroom and was merely stopping by to see what the big commotion was all about.

Judge Gooding regarded him with interest for some moments. "Your legal name is Ferdinand Banthorp Hartzler. Is that correct?"

"Yes, your honor," he replied in a deep baritone voice.

"I understand that you have a nickname."

"Yes, your honor."

She waited.

"Froggie," he added with what I can only call dignity.

"In this courtroom," she said, "members of the bar and all government representatives will refer to you as Mr. Hartzler. Your own lawyer will do so. Other witnesses can call you Froggie as they wish."

She looked pointedly at the gallery.

"Mr. Hartzler, you are charged with five felonies: drug trafficking, running a criminal organization, aiding and abetting the flight of other named suspects of said organization, tax evasion, and child endangerment. Further charges may be lodged against you as the investigation continues. Do you understand the general nature of these charges?"

Froggie turned to his lawyer, who waved him off and addressed the judge. "Your honor," he said, "before we proceed with this hearing, I must withdraw myself as counsel for the defense."

Froggie looked at his lawyer with astonishment. Many others in the spectator area broke into furious whispering back and forth.

"Explain," said the judge.

"I apologize to the court for the last-minute change, but decisions were made at the corporate level late last night. They prevent me from defending Mr. Hartzler."

Judge Gooding gave him a skeptical look.

"I am one of the litigators for Castilia Development Corporation, who originally assigned me to represent Mr. Hartzler. His relationship with Castilia Development is somewhat complex, so I ask your indulgence. First, as an individual, Mr. Hartzler works as an employee, who provides goods, services, and consulting to us. Secondly, Mr. Hartzler is a member of BTC Enterprises, a commune that rents houses from Castilia Corp. So, you can say that we are his landlord and he is one of our renters. Ordinarily, either relationship would mandate us to represent him. However, two weeks ago, Mr. Hartzler and other members of BTC Enterprises sponsored the Flaming Trout Festival, which was raided by various agencies of the U.S. government. The festival was not sanctioned by Castilia Development; in fact, it violated several of our policies for both employees and renters. Today we are firing Mr. Hartzler as an employee and evicting BTC Enterprises as tenants. It is now inappropriate for me to represent him. Or more than that. I am legally prevented from doing so."

The judge glared at the lawyer. "Mr. Lennox, I live in this community, and I follow the news like any other citizen. I am fully aware of the festival, which I note has been taking place for years without objection from Castilia Development. Now, suddenly, you want to take no responsibility for it. This is one of the most disingenuous petitions I have ever heard. I want to decline it out of hand, but first, I want to hear directly from the defendant. Mr. Hartzler, please rise."

"Yes, your honor?"

"Given what you just heard, do you still want Mr. Lennox to represent you?"

Froggie looked around until he locked eyes with Franklin Bucher, who vigorously shook his head. *No!*

"No, your honor."

"I think that is wise," she said caustically. "Mr. Lennox, you are excused from representing Mr. Hartzler. Please leave the courtroom.

"Your honor!"

She waved him off. "Strike that from the record. Please leave the defense table. You may, of course, stay in the spectator section."

"Thank you, your honor," said the lawyer. He gathered his papers and walked to the back of the courthouse, sitting down quietly. Never once did he make eye contact with Froggie.

Judge Gooding asked the defendant if he had any other legal counsel. He pointed to Franklin Bucher. "Mr. Bucher is our own lawyer."

"Our own lawyer? Please explain."

"He is the lawyer for the commune, BTC Enterprises."

The judge nodded. "Is Mr. Bucher in the courthouse?"

"I am, your honor."

"Are you willing to represent Mr. Hartzler in this hearing?"

"Yes, your honor."

"Good. But here's the more important question. Are you willing for this hearing to continue right now, or do you need time to consult with your client? If you want a recess, I will grant it. The downside for your client will be that he will be returned to the confinement center until we can reschedule the hearing. That could take several days."

"Can I have a moment?"

"Of course."

Franklin moved up to the defendant's table and had a short, whispered conversation. "My client wishes to proceed."

"Very well, counselor. Please sit." She turned to her clerk of court. "If you would read the charges, please?"

"The State of Ohio charges Ferdinand Hartzler with five felonies.

Felony 1: Aiding and abetting the sale of illegal drugs.

Felony 2: Aiding and abetting the wholesale distribution of illegal drugs.

Felony 3: Endangering public safety by burning a sculpture close to a large gathering.

Felony 4: Participating in a scheme to defraud the IRS by hiding illegal money transfers from HSBC Bank in Delaware.

Felony 5: Child endangerment."

Judge Gooding turned to Froggie. "Mr. Hartzler, do you understand these charges?"

Froggie turned to his new lawyer, who spoke on his behalf. "Your honor, my client says he doesn't understand the child endangerment charge."

She consulted her notes. "The charging document lists the following specifics: raising children in unsanitary conditions; in proximity to known felons; exposing them to drug dealing; homeschooling without proper permission from the state; failure to vaccinate children; malnutrition; suspicion of sexual abuse."

Again, Froggie consulted with his lawyer. "Your honor, my client denies all charges and will vigorously defend himself, but he acknowledges that he understands them."

"I'd like to hear that directly from the defendant."

"Your honor," Froggie rumbled from deep in his chest, "I declare that I am not guilty of any of these vile, ridiculous charges."

She looked him over. "In the State of Ohio, we have guidelines to establish the risk to the community and the risk of flight if you were to be released from jail pending your trial. Your case is a bit unusual. You have been charged with two felonies in the past, both involving peaceful protests and thrown out due to a lack of evidence against you. This bothers me. I could interpret this as evidence against you. Still, at the same time, I could interpret this as evidence ..." and here she raised her eyes to stare directly at the prosecuting attorney ... "of a pattern of government overreaction to your political views and legal activities as an activist. After a great deal of

191

thought, I used my discretion to keep these earlier charges out of the formula. I have, however, included all five felonies you are charged with, at least for now. These argue for either no bail or for a very high level of bail. I have also entered into the database that you have lived your entire life in the community, and have an unblemished record outside of legal, political speech. You also have a family here."

"As you know, the prosecution asked that you be held without bail until additional charges can be filed. I agreed to that, due to the seriousness of the existing charges. Today we are here to reconsider your application for release on bail. The prosecution has not brought additional charges. They requested that you continue to be held without bail, saying the original charges are more than sufficient to make you a flight risk.

"I have rejected that motion."

"In response, the prosecution today asks that I set bail at $250,000 per felony, which amounts to $1,250,000. This is consistent with the state guidelines, albeit at the upper end. Do you wish to contest this level of bail?"

"That's outrageous!" came a loud voice from the back.

"Bailiff, remove that man," Judge Gooding said, calmly.

The bailiff did so, arousing considerable muttering from the others.

Franklin Bucher stood. "We object to this level of bail."

"On what grounds?"

The lawyer didn't even hesitate. "Because my client is not a risk to the community. Nor does he present a clear risk of flight."

The judge consulted her notes. "It says here that Mr. Lennox had a character witness lined up. A certain Marcus Elliott."

"That would be Father Marcus Elliott," said the lawyer,

gently correcting her. "Father Marcus is an ordained priest and serves as rector of St. Alban's Episcopal Church."

"The one here in Sandusky?"

"Yes, your honor. Just two blocks away."

They went through the formalities, and Father Marcus took the stand.

This should be interesting, I thought: church and state lined up against each other.

Franklin asked a few questions to establish Father Marcus' relationship with Froggie, being careful to refer to him as Mr. Hartzler.

"Froggie has been a dues-paying and regularly attending member of St. Alban's for many years," Marcus said, speaking carefully and formally. "This means that I am his priest, and as such, I cannot disclose confidential information we may have shared in that context. I have a second relationship that is not protected by confidentiality, and it is from this relationship that I'd like to speak to Froggie's character."

"And what is this second relationship?"

"I am the current President of the NW Ohio Organic Farmers' Association."

The government lawyer frowned and made a note.

There was a bit of back and forth to establish the legal identity of the organization and proof of Marcus' standing as its president. Once the judge and prosecuting attorney were satisfied, Franklin proceeded by asking the most open-ended question in the world. "What would you like the court to know about Mr. Hartzler?"

Father Marcus squared his shoulders and addressed his comments to the entire courtroom as if the witness stand was his pulpit, and they were his congregation. "I would start with this: Froggie is the least mobile person I have ever known. If you know him as I do, you will understand that the very idea of him fleeing is inconceivable. In over twenty years, I've never known him to go more than twenty miles outside of Castilia except for two occasions. One was a trip out west from which he returned. The second is a business trip authorized and paid for by none other than Castilia Development, the same people who are abandoning him. I've been thinking about this ever since Mr. Lennox asked me to speak on his behalf last week. I really hadn't thought of it before, but Froggie is deeply connected to this particular place. Froggie is just there. You don't question his presence any more than you would that big old oak tree at the corner of Lake and Pleasant, where my church is. You'd never ask an oak tree to post bail or bother to erect a fence around it to prevent it from running off. It's rooted in the soil. The same thing goes for Froggie, who is as rooted to the land and especially the trout farm as any oak tree. I was told that the arresting officer said that Froggie's main concern when he was being led off in handcuffs was who was going to take care of his trout."

A murmur of agreement came from the back of the room.

"Froggie is widely known in this part of Ohio because of his environmental activism, so if you don't believe me, there are literally hundreds of others who can vouch for him. Here's the thing, though, that they all would tell you: if they live far away, they come to see him; he doesn't go to see them. He has spoken in Sandusky and Toledo, but never in Cleveland or Columbus. He's been invited by my organization and groups like the Sierra Club and the Audubon Society. His response is always the same: 'Who will take care of my trout?'"

Judge Gooding interrupted him. "Are you suggesting that Froggie only cares about his trout?" she demanded. "Isn't he a family man as well? Or doesn't he care about them?"

What followed was one of those moments that the legal system seems invented to prevent, and yet, which often determines the outcome of a case. Marcus stared at the judge, open-mouthed, realizing the trap he'd been making for his friend, and then burst out laughing. This wasn't any little chuckle or dignified sniff of suppressed amusement. No, this was a full-throated expression of complete surprise and delight. "Oh, my goodness!" he managed to say. "Froggie not caring about his family? Or other people?" He had to wipe his eyes. "Forgive me, your honor. I was so impressed with myself for coming up with that image of an oak tree that I totally distorted my portrait. Froggie is the most social being in three states, and his love of Janey and Elroy, and the younger ones, Spectacula, Jaydon and Boh-Boh. If the criterion is how much he loves his family, there's nobody who could top him. Please, your honor, forget the trout. I'm sorry I brought them up. Froggie would never leave his family. That's another reason why he's not a flight risk. They're not going anywhere, and neither is Froggie."

Judge Gooding asked the prosecuting attorney if he had any questions for Father Marcus before she dismissed him.

"I do, your honor."

"Your witness, then."

From the look of him, the prosecutor was no rookie. Just as Father Marcus struck me as a man totally at home in his body, Donald Phelps was totally at home in a courtroom. I'd been watching him as best I could, and as far as I could see, he had taken no notes or consulted any documents. He approached the priest, stopping quite some distance from the stand.

"Father Marcus, have you ever visited the commune?"

"Yes, I have."

"Did you do so in your role as a priest or simply as a friend?"

"I suppose as a friend."

"So your interactions there are not covered by priestly confidentiality."

"No."

"Good." He took two rapid steps forward as if he was going to physically assault the priest. "As a friend of Mr. Hartzler, did you take drugs with him? Were you ever offered drugs? Did you see others using drugs?"

"I object!" Franklin cried.

"On what grounds?"

"Intimidation. Father Marcus is not a defendant."

The judge was less ruffled by the aggressive approach than I might have thought. "Objection is sustained," she said, mildly, "but if the prosecuting attorney would like to restate his questions one at a time in a calm manner, I will not hinder him."

The attorney gave a slight bow to the judge. He'd already succeeded in altering the tone of the proceeding, setting everyone on edge. He backed away from the witness stand and asked in a respectful voice, "Father Marcus, did you ever observe people using recreational drugs on the commune?"

"Yes."

"Was it widespread?"

"I'm not sure what you mean by widespread."

The prosecutor waited for a beat or two, letting the priest fidget. His tactic didn't work. I made a note in my notebook: *Father Marcus = experienced witness.*

"Let me rephrase. Did you observe more than one person using drugs?"

"Yes."

"Did you observe one or more people using drugs on more than one visit?"

"Yes."

"Was Mr. Hartzler, one of these people using drugs?"

"Yes."

"Can you describe the kinds of drugs you saw Mr. Hartzler using?"

"Marijuana," said the priest, maintaining his cool.

"You sure it was marijuana? Not tobacco?"

"Oh, Froggie would never smoke tobacco. He says it's addictive and bad for the lungs."

"And marijuana isn't?" the prosecutor shot back.

"Sure, it is. The difference is how much you consume. You smoke a pack of cigarettes a day, your health is going to suffer. You smoke a joint once a week, it's not good for you, but it's a lot better than a pack a day."

"You do realize that smoking marijuana is illegal in Ohio, don't you?"

Father Marcus allowed himself a quick smile. "A misdemeanor," he said, "not a felony."

For a second, the prosecutor looked like he'd been punched in the gut. "Are you toying with me?"

"Objection!"

"Sustained."

"Father Marcus, are you an experienced witness?"

"Objection!"

"On what grounds?"

"Relevance."

The judge turned to the prosecutor. "Any response?"

"Your honor, when a priest appears as a character witness, especially when he does so wearing a clerical collar, I think we all tend to assume that he is honest and – forgive me – naïve in the ways of the courtroom. I think it's only fair to correct this impression."

"Hmm," said the judge. "So you are telling me that you assumed the witness was inexperienced because he was wearing a clerical collar."

"Yes, your honor."

"And so you verbally aggressively attacked him, thinking he would panic."

"Uh, no, your honor."

"That will be all, Mr. Phelps." She turned to Mather Marcus. "I think I'll ask the question on behalf of the prosecution. Have you ever appeared in court before?"

"Yes, your honor, many times."

"As a witness?"

"As a witness, as plaintiff, as a defendant."

"So, not naïve at all?"

"Not when it comes to civil actions regarding the environment."

She seemed to be taking a liking to him. "How about criminal cases?"

"I'm not sure," he said carefully.

"Would you clarify that, please?"

"A group of us trespassed on the grounds of an Army depot. There was some debate about whether that was criminal trespassing or a misdemeanor."

"I'd think you'd remember."

"It got thrown out of court before the issue got decided."

Froggie made a grunting sound that somehow conveyed vast amusement. It was the first hint of animation he had shown since being seated at the defendant's table.

She thought about it. "I think we're getting off-topic." She thought some more. "There's nothing wrong with a citizen being familiar with courtroom proceedings. In fact, we want regular citizens to observe open sessions and be informed about the law."

She looked at the prosecutor. "Unless you have any further questions, I'd like to dismiss this witness and move to the question of bail."

"No further questions," said the prosecutor.

The judge asked the two attorneys to approach the bench, but she pitched her voice to the entire courtroom. 'While the charges against Mr. Hartzler are serious," she said, "I find that the risk of flight is minimal, and the risk to the community is virtually nonexistent. I am therefore reducing the requested amount of bail by a factor of 1,000. In other words, I am setting bail at $2,500 per felony count, making the total $12,500."

"Your honor, these are not trivial charges."

"Mr. Phelps, I in no way consider them trivial. Your problem is that you are trying to attach them to the wrong man. You bring me one of the named suspects – one of those you allowed to escape in your botched raid – and you will see me quite willing to consider the kinds of bail numbers you suggested."

She hammered the gavel down, stood up, and declared that court was adjourned. A great cheer went up in the courtroom. The judge demanded order, but she did with a gleam in her eye. The bailiffs escorted Froggie out while Franklin Bucher headed to some office in the courthouse to arrange for paying Froggie's bail.

CHAPTER 26:

The Four Horsemen of the Epocalypse

I called Peter and gave him a quick rundown of the bail hearing. He listened without interrupting. When I finished, he was brusque. "Very interesting, Mouse. Do you have anything about the bikers heading to Cleveland? Or any connection to Cleveland?"

"Not so far."

"Do you at least have a quote that mentions Cleveland?"

"I'm working on it."

"You know what? Why don't you head home now. You've got nothing we can use."

"Can I at least stick around until I can meet Froggie?"

"One hour, then you head back, regardless."

"Okay, boss," I said, understanding that this was the best I could do for now. Why he needed me back was something of a mystery. If I couldn't meet Froggie today, I'd drive back when I could. Really wanted to see this commune and the trout farm. What the hell did a trout farm look like, anyway?

Father Marcus was passing by just as I got off the phone. I managed to snag him. I explained that I only had an hour and still needed to check out of the Crossroads, but if he had a half hour to spare me, I would dearly love to interview him. He graciously accepted. St. Alban's was only two blocks from the court house, so we walked over and met in his office. It was a bit cluttered. The books on the built-in bookcase were half Christian and half environmentalism. He saw me looking at them.

"You're wondering if I have a split personality," he offered.

"The really interesting people often do," I assured him.

He smiled at that. "What can I do for you?"

I had to suppress a moment of panic. I hadn't prepared for this, which ordinarily wouldn't be a problem, but I only had half an hour. "Much as I'd love to ask you about Froggie and the bail hearing, I think what I'd like to hear about is how you see the environmental issues around here. To me, Castilia and Sandusky look clean, healthy, in balance. The Sandusky River hasn't caught fire, to my knowledge. I don't see blight or huge piles of mining debris. Hardly a crisis."

"Appearances can be deceptive," the priest said. "The environment looks healthy, as you say, and if you are a farmer looking to extract the most profit out of the land in the shortest time, then you might say it's flourishing. But the ecosystem is at a critical stage, and the same threats that are operating at a global level are at work right here in humble little Sandusky. Are you familiar with the Book of Revelation? The Apocalypse? The Four Horsemen?"

He was freaking me out.

"War," he said. "Famine. Disease. Death."

I swallowed.

"The Four Horsemen of the Apocalypse. According to Revelation, they show up at the end of the world just before the Savior returns to bring Heaven back down to Earth."

"You, uh, don't believe that stuff, do you? I mean, literally?"

"I certainly think there is a thing called war, and a thing called death, and a thing called disease, and a thing called famine. These aren't mythological beings; these are current realities running rampant around the globe."

"Yes," I said, beginning to get my feet back under me, "but on horseback?"

"Well, that part is figurative, absolutely." He leaned back in his chair. "I wish you were part of our congregation, Mouse. I really do. You'd energize our adult ed program with your questions. But I suspect you have more pressing issues than biblical studies."

"Tell me more about the environment being in crisis."

"Actually, the word to use is ecosystem. The environment is simply that which surrounds us. The ecosystem is all the living things within that environment and how they interact. I am surrounded by an environment, but I am an active participant of the ecosystem."

My confusion must have shown.

"Yesterday, at the rally, you were in the environment of the church basement, but not part of the ecosystem. You were an outside observer. That changed when Fred Williams called you out and you defended yourself. At that point, you were part of both the environment and the ecosystem."

"What was his deal, anyway?"

"Stanhope has been very successful in this region. Most farmers around here use their products. A few individuals like Fred absolutely refuse. So what, you say? Stanhope has 90% of the market and the organic farms have 10%. Or 5%, more likely. But in order for an organic farmer to keep his certification, he has to get his farm inspected on a regular basis. When they inspected Fred's farm back in 2004, they found that he had MowDown™ in his fields and genetically modified alfalfa from Stanhope growing here and there. How did that happen?

Well, it happened because the wind blows across the environment and doesn't respect the boundaries between farms any more than chemicals and patented seeds care about the legal system. His neighbors on all sides were using MowDown™ and MowDown Resistant™ crops. Some invaded his own, carefully managed ecosystem, polluting it. Fred lost his certification as an organic farmer. This cost him a great deal of money because he could no longer sell his corn or alfalfa at a premium rate. He didn't like that, and I think you can guess from how he spoke yesterday what happened next."

"He sued Stanhope."

"True, but actually it was a countersuit. Stanhope went after him first, if you can believe that. They claimed he was illegally using their patented seeds and herbicides."

By this time, I was madly jotting down notes.

"When you think about it in the abstract, it's a very interesting case. The wind scattered the seeds. Was it Stanhope's responsibility to keep their seeds from being scattered? Or was it the job of the other farmers to keep the Stanhope products from spreading? Or was it Fred's responsibility to make sure he didn't use their seeds, even accidentally. Who, in other words, was responsible for the wind?"

"But that's a ridiculous question!" I objected.

"It is, isn't it?" He reached for his Bible, but held himself back. "There are so many ways to go at it. In the end, it comes down to whether genetically modified organisms are pollutants – as Fred maintained – or valuable man-made products protected by copyright."

We sat looking at each other in silence for a few moments as I struggled to let the implications of what he said sink in. "There's something really wrong here," I muttered. It wasn't much of a comment, but it was all I had to contribute. "What finally happened?"

The priest sighed. "We all chipped in to defend him, and he even got some pro-bono legal support, but Stanhope overwhelmed him with a deluge of lawyers filing briefs right and left. They settled after Fred agreed to pay Stanhope $100 for illegal use of their products. Stanhope didn't care about the money, of course. What they cared about was establishing legal precedent. Afterwards, Stanhope went about their merry way, making money hand over fist. Fred lost most of his farm to pay his legal bills and the whole region learned to fear Stanhope and its legal team even more than they had before."

"That sucks," I declared.

"Yes, it does," Father Marcus said, gently. "But that's just one little organic farm. How did you put it last night? A fly buzzing around the next elephant over?"

I gulped.

"Don't worry," he assured me. "There was a lot of buzzing among the flies afterwards, but most of them agreed with what you said and a few even thought you were pretty courageous for telling the truth."

"And how about you? What did you think about what I said?"

He took a breath. "I might have picked a different analogy," he admitted. "On the other hand, what you said stuck. It was memorable, whether you agreed with it or not."

I looked down at my notes. There was so much I wanted to ask him. The Four Horsemen still bothered me. So did the fact that I didn't understand the difference between the environment and the ecosystem. It was clear to me that it mattered to him. What was I missing? I wished I had all afternoon. "Do you know a man named Jeremiah Tennyson? Dr. Tennyson from Cleveland?"

Father Marcus' eyes grew wide. "I know about him, but only by reputation. Never met the man in person. He's one of my true heroes."

For a moment, I allowed myself to feel smug. "I could introduce you, if you ever want to come to Cleveland. I know him well."

"You do?"

"Long story," I said. "I'd be glad to share it another time. You two should definitely meet, though. You're two of a kind."

"That's a compliment," he responded. "And I'd love to meet him."

I glanced down at my notes. "Okay," I said, "back to the Book of Revelation and those Horsemen. I assume that the one you are concerned with is the one called Famine. You want to explain that?"

He considered my question. "Famine comes about when ecosystems collapse," he said. "Let's change our focus from poor old Fred Williams and look at his neighboring farmers. What Stanhope is doing is enabling those farmers to choose one crop – let's say corn – and destroying the ecosystem in order to maximize how much corn you can extract from it in the extreme short term. Let's say five years. Or ten years. Or even twenty, but that's longer than most farmers seem to be thinking these days. They manufacture a poison that is not found in nature – Glyphosate – and spray it all over the ecosystem, which kills damned near every living thing it touches. Worms die. Bugs die. Amphibians mutate or die. Birds die. Rabbits and deer and foxes and groundhogs die. Butterflies die. If they're not careful, the farmers and their families and their pets die. Plants of all kinds die, including ordinary corn. What you have over time is a dead zone where nothing lives. Into that dead ecosystem, you plant the new, bio-engineered strain manufactured to resist the poison in the ground. It grows, and because it is free from having to compete with weeds and pests, it thrives. So you have..."

He cut himself off and looked at me quizzically. "Let's go

back to the Four Horsemen," he said. "You asked me about Famine, but we should have started with Disease. That's the first horseman. In today's world, he's not sitting on a horse. He's driving a John Deere tractor, which lets him spread the disease called Glyphosate poisoning across vast fields. Everything dies. The ecosystem collapses. This is step one. Then new plants invade, and for a short time they thrive. Yields go up. Small-scale warfare breaks out between the farmers of disease and the organic farmers of the ecosystem. It's small scale, but its war, alright. It's biological warfare and it's economic warfare. Initially, the casualties are pretty much all among the small farms. Fred managed to keep his house and a few acres, but most of his carefully tended acreage was auctioned off to his neighbors, who promptly sprayed Glyphosate all over it. It's a war of attrition: picking off one farmer at a time, swallowing up a few acres of healthy ecosystem at a time."

"Another war is being fought out of sight, and this war doesn't reach the news outlets like The Plain Speaker. The ecosystem is fragile up to a point, but it's also incredibly resilient and adaptive. Recently, we are finding that certain insects are developing their own resistance to Glyphosate. So are certain bacteria and fungi. Even earthworms are adapting, becoming tolerant. As these unwanted members of the old ecosystem fight back, crop yields start to go back down. The answer so far has been to increase the amount of poison farmers have to spray on their crops. It's an arms race. The economic advantages are diminishing. Poisons and customized seeds are expensive, and if you need to apply more of them, your profits decline."

"But not to the point of famine," I objected.

"This is where mono crops come in. Nature thrives on diversity and hates monopolies. When there's nothing around but GMO corn, then that crop becomes the only target of opportunity. What happens when some organism evolves that can destroy corn? Let's say it's something new, not just some corn borer that's evolved to be a little more resistant to Glyphosate. Maybe it's some wasp from Asia or Africa. If it gets a foothold in an ecosystem where corn makes up only one tenth of the living organisms, that wasp is going to take hold, but even if it destroys half of the corn, that's only 5% of the ecosystem. But what if the ecosystem consists of 90% corn and extends for thousands of miles in all directions? That wasp is going to thrive and its population is going to expand exponentially. Within five years, it has destroyed 90% of the corn. So, do the math: 90% of 90% equals 81% of that ecosystem has been replaced by a plague of wasps, dead fields, and who knows what other kinds of destruction caused indirectly by that rapid turnover. Topsoil starts to blow away. Erosion sets in. The farmers go bankrupt, so the economic ecosystem collapses. So, soon enough, Mouse, you end up with ..."

"Famine," I said, horrified at the very word.

He nods. "The second horseman, right here in mid-America."

I feel like I'm standing on a girder two hundred feet off the ground. "You don't have to explain the war and death phases," I tell him "I think I get the picture."

Marcus checked his watch. "That's good, because you are out of time, and talking to you is depressing the hell out of me." He chuckled at that, taking the sting out, but I felt it, nonetheless.

I screwed up my face. "Is this the kind of thing you preach about in church all the time?"

At that, he dropped the challenging tone and became pure compassion. "Church is mostly about hope and comfort. And luckily, we have this thing called the Lectionary that tells me what passages to read each Sunday. We hit the Book of Revelation a couple of times a year, but just in little bits and pieces." He stood up and held out his hand. "And you know, ultimately, the Bible, including the Book of Revelation, ends in the triumph of good over evil and the establishment of a new world."

I took his extended hand and shook it. But I couldn't help myself. "Father Marcus, talking with you has been a real revelation."

His eyes narrowed and his smile turned downward. "God loves us all, even smart asses." Then he burst out laughing. "Mouse, please come back. We may look like a sleepy little town, but there's a lot going on under the surface."

I thanked him and headed back to Cleveland, taking Route 6 along Lake Erie again. The Lake didn't look so reassuring this time. I saw it as a target for malignant chemicals and distorted creatures.

I kept thinking about Fred Williams losing his farm because of Stanhope's legal team.

And now here was Froggie, perhaps facing the same kind of large, cooperate forces. It wasn't Stanhope, but it just as well could have been.

I write about the unheralded, common folk all the time. I could do something with this, I thought. It wouldn't change a thing, but it was still a real story, an important story. The biggest story in Ohio? No. I leave that stuff to the real reporters. This is my niche, and why not venture outside the city limits every so often?

CHAPTER 27:

Brooding on the Banks of the Vermilion River

On my way back to Cleveland, I stopped at the Vermilion River, parked the car, and walked over to the bank where I could look at the water serenely flowing past me on its way to Lake Erie just downstream from Route 6. My father took me fishing there once. The river is famous for steelhead, but we were after small mouth bass. "Pound for pound, Marky," he said, "smallies are the fiercest fighting fish in the world." I remember distinctly the sound of 'fiercest fighting fish.' There was an anger in him that propelled those f's like boxing gloves hitting a bag. What he was angry about, I don't know, but it was shortly before he abandoned my mom and us kids and went off to Colorado to live with the bears. That's how Mom put it. We didn't believe her, until it was time for bed and she turned out the light, leaving me staring into the darkness, picturing him being eaten by a huge grizzly. No doubt my older brother Ben had his own images to deal with. He was two years older and his fears loomed larger and sharper than mine. I closed my eyes and allowed myself to imagine the back end of a bear moving away from me. "Help me, Marky!" my Dad cried.

"Come back!" I yelled. Then I heard a crunching sound.

The memory of that night without Dad was with me,

triggered by where I was standing. The emotion in that vision was the strongest feeling of my life.

My father used to tell us stories about the Native Americans who lived here and were driven out by the white man. This, he said, was nonsense for number of reasons. First, it ignored over eight thousand years of history to concentrate on a couple of hundred years when the Europeans arrived. We were fishing here at the Vermilion, a year before he ran out on us. Ben didn't like fishing, so he stayed home. "Think of it, Marky," my dad said, gesturing around in all directions. "Way, way back in time, way before the Egyptians or the Chinese had any kind of civilization, there were Indians living here. We don't know much about them, but we do know this: they didn't always get along. Who knows what battles took place along this river? There could have been hundreds."

He loved reading about the frontier and the adventures of the settlers and the Indians. He told me there were two main languages in these parts: Algonquin and Iroquois, and a number of tribes that spoke one or the other. They fought each other constantly, one tribe extending its territory, another pulling back or even leaving the area entirely. "Thousands of years," he said, as if he could see them all laid out on the surface of the water, passing in front of us. "And then the Europeans came, but it wasn't as simple as the white man versus the Indians. All around the Great Lakes, the white men were also separated by two languages: English and French. They fought each other constantly. "Ever hear of the French and Indian Wars, Marky?"

"No."

"What do they teach you these days?" he asked in disgust, though I don't see why, given that I was in third grade. I listened, though, entranced.

"There were wars or skirmishes before the War of Independence, when the Americans parted ways with the British.

210

So, now, there were French troops, French Canadian troops, British troops, American troops, Algonquin tribes, and Iroquois tribes all forming alliances and killing each other. You had tribes switching sides all the time. In the end, it wasn't the British who won, and it wasn't the French. It was the Americans. We're the ones who pushed the last Indian tribe, the Wyandots, out of Ohio."

"Where'd they go?"

"Kansas. Others went to Oklahoma."

It was too much for my young mind to comprehend. "Why?" I asked.

"Why? Better weapons," my dad said. "But here's what really matters. I bet over the last eight thousand years, fifty different tribes lived along the Vermilion and the lake shore, but the rivers and the lake never changed. They had the same fish, the same trees, the frogs, the snakes, the deer, the buffalo. All the trees stayed the same. We used to have chestnut trees all over this part of America. It didn't matter whether the Indians in one location spoke Algonquin or Iroquois; they all lived with nature, not outside of it. When the Europeans came, they changed the rivers and the streams, the lakes and the lands and it didn't matter whether they spoke English or French. They brought diseases and they changed the land, and built dams and cut down forests and started polluting the air and water and ground."

It was quite a lecture from a man who was usually rather taciturn. I hadn't thought about that moment in years. It surprised me that I could recall it at all.

"What are we supposed to do?"

"Get the hell out of Dodge," he said.

The phrase meant nothing to me.

"Move to the mountains," he continued, which did make sense. It made a lot more sense a year later when he did just that. I'd have gone with him if he had offered to take me. We could have lived like the Indians in harmony with the land, up in the mountains somewhere out West.

This didn't mean he was an environmentalist. I'm not sure the term even existed back then. He was a dreamer, a wanderer. He'd have fit in with the commune in Castilia if it had been around when he headed out of town. And who knows, maybe he passed through there a time or two as one of the bikers.

I threw a pebble into the river. Its impact disturbed the surface for less than a second. That's him, I thought, a momentary splash in my life. I threw another pebble. That's me.

I was heading back to Cleveland, my home base, my place of stability, where the biggest drama in my life was the occasional flare-up with Peter. Peter was my father now. He had guided me for the past ten years. He wasn't going to like what I had to tell him about Castilia and how important I thought it was.

I looked at the water, flowing endlessly. It was flowing before I was born, it would be flowing after I was gone and everyone who ever knew me was gone, and all my columns were long forgotten, and the Cleveland Plain Speaker wasn't even worth a footnote. The truth was, I didn't matter. Neither did Peter Zenger. Castilia and Sandusky and even Cleveland would all pass away just like those ancient Indian villages we know nothing about. The Vermilion River, now, that mattered. It endured. The Cuyahoga mattered. Lake Erie mattered.

It was all too easy to imagine the Four Horsemen rising up out of the water, heading for Cleveland. A stronger man would have put those thoughts out of his mind. And do what: fly to Cleveland and ward them off with a meat cleaver? How was that supposed to work out? If only I hadn't sat down with Father Marcus face to face, I could have distanced myself from the horror of the Horsemen. What was Cleveland to them? A spot on the map, a little clod of soil that could be obliterated by a single hoof. I could no more escape the destruction of the world than I could the devastation of my father's abandonment. I remember my grandmother singing an old hymn with the chorus that asked, "Where you gonna go when the land goes under the water?" My mother was an only child, so there were no uncles around to give me and my brother male guidance and reassurance. I found myself wanting to run back to my car, drive back to Sandusky, and knock on the church door. "Tell me it's going to be okay. Tell me you were just kidding."

The world is not supposed to end.

The Great Lakes are not supposed to end.

I'm not supposed to end.

CHAPTER 28:

Mouse, Reporting from Castilia

Things were tense back at The Plain Speaker. I had no idea what happened at Monday's staff meeting, but it was pretty clear that it hadn't produced any break-throughs. I felt a little guilty about goofing off that morning, even though it had been at Peter's insistence. The first thing I did was get a cup of coffee and look around for someone to chat with. There was no one. Oh, there were people around, alright, but people open to a little casual conversation? Forget about it.

I called Dorothy to see when I could debrief with Peter.

"Oh, hi, Mouse. He hasn't asked about you. Where've you been, anyway? Taking a couple of days off?"

I puffed myself up. "I'll have you know I've been on a special assignment from Peter."

"Well, how about that? Special assignment. You sure he didn't just tell you to get lost?"

"You make me feel so special, you know that, Dorothy?"

"Oh, dear!" she replied, not missing a beat. "Don't tell Peter."

"Can you just check with him, please?"

She called me back an hour later, saying Peter was

available.

When I got there, he greeted me cheerfully, which made me put my guard up.

"Well, if it isn't our foreign correspondent," he said. "We were all worried about you, out there in Castilia without an armored car."

Ha, ha, ha.

"Your phone call was kind of sketchy, but I did appreciate it. So: no news on the bikers, eh? What did you find out that's newsworthy?"

"A great deal," I told him, honestly. "Nothing we can print right now, but a whole lot of interesting stuff to keep watching over as it develops."

He seemed more interested than I expected.

"Tell me," he said. "Go ahead and take your time."

My jaw dropped. "Peter, are you feeling okay? I've never heard you say that to me. Ever."

"Let's just say there are wheels within wheels in this situation, and I think it's fair to say that nobody sees the whole picture. That's one reason I decided to send my most nonlinear reporter to look around. Anybody else, I'd start with one of two approaches: either I'd say start at the beginning, or I'd say start with the headline and a few bullet points under that. Since it's you and it's so fluid, pick any point you found interesting, and let's see where it takes us."

I took a deep breath. "Okay. Here's as good a moment as any. Froggie is the only guy in jail, and the FBI wants to pin something on him – anything at all – just so they can say they got some result to justify all the manpower and negative press. But before things get started, his lawyer recuses himself. Says he has a conflict of interest." I described the scene in front of the judge and her displeasure with the sudden announcement. Peter asked for the names of the individuals and the confusing, overlapping corporations. He was particularly interested to hear that the Treasury Department was involved.

"How big is this commune, again?" he asked.

"Six people, depending on how you count. If you include Froggie's kids, you're up to ten."

"Six adults in a village nobody has heard of, and you have the FBI, the ATF, and the Treasury Department mounting a large, coordinated raid on a festival about trout. Does that seem as odd to you as it does to me?"

"I agree with you, Peter."

"It suggests that somebody is really connected. But who? How? Why?"

"I'll tell you one name that came up: Stanhope."

"I can't believe it," he said. "I tell you to keep your ears open for news about them in Cleveland, and you give me zilch. I send you to Castilia to cover something completely unconnected, and that's where you hear about Stanhope. I'm trying to see the humor in all this, but I'm struggling."

"I never once brought them up," I pointed out. "It was always someone else who plucked them out of thin air and threw them into the conversation. I never made the connection to Stanhope; they did."

"You're sure about that, Mouse? You sure you didn't go there looking for Stanhope?"

"I swear to God, Peter."

He scowled.

"There's this association of organic farmers that Froggie is involved in, and they are always taking on Stanhope. That's the only connection I can come up with. Otherwise, it's all about this Castilia Development Corporation and the festival, just as you said it would be."

"No connection between Castilia and Stanhope?"

"None."

He rocked in his chair in frustration. "Alright, get out of here. Go write an article about something quirky in Cleveland."

"Don't you want something about Castilia?"

He shook his head. "What's there to write? What could you say about your trip that has any relevance or even interest to a resident of Cleveland?"

"Can I at least try?"

"You know what? Don't even bother. I'm not mad at you, and I don't want you to think you've failed the assignment. Just let it go."

He saw my disappointment.

"Didn't you tell me you were going to interview that friend of yours? Go do that."

PART V:
THE COMMUNE

[2009 – looking back to 1965]

CHAPTER 29:

How I Got Involved with Castilia

My name is Arne Price. I work with Mouse, and it's his fault that I am writing this history of the Bite This Commune in the year 2009.

Just how Mouse got me involved is a story for later. All I want to say at this point is that I consider Mouse one of my best friends and that's the only reason I agreed to go meet these strange people. It wasn't out of genuine interest; it was all about loyalty. Once I got there, I became as hooked by the place as Mouse. Our interests are different. He is all about the environment and organic farming; I am all about Stanhope, corruption, and greed. He's the cheerful optimist; I'm the suspicious, cynical pessimist. We get along fine.

The history of the *Bite This Commune* starts in 1965 with the births of Froggie and Hildy.

Just to put things in perspective, 1965 was the start of President Lyndon Johnson's first elected term as President after Kennedy was assassinated. The first American combat troops arrived in Viet Nam, a total of 3,500 that grew to 180,000 by year's end. Johnson announced the "Great Society" initiative; the antiwar movement ramped up in response; and Martin Luther King led the march to Montgomery. Race riots began in Watts, followed by similar riots across the country. (On a personal note, the riots in Cleveland's Hough neighborhood followed in 1966. My involvement in them led me to "voluntarily" join the Army and got my ass sent to Viet Nam as soon as I cleared basic training.) Bob Dylan went electric, the Beatles performed at Shea Stadium, and Jefferson Airplane debuted in San Francisco. It was one of the most tumultuous years in American history, the beginning of fundamental changes that affect us to the present day.

Not in Castilia, though. Castilia is a farming community that revolves around the seasons of the year, not the ups and downs of politics and protest. Froggie and Hildy were born into a society that talked much more about the price of corn and local gossip than to the events in Washington and San Francisco.

The boy who became known as Froggie was legally named Ferdinand. He was the fifth child and only male offspring of Ray and Linda Hartzler. They were good, decent folk living good, honest lives, not exactly poor, but close to it. Ray managed a hardware store; Linda managed to keep the family of girls more or less in line. Then along came Ferdinand. There was just something different about the child that went far beyond just being a boy. Early on, he picked up the nickname Froggie, which is what he is called to this day. I don't know what he looked like in kindergarten (large even then, I imagine), but by the time he reached high school, he was a full-grown bullfrog, the most massive defensive lineman on the football team, a ferocious disruptor and tackler. Off the field, he was amiable and gentle and a bit of a dreamer. In fact, it was more than a bit; his daydreaming almost kept him from graduating.

The girl, born a few months later, was named Hildegaard Bosch, the only child of Stanley and Phyllis Bosch. Stanley was the town dentist; Shirley came from a wealthy family in Detroit. Together, they were the most affluent couple in Castilia, but you wouldn't know that by talking to them. They lived comfortably, but not ostentatiously. When

Hildy was ready for kindergarten, they sent her to the local school rather than the prep school in Sandusky. They did so because Froggie was enrolled, and wherever Froggie went, Hildy was sure to follow. She was his beautiful princess, and he was her frog prince.

Their parents got along as well, despite the difference in their wealth. In a town the size of Castilia (which was bigger back then than it is now, but still a very small place), the birth of a child was a big deal, and the two sets of young parents quickly made contact for mutual support. The babies met when Hildy was only six weeks old. They were best friends from that moment on.

Forty-seven years later, Froggie and Hildy were still living in Castilia when half the federal government (or so it seemed) descended on the Bite This Commune, arresting everyone in sight. Unfortunately, the ones they were looking for had departed the day before. The people arrested were innocent bystanders. The date of the raid was March 21, 2006. That was the Spring Equinox and the climax of the commune's annual Flaming Trout Festival. As fellow reporters at the Cleveland Plain Speaker we heard about the raid, but paid it little attention. We were after bigger stories involving the lawsuit against Stanhope Chemicals. It never crossed our minds that Castilia might be part of that bigger story. To be honest, few of us had ever even heard of the place.

That changed a couple of weeks later when Peter Zenger sent Mouse to Castilia to cover the aftermath of the raid. It cracks me up when I think of how clueless my buddy Mouse was when he more or less parachuted into Castilia and made his way to the Cardinal Café. In my imagination, he was like me when I was dropped off in Viet Nam, except that I at least had basic training and a platoon of fellow soldiers surrounding me. Mouse was on his own with no map. In retrospect, it was amazing how much he uncovered in the space of twenty-four hours.

I'll let Mouse describe how he hooked me into coming with him on his second trip to Castilia. It's more his story than mine. He'll tell it better, in any case.

Me? I'll do what I usually do and stick to the facts, keeping myself out of it. Between the two of us, maybe we can tell a coherent story. It's going to be a challenge, though, given what I've turned up so far and the sheer number of characters we've met along the way. The people living in northwestern Ohio are way more interesting than I expected, every one of them.

CHAPTER 30:

The Presentation

Throughout the 1960s and 1970s, back-to-the-land hippie communes sprang up across the country. Many crashed and burned after a few years, and the whole movement was in significant decline by the time Hildy and Froggie reached high school. Still, they wanted nothing more than to join one after they graduated in 1982. By then, there were hardly any left. They figured the only thing to do was to start one of their own. They pulled in half a dozen kids around the same age and managed to rent a house scheduled for demolition in six months. People drifted in and out like seaweed. Hildy and Froggie stayed. They became lovers, experimented with drugs, and tried on all manner of religions and spiritual practices. Why? Because that's what you did when you joined a commune.

Their parents didn't approve. They figured it was just a symptom of the times, a phase the kids would outgrow after six months. Froggie got a job at the Cardinal Café washing dishes and clearing tables. After a few months, the clients got used to him and his outrageous clothes, and he became a kind of draw. What would he wear today? They teased him about it constantly, and he never took offense. Just by being his authentic, young self, he cheered the place up. In time, they let him do a little cooking, and then, when the junior cook quit to go to the community college to learn to be an auto mechanic, they asked Froggie if he wanted the job. He jumped at it. It turned out that he was a natural. Despite his size, he worked well in the cramped kitchen, maneuvering out of people's way, never getting upset, rarely messing up an order.

He had found his niche. He began to see himself opening up his own restaurant, a place where he could experiment with his own recipes. It would be vegetarian and serve only organic produce from the immediate region. If that didn't work out, it would be mainly vegetarian with a few meat dishes added, just enough to get by.

Hildy, on the other hand, was adrift. She was madly in love with Froggie, but she had no clue what she wanted to do with her life when they were apart. Her parents became ever more frantic. They stopped worrying about where and how she was living. As far as they were concerned, she was married to Froggie, and when the right time came, they would get married. So they let those concerns go. What they couldn't let go was the need for her to get a college education. They would pay for it willingly. She countered their offers by saying that she didn't want to waste their money by taking a bunch of classes that didn't interest her or lead to a job. She had friends who did that and ended up dropping out, feeling like failures, and carrying loads of debt. College, her parents told her, was exactly the place where you find out what you are interested in. It was one thing for Froggie to discover his love of cooking by stumbling on it through an entry-level job, but they had a hard time imagining the same path for her. She went out the next day and got a job clerking at a sewing goods store in Sandusky. She was miserable there. Then she found a job in a Sears store ringing up sales. She hated it. She tried being a receptionist at a hair salon. It bored her stiff.

One day, a new girl wandered into the commune, saying her name was Blossom and that she was a food artist. That took a bit of explanation. She drew and painted plants. Some of her artwork ended up as calendars with a different plant featured for each month. Some turned into painted vases or glassware. So far, so good. But she also painted plants – as in painting pictures on plants. Some were geometric patterns or large swirls of color, some were fairies or little forest folk, and some were hilarious: she'd paint worms coming out of apples, stairways leading into squash, parades of ants marching along a zucchini. Nature infused all that she did. She made dyes and inks from local plants and used them to decorate clothes. She loved to garden, and she loved to gather edible weeds and forest plants to add to soups and salads. She was on her way to Tennessee after spending a few years in the Pacific Northwest in a commune that ran an organic farm. She'd been hitchhiking her way east, taking her time. A farmer in Toledo told her about an art fair and community market in Sandusky, where she might be able to sell some of her work. He was on his way to Castilia to see his brother and offered to take her that far. He dropped her off at the Cardinal Café and wished her luck. As luck would have it, Froggie was sitting at one of the tables, taking a break after the lunch crowd cleared out. She took one look at the way he was dressed and knew she'd found a kindred spirit. That night he brought her over to the commune and the home she never knew she'd been looking for. She moved in and never left.

Blossom was drawn to Froggie, but more as a brother than anything else. The person she was most drawn to was Hildy. A strange chemistry bonded them. It was almost as if they were sisters separated at birth. Each was completely relaxed and comfortable around the other. Hildy took one look at Blossom's art and immediately began taking her around town, introducing her to every shop owner, every customer, every diner at the café. Soon, Blossom's artwork was on display all over town, and she began taking orders for custom calendars, one of a kind birthday cards, a new sign for the florist shop, a new menu for the café. And yes, she even got her father to display a large painting of daffodils in the waiting room of his ophthalmology office. Initially, it was on loan with a small for sale sign underneath it, but after Dr. Bosch heard enough compliments, he bought it outright. It hangs there, still.

Hildy, Froggie, and Blossom began to dream about

opening a combined restaurant and revolving art gallery. Froggie would be the chef, Blossom would decorate the food, Hildy would wait tables, run the cash register, and be the business manager. It could work; they just knew it. All they needed was some money to get things started. They tossed ideas around and came up with a plan. They would make a presentation to their parents (not Blossom's – she didn't seem to have any) and to a couple of other influential people who were friends of Hildy's parents. One was Elliot Washburn, the president of the First Bank of Castilia and the other was a local lawyer named Franklin Bucher (pronounced "Booker.") They would make their presentation on a Sunday night when the Cardinal was usually closed. Their guests wouldn't have to imagine a thing; they would experience the vision directly.

The first roadblock they hit would have been obvious to any adult with the least experience of business. Christine Nichols, the owner of the Cardinal Café, asked Froggie a disturbingly direct question: why would she want to help them start another restaurant in town, one that would compete with hers? Froggie gaped at her, open-mouthed. He had no idea. He hadn't even thought about it. Christine suggested that he needed to find an answer, and if he did, she'd reconsider. But for right now, no. Sorry.

The next was Hildy's father. He was more than happy to attend, but he wasn't so sure he wanted to ask Elliott or Franklin to come. Hildy was astonished and deeply hurt. It didn't make her feel any better when he explained that he was afraid the proposal would make them – and him – look foolish. He wasn't scared of the dinner or her ability to speak with confidence, but what did they know about financing a business? Did they even know what a business plan was? Or a loan? Or collateral? He suggested that they do a dry run just with the parents, and just about the business proposal. At this point, there was no need to host a dinner and go to the expense of renting out the café and paying for the food. She hadn't even gotten around to mentioning Froggie's setback with Christine, and their inability to come up with an answer to why she should let them hold the event at her restaurant in the first place. Her father came up with an alternative proposal of his own. Why not come to dinner at their house instead? They'd already met Blossom and rather liked her. It could be a lovely evening, and it would allow them to talk about what went well and what they might want to work on before calling in the real businessmen. Hildy burst into tears, vowing never to speak to him again.

For the three would-be entrepreneurs, the world stopped turning, the sun stopped shining, and a new ice age descended upon them and all their dreams. Little did they know all that was happening behind the scenes, nor how lucky they were to live in that particular town with those specific parents. Hildy's father Ray told his wife Phyllis about the conversation, which triggered an emergency meeting with Froggie's parents Ray and Linda, which in turn led to a discussion with Christine Nichols, who began to see the humor in the whole thing and the reality that she had nothing to fear. Quite the contrary, this could be an excellent learning opportunity for the kids and maybe make them appreciate what running a small business was like. The one thing they asked her was not to let them use the restaurant for free. They talked about a suitable number. It had to be high enough to challenge their meager resources, but not so high that they would just give up. They settled on a price of $25.00. Christine was a little nervous that that might be too high, but Froggie's mother suggested that she tell him he could work it off by picking up an extra shift. But let them come up with the money if possible. They began to take a certain guilty pleasure in maximizing this opportunity for learning. It had nothing to do with getting even with their rebellious kids. They were only operating out of love and concern for them.

Bringing the banker and the lawyer was a matter of

contention. Stanley was reluctant. He had a certain standing in the community and didn't want his business friends to be critical behind his back. Phyllis was having none of that male ego nonsense and went straight to Elliott Washburn's wife, Clarissa. The parental plot thickened when Clarissa agreed to talk her husband into attending (and not ridiculing the kids), but only if they included her son Thomas. Thomas was two years older than Froggie and Hildy and knew them enough to be friendly. Thomas's lack of enthusiasm for finishing college and following his father into the banking business was an issue. She thought the experience might be eye-opening for him, no matter how things went. He might be inspired by the enterprising attitude of the kids, or he might see how unprepared they were and how much he, himself, had to learn. Either way, it would be a win.

Two weeks and a hundred conversations later, Froggie, Hildy, and Blossom hosted Froggie's parents, Hildy's parents, Franklin Bucher, and Elliott and Clarissa Washburn and their son Thomas for a sit-down dinner at the Cardinal Café. With help from friends and members of the commune, they completely rearranged the seating area and put up Blossom's food art everywhere. The menu was fixed because offering multiple dishes just wasn't possible under these circumstances. Still, it was beautifully illustrated, and each guest had their own, one of a kind, inscribed menu to take home with them. The food wasn't particularly fancy, but the ingredients were fresh as of that morning, and the preparation, cooking, and decorating of each item was first-class and novel. Hildy performed her role as hostess with graciousness and confidence that surprised her guests. All three of the entrepreneurs served each course and kept a mostly discrete watch over the guests, bringing fresh water as needed. The meal was a grand slam home run. A triumph, all the sweeter because it was so unexpected.

What followed was a disaster. The business plan was a

dreamscape seen through a soft filter with nary a hard edge to be found. They had some numbers in it, but upon gentle probing, the numbers were nothing more than optimistic guesses plucked out of the air. In this dream world, there were no accidents (and thus no thought to insurance), no bad weather or failing roofs, no disruptions in supply chains, no ups and downs in customers, no seasonal changes other than available fresh food, no turnover in staff, no time to set up the books or handle any of the legal requirements (and no budget to pay for having this done), no health insurance or vacation for staff, no extra staffing for peak events like Mother's Day, no spoilage of food, no business taxes, no budget for phone service, water, electricity, let alone property taxes and assessments.

Then came the marketing questions. Did they know how far people would be willing to travel to go to their restaurant? Did they know how many people lived within this distance? Did they know the age distribution or average family size? Did they know how much people around there spent on restaurant meals on average? Did they know the average profit margins of small restaurants or how long new restaurants tended to survive? Had they performed any kind of survey to gauge people's desire for vegetarian food? Did they have an advertising budget? Did they have plans for a grand opening? Did they have a formula for how to price their meals? Who would they be competing against (in addition to the Cardinal), and how would they go about it? What would they do if a new, vegetarian restaurant opened up next door to them if they were successful enough?

The adults were all careful to keep their tone of voice sympathetic and respectful. When the kids flailed around to answer or simply gave up and said they didn't know, the response was some variation of "well, that's something you'll have to think about before you open your new restaurant."

The one person in the room feeling the most pressure turned out to be young Thomas, the banker's son, who was caught between his allegiance to his classmates and their shared generation on the one hand and to his parents on the other. He held back, maintaining a careful silence throughout the excruciating Q and A. The adults let him do so until the very end, but then his father singled him out and gave him a Hobbesian choice: his son could either announce whether or not he would grant them a loan or he could ask a serious, meaningful question that the others hadn't thought about. It was one or the other.

Thomas looked like he was going to puke as he struggled to come up with a question. There was no way in hell he was going to say yes or no to a loan. What could he ask that wouldn't make him look like as big a fool as the hippies but not seem cruel? His brain went on strike, refusing to work for him. Time slowed down, and the pressure he felt increased. At last, he came up with what turned out to be the most devastating question of the evening. "How much would you charge for the dinner you just served us?"

Hildy looked at Froggie, who looked at Blossom, who looked back to Hildy, who put into words what was obvious. "We, ah, haven't talked about that."

Phyllis (Hildy's mom) stood up and addressed the room. "I think we should give these kids a round of applause for their courage. I imagine we've all learned things tonight. I know I have. And I know we'll be having our own conversations in the days to come. So, how about it? How about a standing ovation?"

And so ended chapter one of the commune.

CHAPTER 31:

Skullman

T he young entrepreneurs responded to the crushing experience of their presentation in ways that would influence the next twenty-three years of their lives.

Of course, their first reaction was to get thoroughly wrecked together and reaffirm that nothing was fundamentally different. All they had to do was a bit of homework to flesh out their business plan and then resubmit it. They figured they could pull that off in six weeks, max. The next morning, things looked a little grimmer. Froggie went back to the Cardinal, tail between his legs. Blossom went hiking, picking wildflowers and herbs. Hildy sulked in her room, reliving the humiliation dished out by her parents and their capitalist friends.

The first one to recover was Blossom. In her gentle, earth-motherly way, she helped the others to see that their vision was filled with enough positive energy that the universe would support them and make it come about in astonishing and wonderful ways. The only thing they had to do – *and this was important, guys* – was to understand that the journey was just as important as the goal, and that every apparent setback was simply the perfect unfolding of the steps they needed to take next. Yielding to the flow was the quickest path to fulfillment, and if they did so, the universe would send messengers and helpers to guide them and bring about a manifestation more magical than their current, troubled minds could even contemplate. If, on the other hand, they tried to bull ahead according to their plans and try to force things to happen more quickly, all they would achieve was unhappiness and failure.

The others asked her what that meant, like, you know, specifically?

Blossom replied that she couldn't possibly tell them what they should do. As for herself, she had gotten visited by a spiritual guide in the guise of a sea turtle that showed up in the middle of a dream. What the turtle told her was that she lacked the earth element and was too influenced by water, air, and spirit. It was time to stop wandering around and put down some roots, time to stop gathering blossoms and start sowing seeds, stop firing up her imagination and observe how real plants grow in real soil.

Okay, but what was she going to actually do with that advice?

Blossom announced that she was going to start working at an organic farming co-op a few miles away.

Did that mean she was going to leave the commune?

No. She liked it here just fine.

Hildy's new journey started a couple of weeks later. Her parents let her stew for a week and then began to pester her about talking with them. Come over for dinner, they pleaded. Just her, not Froggie. They had a gift for her. She delayed long enough to establish a certain measure of dignity and relented. Her parents told her they wanted to support her path to opening a restaurant with the others, but only if she was serious about it. She assured them that she was.

You need a business degree.

She had come to much the same conclusion a week

earlier.

They were delighted to hear it and asked if she had done any research into programs nearby. She had not.

No problem. We have.

They told her there were several options. She could get a general business degree, either at the associate level (two years) or the bachelor's level (four years). That was one way to go. Another would be to get a culinary arts degree (again for two years or four years). Yet another would be to get a degree in marketing or sales.

It didn't matter what path she chose; they would pay for it.

Hildy accused them of using the presentation as a sneaky way of convincing her to get a college degree so they wouldn't have to apologize for her to their snooty friends. It stung them, because there was a sliver of truth to what she said, and her mother even admitted to it. The larger issue, her father said, was that they truly wanted her to be happy and if running a restaurant was what she wanted to do, then that's what they wanted for her.

We want what you want.

She believed them, but why not invest in a restaurant right now? Take whatever it would cost to pay for a college degree and give her the money. Why make her delay her dreams by four years? That way, she wouldn't have to ask the bank for a loan and have to learn all the right answers to the stupid questions they flung at her.

They kept their cool and explained that the questions a bank asked were the questions she and Froggie would need to ask themselves even if they were simply given the money the way she wanted. They would need to figure out how to price their meals, how to advertise, how to set up their books, what kind of insurance they needed, what kind of regulations they had to follow, what taxes they would have to pay. The quickest and safest way to figure that out was to go to college for a couple of years or more.

It's better to make a mistake on a test than in real life.

Much as she didn't want to admit it, it made sense. The conversation moved on to what kind of program would be most useful. She thought culinary arts would be the most relevant, but when they talked about the kinds of courses she would take, she saw that a culinary arts degree would be much more valuable for Froggie to get. Her mother pulled out a brochure from a community college in Loraine and showed her the description, which said that their program would equip her to manage a commercial kitchen, set up a catering business, or run a food service in a nursing home or hospital. That didn't sound like Froggie at all. Nor did it appeal to her.

A general business degree might be better, but that probably meant waiting four years to get going—an eternity in her mind. Her mother pulled out more brochures, showing her that two year programs might be all she needed, with the benefit that if she realized she needed a four year degree, she could transfer her credits. They looked at various specialties within the general area of business. The one that Hildy found most interesting was marketing, except for one thing; all that math. She wasn't sure she could handle it.

If you have trouble, they have support programs. If worse comes to worst, we'll find you a private tutor and pay for it.

Nothing got decided that night, but in January Hildy enrolled in the marketing program at Loraine Community College. It was thirty-five miles away. Her parents bought her a five year old beater and even paid for the gas. They pretended it was a loan, but one she didn't have to repay right away – or ever, for that matter.

Froggie's path was apparent only in retrospect. Following the presentation, he admitted to Hildy that there were only two things he wanted to do -- besides spending the rest of his life with her. One was to smoke dope and the other was to invent recipes and cook food that nourished the bodies and souls of hungry people. This sounded suspiciously like a re-wording of Blossom's vision rather than his own, but that's all he had for her. Sorry! Hildy wanted to know what that meant in terms of things he was going to do that were different from what he'd been doing. He improvised an answer which turned out to be an actual plan (in retrospect). He would continue to work at the Cardinal, but he would start cooking most of the meals at the commune and experiment with new recipes. He was especially interested in incorporating marijuana and *psilocybin* mushrooms as active ingredients. Hildy was skeptical, but agreed to let him try. The other members of the commune were more receptive. They didn't care what they ate as long as they didn't have to cook anymore.

Froggie followed through spectacularly. Working at the Cardinal gave him stability and showed him how to be efficient in the kitchen. Blossom began bringing home organic produce and continued to gather wild plants, which Froggie learned to include in his daily offerings. There were mushrooms out there free for the gathering, and not just *psilocybin*. There were *morels, puffballs, chanterelles* and the well-named *shaggy manes*. Then there were the tubers like *Jerusalem artichokes*, the roots of *Queen Anne's lace* and Froggie's personal favorite, the water covered roots of *cattails*.

It was a time of stability in the commune. Their landlord kept putting off the renovation of the property and let them stay there for a pittance, glad to keep the place occupied. Hildy, Froggie and Blossom made up the essential core. New people came and went. A leather worker named Terry settled in for the long haul. Their neighbors got used to the hippies and realized they might be strange, but they were essentially harmless.

As Hildy was getting ready to start her second year at the community college, Froggie began feeling restless. He yearned for new tastes, different cuisines, wild plants that didn't grow in Ohio. By this time, the commune shared three vehicles: Hildy's car, an ancient Buick, and a customized VW camper. He convinced the others to let him take the camper out west, promising to return with a full load of wild plants and new cuisines. Hildy asked him how long he planned to be gone. *A month,* he said.

He was gone for three.

The camper was filled with dried mushrooms and other wild plants from Ohio, along with enough marijuana to keep a prison mellow for a year. There were two locations he most wanted to visit: the region around Santa Fe and Taos, New Mexico and the region around Boulder, Colorado. He went to the Southwest first, and ended up staying at several meditation centers, helping out with food prep and exchanging recipes and local ingredients. It was an eye-opening, mouth-watering, consciousness-raising experience all around. The whole world of chili peppers opened up to him. He experienced dozens of traditional dishes from the Southwest for the first time. What he expected to be a one week stay turned into six. It wasn't all one way, either. Froggie brought out wild plants from Ohio and demonstrated his own special recipes. The local cooks were impressed enough to share their knowledge and take him with them to harvest wild plants of the desert and high mountains. And, crucially, they taught him to fly fish and exposed him to the wonderous taste of freshly caught trout. He wasn't a natural fisherman, but he was born to bring out the subtle taste of trout in new ways. By the time he left New Mexico, he was capable of catching the occasional trout and carried with him a fly rod and tackle given as a parting gift from a Buddhist meditation center outside of Taos for which he invented a recipe they called *Froggie's Dreamer* forever after. In addition to the fly fishing outfit and a long list of recipes, his camper was now half filled with various peppers and cactus flowers where his rapidly depleting stock of Ohio edibles used to be.

In Colorado, he spent time at the Naropa Institute and some local communes more or less affiliated with it, exchanging recipes and ingredients, cooking alongside local cooks, foraging for new plants and fungi. There were trout up in the mountain streams, and once he gained the trust of some commune members, he learned where to find them and how to catch them, at least at a basic level. He traded recipes and cooking techniques he'd picked up in New Mexico as well as ones he had developed back in Ohio.

He was preparing to head back to Castilia, but his new friends insisted that he had to see Yellowstone Park at the very least. He could get there in a day they said, but after inspecting the VW camper, they amended that to two or three days. He allowed himself to be persuaded, and off he went.

One night he was camping in a remote area of Yellowstone Park when a biker dressed in full leathers and riding a Harley showed up just as it was getting dark. Froggie waved him over and bid him sit down by his fire. No words were exchanged. The biker pulled out a joint, lit it and offered to Froggie, who took a deep, slow, practiced toke, the way some alcoholics will start a long night drinking.

"That's nice," he said. "Name's Froggie, by the way."

The biker just nodded. "Skullman." They passed it back and forth as the twilight deepened and stars came out. Then it was Froggie's turn. He rolled one of his own special blend and watched closely as his new friend took the first toke. It was smoother on the throat, had some intriguing tastes mixed in, and lifted the biker to places he'd never visited before. "Whoa! That's some fine shit."

"It's different, isn't it?" Froggie prodded.

"It's unique."

Froggie was a hundred pounds lighter back then, but still hefty enough to suggest that he was a direct descendant of the Buddha. "It's one of my private blends."

"You grow this stuff?"

"Skullman, my new friend, if I told you, I'd have to kill you."

"Tell me."

"I don't grow anything. Nature grows things. Things grow themselves. I notice. I notice what grows and where it grows, and when the season is right, I gather a few plants here, a few leaves there, and an occasional mushroom if the moon is right. I found a small antler once that I still use. I grind a bit off and mix it in like cinnamon. I like to stay local, gathering things that live together in harmony. For example, right now I have a tuft of mountain goat fur in my camper, along with some glacier lilies and some small flowers I'd never seen before. I asked a ranger what they were. Pinesaps. Nice name. And guess what? They don't have any chlorophyll. They're parasites, sucking nutrients out of the roots of pine trees. But they aren't mushrooms because they produce a flower and seeds, rather than spores. Now, some people would think of grinding some pinesap seeds into a powder and add it to some blend of marijuana grown in Mexico or Columbia, and I'm not saying that's wrong—it being a free country—but it's not, you know, natural. What I'm going to do is see if I can get these pinesaps to grow on my land in Ohio. We have plenty of pine trees there, so maybe it works, maybe it doesn't, but if it does, then I am going to try adding a pinch to my next custom blend and see what happens when I smoke it."

The Milky Way stretched across the night sky like God's favorite head scarf. The two men lay on their backs, falling into it every time they breathed out, pulling themselves back to earth when they breathed in, travelling untold distances with each full breath. Time purred like a house cat.

"Froggie?"

"Yes?"

"What are you going to do with the mountain goat fur?"

"I have no idea."

"You're not going to plant it, are you?"

"No, it belongs above ground where it can feel the wind. I might hang it on a low branch over the spot where I plant the pinesaps. You know, to keep them company."

"That's a fine idea with a touch of madness."

The two men buddied up and spent the next six weeks together in a state of altered consciousness. Skullman had his own traveling kit of hallucinogenics, which they experimented with throughout the backcountry of Yellowstone and on to the Grand Tetons. They parted ways as winter settled in and the high mountain passes began to close. Skullman headed west from the Continental Divide to California; Froggie headed the opposite way back to Castilia. Each vowed to stay in touch.

They didn't.

CHAPTER 32:

Janey

W hen Froggie returned to Castilia, he found things had changed, and not for the better. In his absence, a new woman – don't even think of calling her a girl! – had taken his place and was running the show with the full support and complicity of Hildy. He learned that her name was Janey Kiser, the angriest woman in Castilia, and boy did she have reason to be. She was an artist from the East Coast on the lam from the phonies and parasites who hadn't appreciated her talent at the Rhode Island School of Design. Oh, they had fucked her over, every last one of them. The teachers were the worst, preying on the vulnerable would-be artists, desperate to be recognized in the tribal, cut-throat world of postmodern art dominated by Jean-Michel Basquiat, Willem de Kooning, Jeff Koons, Keith Haring, and Richard Prince. These rock stars of the East Village were a disparate lot, but the one thing they all had in common was that they were men, goddamned men.

Like most new members, she was on her way elsewhere, stopping by for a night or two with the intention of moving on. Two things – well, people – kept her there. The first was Terry, the leatherworker who made belts and vests for people, but was just as happy making tackle and even saddles for horses. Some of his best customers were Amish and Mennonite farmers from Ashland and Mansfield fifty-some

240

miles south. Terry knew absolutely nothing about the New York art scene and didn't particularly care to learn. And why should he? He was not an artist. He was a leatherworker, a craftsman. He didn't even know what the word *artisan* meant, for Christ's sake. But here was the thing: he was an artist, every bit as good as the RISD students Janey had gone to school with. And when she showed him Polaroid prints of her sculptures, some of which included leather straps and braided ropes, he was honestly impressed and told her so in no uncertain terms. He didn't understand it and lacked the vocabulary to even describe what he saw, but the important thing was that he responded to it, strongly. That made her respond to him, just as strongly. They became lovers the night she arrived and were still sharing his room when Froggie showed up two months later.

The second person who kept Janey there was Hildy, a soul sister being treated cavalierly by her man Froggie, a classic chauvinist pig if she ever heard of one. Within a week, she had poor Hildy convinced that Froggie was screwing every woman out west, probably picking up a dozen diseases in the process. Her tirades about faithless men almost destroyed Hildy and might have done so if Terry and Blossom hadn't been there to reassure her. Her parents and Froggie's parents were unhappy with his lack of communication, but they reminded her that Froggie had never had eyes for any woman other than her, and they couldn't imagine that changing.

There was a lot more to Janey than anger and bitterness. Softer, gentler, more caring sides began to appear as Terry's uncomplicated sensuality and honest admiration calmed her physically. At the same time, Hildy's goodhearted concern and empathy began to stitch back together her torn spirit, which had been like a quilt mangled by a lawnmower when she first appeared. Janey started to perceive the others as something more than unsophisticated Ohio rubes. She asked if she could draw portraits of them, and in the process of doing so, she saw more of their deeper truths and was moved. She took a part-time job bagging groceries and was gratified when a few of the shoppers smiled at her or thanked her by name, reading it off the badge they made her wear.

The only person she couldn't stand – other than Froggie, who was nothing more than a stand-in for all the other bastards who'd hurt her and her career – was Blossom. To Janey's eye, Blossom's art was pure, unadulterated crap and her airy-fairy new age spirituality made her want to puke. Blossom was equally repulsed by Janey, whose aura looked like she'd gotten third-degree burns in a nuclear accident. She took one look and fled the commune. Hildy tracked her down and talked her into returning, but the two artists avoided each other like feral cats. There was no portrait of Blossom. Never would be, either.

Enter Froggie, oblivious to all these changes and eager to share his adventures with the others, hold Hildy in his arms, reclaim their love for each other, and then start cooking up a storm. He got the storm part right, but that was it. Blossom seemed the only person glad to see him. The others were clustered around this hard looking, black-haired, spidery woman glaring daggers at him as if he'd done her some vast and unforgivable wrong. He'd never met this furious stranger, so how could he have hurt her? The coldness of the reception, especially the frost emanating from his beloved Hildy, hit him almost as hard as the debacle at the Cardinal when they presented their business plan. Hildy did allow him into her bed but kept herself as far from him as possible. She wouldn't so much as hold his hand. It took an eternity for either to fall asleep and when Froggie woke up in the early hours of the morning, he was aghast to hear Hildy sobbing into her pillow. He knew better than to reach out for her. In the morning, she had gone off to her community college for the day.

Blossom took him aside and filled him in as best she could. Froggie begged her to act as a go-between to help him figure out what he could do to make amends to Hildy for staying away so long. Blossom told him about Janey's many insinuations about his sexual adventures. It was all he could do to remain standing. Anger at Janey came later. For the moment, all he could do was imagine the pain Hildy had been feeling.

"You know it's not true," he said to Blossom.

"Of course it's not, and deep down, Hildy knows it, too."

"Let's take a walk."

"There's a special little glen I discovered while you were gone. Want to see it?"

"I have a gift for you," he said mysteriously. "I'll give it to you there."

He went to the camper and pulled out the pinesaps and the fluff of mountain goat hair, well-hidden and kept moist in a container of moss. She looked at it, wondering what was inside. She had missed Froggie something terrible and felt that she was rapidly losing Hildy as her best friend. They walked along the roadway a couple of miles, their shadows elongating in front of them and their auras melting into each other like the colors of a rainbow. Without a doubt, they loved each other, but there was nothing sexual about it. Even the word *romantic* was wrong. They were brother and sister soulmates wandering through paradise.

When they reached the glen, Froggie gave her the box of moss and explained what was inside. She had never heard of pinesaps before or Dutchman's pipe, another name for them. They were lovely, a kind of curled over asparagus rendered in watercolor. She uncovered them the way she would a nest of baby robins. He let her select a pine tree to plant them under, and together they dug a shallow hole and gently put them into it, covering them up with just enough soil to secure them in place.

"And now this," he said. He handed Blossom the mountain goat fur. She asked a question with her eyes, and he responded with a tiny motion of his hand. *Do with it as you wish.*

She hung it on a low bough extending from the next pine over.

When they got back to the commune, Hildy's car was parked on the street.

"Stay here," Blossom said. "Let me go talk to her. I'll let you know when it's time to come inside."

He stood there, a man of straw, miserable from head to toe, completely immobilized. At last, the front door opened, and Hildy walked out. She came up to him so close he could feel her breath. She looked deep into his eyes, more deeply than he ever remembered. And then she slapped him full across the face, burst into tears, and hugged him as if she was afraid of drowning.

CHAPTER 33:

New Alliances

The next year and a half (1982 – 1984) was a difficult time for the commune. Janey's arrival stirred things up, but there were forces already in play. You could argue that Froggie's road trip was the real beginning of all the troubles, but you could just as easily say it began with Hildy's internship at the First Bank of Castilia.

The business program at the community college encouraged the students to take an internship at a business of interest. They granted up to two credits at the discretion of the professor. Hildy approached Elliott Washburn, the bank president, who had destroyed her self-confidence a year and a half earlier. It was an act of courage on her part, and Elliott recognized it as such. He was also impressed with her decision to get a business degree, even though it was at the associate level rather than a bachelor's or master's. They talked for some time, exploring options for what she could do at the bank, and the longer they talked, the more impressed he became. Neither of them had forgotten the presentation at the Cardinal. They chewed it over a bit, and in the course of that, Elliott had an idea. How would Hildy like to make a new presentation, using the knowledge she had picked up from the college? What he had in mind was a plan to develop the burned-out YMCA camp that the bank still owned and could not sell for close to two years.

Do you mean, develop it as a new camp?

Pretend you are a real estate developer. A summer camp is just one option. There are thousands of others, including breaking it up into smaller parcels.

Hildy's mind raced ahead like a greyhound until his next words stopped her momentum like a steel linked chain.

I think I'm going to pair you up with Thomas. Both of you must learn how to collaborate in a business setting.

She took a deep gulp and pretended to be happy with the arrangement. Before she could take a second breath, Elliott called his son into the office and explained what he had in mind. Thomas looked shell-shocked more than anything else. The three of them spent another hour sketching in the basic shape of the project. Elliott wanted three options, ranked in order of feasibility, and he wanted the two of them to agree on the ranking before submitting it to him. They had three months – the deadline determined by Hildy's schedule at school.

Any questions?

Who's in charge? Thomas asked.

Since you asked, you are.

When Hildy told Froggie about the internship, he was not pleased. The best he could say was *good luck*. There was tension between them these days arising from the hurt feelings surrounding his extended trip and the reception she gave him when he returned.

The next day, Thomas and Hildy spent the morning walking around the property. Developing it was going to be a real challenge: the cabins and dining halls were a wreck, the pond was too small for boating, the land too uneven and rocky for farming. As far as they could tell, no electricity or telephone lines were running into the property, and the access road was deeply rutted. The tennis courts were cracked and weed infested. It was no wonder the bank still owned the property.

That was the bad news. The good news was that the two of them got along just fine. Away from his father, Thomas relaxed and became a normal human being. He was quite a bit smarter than he let on, and far from the slacker his father seemed to think he was. To top it off, he didn't boss her around.

They settled on three options that very first day: a commune, a golf course, and a nursing home and rehab center. That was the easy part. In fact, the only easy part. Their initial plan was for Hildy to sketch out the commune option and Thomas to look at the golf course. The issues that came up would inform how they approached the nursing home option. That plan lasted less than a day and proved to be a valuable learning experience. They realized that certain pieces of information were fundamental to any proposal and needed to be addressed right up front. The first was a map of the property, showing the precise boundaries. They also required a second map, they decided, that showed the contours of the surface. They needed the title history and an understanding of any liens or other impediments that could tank any project before it started. They began making a list. In addition to what they already had, they needed the building codes applicable to the property in general. Then, if they wanted to build a nursing home, they would need whatever additional codes that would entail. They also needed to understand any environmental issues that might arise, especially with that pond sitting there. What else? The village council. What power did they have to approve or reject any plan? And were there county or state agencies that might have similar authority? Who owned the road? Who plowed it? Who would pay for bringing utilities into it? The list swelled like a loaf of bread in a warming pan.

Thomas felt overwhelmed but fascinated at the same

time. Hildy felt energized, seeing the silver lining in each challenge and eager to get going. They worked on their list, revamping it and prioritizing the information they needed, based on Thomas' experience working for his father, who insisted on prioritizing everything.

Elliott had his own set of priorities, and it became clear that educating and motivating his son was near the top of the list. When Thomas asked to meet with him and explained what it was about, he was hoping for half an hour and expecting fifteen minutes. His father promptly set aside two hours – an almost unheard of amount of time. He had Rachel, his executive secretary, sit in as well. By the time the meeting was over, her list was as long as theirs and almost the same. She accepted it calmly and proceeded to demonstrate what an experienced executive secretary was capable of doing. By the end of the day, Thomas had multiple maps, legal codes, zoning ordinances, quit-claim deeds, and insurance documents piled up on his desk. In half a day, Rachel had found and retrieved what would have taken Thomas and Hildy weeks to even locate. Thomas thanked her. Hildy did a lot more than that. She bought flowers, had Blossom create a one-of-a-kind thank you card, and topped it all off with a small box of chocolates attached to a helium balloon. Thomas thought it was way over the top, but he signed his name and insisted on paying his share. They presented it all to Rachel, who just beamed.

You need help with anything else, you just come to me. Don't hesitate.

Hildy did her best not to smirk.

Froggie had mixed feelings about Hildy's sudden animation. He was delighted to see her so happy, a little worried about this new guy in her life, and more than a bit worried about the direction some of her latest thinking was taking her. A golf course? A for-profit nursing home? She told him about the idea of the whole commune taking over the property on a long term lease. He was not as pleased as she expected.

So, were you planning on asking the rest of us for our thoughts?

It's just an exercise. Obviously, I would if this was real.

So, you're not.

No, she was not. This was her project, not Froggie's. Well, hers and Thomas', and to some extent Elliott Washburn's and Hildy's faculty supervisor. That was more than enough feedback, thank you very much. And forget about telling Janey. As much as she had come to like her, Janey was the last person she wanted butting into her project. She made Froggie promise not to tell her a word.

Janey was a special friend, but she had opinions about everything. She had opened Hildy's eyes to the power everyone at the commune had given to Froggie without a second thought. His charisma, his sense of entitlement, even his physical size grated on her. She found herself talking to Janey more and more. In turn, Janey began opening up to her. All was not well between Janey and Terry. She wished there were more bedrooms in the house so she could have one to herself. That alone might be enough to fix their relationship, she thought. Hildy began thinking along the same lines in terms of Froggie and herself.

Froggie began to take complete control over the kitchen and the meal planning for dinner. There was no resistance in the beginning. The others were more than happy to let him do it until they began making requests or suggestions and getting turned down as a matter of course. He was becoming an accomplished chef and using the others as his taste testers. As long as he got to create the recipe, he was gracious in accepting honest feedback and willingly made adjustments. This diluted the grumbling about the way he was making all the decisions. They were the best-fed commune in the country, they figured. But, still, sometimes you just want something ordinary that you grew up with: mac and cheese, hamburgers, tuna fish casserole. Eating at Froggie's restaurant felt like meeting new people every day of your life.

Here, bite this, Froggie would say, as he presented his latest concoction.

It became a running joke among them. Any request for helping out with a chore would be answered with, *bite this*, or *bite me*. It was funny, but underneath the banter, resentment was building. One night, after a disagreeable day with Terry, Janey had had it.

Here, bite this, Froggie said, shoving a forkful of braised turnip greens mixed with some ferns at her mouth.

Fuck you, she replied.

Oh, come on, he said, *give it a try*.

You can bite this whole commune!

Froggie's eyes grew big and bulbous. He took a step back, breathed in a mighty breath and ... hesitated. He thought about what she'd just said and broke into a glorious grin. It was daybreak in the pond. *That's it!* he cried in exultation. Turning to the others, he put it to them. *What do you guys think about calling ourselves the Bite This Commune?*

The response was overwhelming. They loved it. The only one voting *no* was Janey, who vowed to leave in the morning.

You can't leave now, Froggie announced. *You just named us. That makes you family.*

Janey looked like she was going to spit in his face.

Later that night, Hildy and Froggie talked about it. Hildy confessed to loving the name, but she also understood where Janey was coming from. *You need to come down from your throne as the king of food.* Froggie relented, but grudgingly. In the morning, Hildy convinced Janey to stick around, and things settled back down. In a face-saving move, Froggie asked if he could cut back his cooking schedule to five nights a week and let others plan and prepare dinners on Mondays and Tuesdays. Janey promptly signed up for Mondays, and Hildy did for Tuesdays. Old, familiar foods quickly showed up, and to his credit, Froggie never complained. In fact, he enjoyed it. Janey began to soften her blanket opposition to everything he said or did. The whole Bite This Commune started to experience a tentative sense of stability.

As part of achieving that stability, Froggie stopped complaining about Hildy and Thomas not consulting with him as they planned a hypothetical commune at the YMCA camp, even though it bugged him mightily. One night, he found himself alone with Janey when she was in a good mood. They got to talking about her sculptures and the frustrations she felt in not being able to explore larger pieces. He shared his own frustrations with the kitchen's size and the overall limitations posed by the house. This led to him asking Janey what she knew about Hildy's plans for the commune leasing the camp.

What plans?

The ones she and Thomas are presenting to the bank next week.

This was news to Janey. She knew about Hildy's internship, but not about any plans for the commune. Apparently, that little detail never came up. She felt betrayed, and for the first time ever, she found herself in the same boat with Froggie. He could play the martyr (peacemaker was the term he preferred), but she was not going to let this secrecy stand.

Leave it to me.

Froggie immediately wished he'd left it alone. Janey stomped off like a bull in search of a red cape. He wandered off by himself, thinking hard. It might be a good idea if he did a little noodling about the kind of commune he would build at the camp if he had some miraculous bank loan to play around with. The time would come when Hildy showed her plans to the commune. Now that Janey knew about it, that was a given. Froggie would never forget the humiliation at the Cardinal, and he was unwilling to switch sides and become one of the nay-sayers whose only role was to pick apart this new proposal.

He turned to Blossom for advice, suggesting that the two of them come up with their own plan.

Who knows? It might be very similar to Hildy's, he suggested.

Tell me the truth, Froggie. Are you jealous of all the time she's spending with Thomas?

No.

Because, if that's the case, I won't help you. But if it's not, maybe we should call a special meeting where everybody who wants to can present their ideas for expanding. We all know we have to do it.

You don't want to collaborate with me?

Of course, I do, but after that meeting.

Why not?

Because if it's us against them, it will destroy the commune.

This was a shocking thing to hear, and if anyone other than Blossom had said it, Froggie would have dismissed it out of hand. But she had an intuitive sense of force fields and auras he lacked, and he respected that. If she thought they should submit individual plans and collaborate later on, he'd be wise to do so.

Anybody else we should talk to? he asked.

Terry.

Anything I tell him, he'll tell Janey.

You still have to do it.

Froggie sighed, realizing she was right. The next day, he

pulled Terry aside and learned that Janey hadn't clued him in at all. He agreed that she was going to make a scene, but he had no idea when or where or exactly how she was planning to do it. The concept of everyone having a chance to present their ideas appealed to him. He had been thinking of options for the future for some time. So, yeah, it was a good idea.

I don't want to put you in a bind with Janey.

I'm always in a bind with Janey.

So, are you going to tell her?

Beats the fuck out of me.

Before he could decide how to approach Janey, she beat him to the punch. It was Monday, her night to cook, which gave her a natural opening. Over the past few months, Froggie established a tradition of announcing the menu and explaining something about the food and what he was trying to accomplish with his latest recipe. When Janey asked for everybody's attention, they assumed she would follow that pattern, but what she had to announce was not about the evening's meal. It was about secrets and powerplays. It was addressed to the whole community, but it was aimed at Hildy. *Was it true*, she asked, *that Hildy and the banker's own son were hatching a scheme for the bank to take over the commune?*

Hildy was visibly startled, and her first response was to glare murderously at Froggie for breaking his promise not to tell anyone. Then she stood up and addressed them all.

I can see that my dear friend Froggie can't keep a secret, so my surprise is spoiled now. Thanks, Frogman.

She went on to tell them about the assignment she'd been given by Elliott Washburn and how she and Thomas were going to present their options next week. Right after that, she was going to tell them all about it and show off the plan for a commune at the camp, which she assumed would lead to a larger conversation that included everybody. It had

253

never, ever been her plan to exclude anyone from a conversation about their future. She apologized if it seemed that way.

Well, isn't that unfortunate, Janey declared, *but since the word got out, perhaps Hildy should give the rest of them at least an overview right now.*

Blossom stood up. *Can I offer up a different idea? Why don't we all come up with our own plans? I know I'd like to, and waiting a week is no big deal.*

Now it was Janey's turn to be startled. She tried to read the room, but couldn't tell what was going on in people's minds. She told herself to forget about what the others thought; what did she feel about Blossom's suggestion. She decided she liked it. She said so, too. Then she took it upon herself to call for a vote. Should they have a special event one week from now where anyone could present a plan for their future?

Can we make that two weeks? Hildy asked, plaintively. *Our proposal to the bank isn't until a week from Wednesday.*

Janey was about to object, but Froggie seconded Hildy's motion.

It was unanimous. The big meeting would take place in two weeks. As soon as the vote was taken, Hildy left the table and headed for the door. Froggie chased after her. Where was she going? Could they at least talk about it? She informed him that she was going to spend the next night and maybe more at her parents' house. She had a lot of work to do.

Aren't you going to at least take a change of clothes?

I'll get my mom to take me shopping. It's been a while since I had anything new to wear.

And off she went, taking his future with her.

CHAPTER 34:

The Vision Quest

Twelve people attended the Vision Quest at the Bite This Commune. Five members presented plans: Hildy, Froggie, Blossom, Janey, and Terry. In addition, Thomas presented the other two options he and Hildy had given to the bank on Wednesday. The other six people were transients or friends, who were welcome as bystanders. Janey – since it was, technically, her night to cook and because she insisted on being in charge – laid out the ground rules.

1. Pass the piecepipe before each presentation.

2. Draw lots to determine the order.

3. Applaud, but don't comment.

4. Presenters don't talk more than 10 minutes.

5. Keep an open mind. If that's hard for you, additional drugs are available.

6. Open discussion at the end with no leader.

One of the visitors asked for a bit of background. Janey referred the question to Hildy, who explained her internship at the bank and the three proposals she and Thomas developed together. She emphasized that this was purely a school project and that the only thing real about it was the camp and the fact that the bank owned it and didn't want to. That did not mean that their plans – or any plans others might be presented tonight – would be approved by the bank.

So, what's the point?

It's a great way to think big and creatively about our future.

Janey inserted herself before any further questions could arise.

Let's pass the piecepipe.

The piecepipe was one of the functional sculptures Janey brought with her on her way west to San Francisco. She constructed it out of four found objects: a 9-inch length of copper tubing, a small kitchen funnel, a pair of ruby red lips with plastic feet that made them jump around on a table, and a keychain with a plastic lanyard and a peace symbol in rainbow colors at the end. The windup mechanism still worked. The pipe offended everybody who had ever seen it, which was precisely Janey's intent. But then some fool at one of their impromptu parties decided to use it to smoke some hashish, and – holy mother of god! – the combination of the hash and the chattering lips pressed against his own blasted a kaleidoscope of unspeakable insight into his addled brain. Before Janey could pull her stoned self off the couch, the piecepipe had already been passed to two others, and somewhere along the line, she lost control over its meaning. Instead of a blunt challenge to the sensibilities of East Village artists, her pipe transformed into a sacred object of counter-culture weirdness. Janey felt herself being snatched away by some trickster spirit, forced to let go. Let go of what? Of intentionality. Of ownership. Of her belief that she was the creator of this thing. In her mind, the piecepipe was now a symbol of unintended consequences and possibly even a doorway to the realm of flowing, cosmic contortions in more than three dimensions. In all honesty, she became a little frightened of it, but she was damned if she would allow others to see that fear. Passing the piecepipe had been Froggie's idea when the core group came up with the rules. She agreed, despite her wariness.

Now, the time had come, and, in front of everyone, she fired up a bit of hashish, put her lips to the plastic ones, and took the first toke. According to the unwritten rules, the person smoking the pipe had to hold the smoke in until the next person inhaled. When the pipe reached Thomas, he almost passed, but Hildy jabbed her elbow into his ribs as a not very subtle hint that passing was not an option. He took a small hit and quickly passed it to Blossom, who serenely took her time before inhaling. By then, Thomas felt the room tilting a bit to the left. The visioning began.

Later on, nobody could agree on the exact order, except that, purely by chance, Hildy went first. And wasn't that interesting? She unrolled a plat map showing the boundaries of the camp, the county road that bordered it on one side, and the boundaries of the adjacent properties. The map had almost as much mind-altering power as the piecepipe. Vague, gauzy visions gave way to precise lines and legal concepts like ownership, legally defined boundaries, deeds, laws, taxes, and money. Knowing full well how alien this kind of thinking was to her audience, she alluded to the fact that she and Thomas had included a business plan filled with numbers to the bank. She would be happy to share that material later on if anyone was interested. For now, she wanted them to imagine a day-care center that would be eco-friendly, communally staffed, and have its own organic gardens and greenhouse, along with a dining hall and kitchen where Froggie could make lunch for the kids and staff and dinner for the entire commune. The vision included several small cabins for the cooperative to live in. Finally, there would be a boardwalk surrounding the pond, with a small gazebo attached to it. This, she explained, was where they would keep the fishing poles to catch the trout they would stock the pond with. The older kids could go fishing there, and Froggie could use the trout in his meals.

She got an enthusiastic round of applause.

The piecepipe went around again, and the next speaker

stood up. Let's say it was Terry. His vision was for a center that produced, sold, and taught people how to make traditional, handcrafted products such as saddles, furniture, cabinetry, and possibly quilts or pottery. He had his own set of show-and-tell materials. He passed around pictures from magazines and travel brochures showing a Shaker village near Lexington, Kentucky; a woodworking school in Vermont; a saddlery school in Las Cruces, New Mexico; a quilting museum in Bucks County, Pennsylvania; and a pottery collective in Berkeley, California. He reminded his audience that these were just basic ideas, not blueprints.

Another round of applause. Another round of the piece-pipe.

Janey's vision overlapped a bit with Terry's. She had in mind a fine arts studio that would make, sell, and teach classes in sculpture, fiber arts, ceramics, and painting. The pond would be the central feature in the middle of a large sculpture garden, where students or working professionals could create large-scale works, exhibit them, and hopefully sell them. In any case, no sculpture would remain on site for more than five years. She described a group of three or four barnlike studios and a gallery to display the smaller items. Proceeds from the sale of any artwork would be split between the artist and the center at some agreed-upon rate that took into account material costs, time of construction, how long it took to sell, and no doubt other considerations she hadn't figured out, yet.

Applause; piecepipe.

Blossom's vision was of a communally run organic farm. Like Hildy, she had visited the camp and made her own kind of map. Hers was a watercolor landscape with two large greenhouses, a store, a barn for horses, a second barn for farming equipment, and a longhouse made of logs where the commune would live. There wasn't a boundary in sight, not even a hedge. Birds flew overhead, and if you looked closely, you could just make out a little beaver swimming in the pond.

Applause; piecepipe.

Thomas took one of his turns. Referring to the same plat map Hildy used, he talked about a senior citizen complex that included a social center, a dining hall, apartments, a rehab center, and a nursing home, all interconnected. It was something the village needed, and much of the construction costs would be paid by taxes. He kept his presentation very brief.

Applause; piecepipe.

He used his second turn (whenever that was) to present the only vision that flopped. It just plain flopped. It was a golf course. The pond would be a water hazard. Instead of a longhouse for communal living, he described an opulent clubhouse. And the less said about that, the better.

Half-hearted applause; aggressive use of the piecepipe.

Froggie came last (by most accounts, anyway). To the surprise of no one, he envisioned a restaurant supported by an organic farm with a large vegetable garden, some fields, and one small greenhouse. He talked about a small grocery store or roadside stand. He described a small building for farm equipment and a similar one used as a fish house for cleaning trout taken from the pond. His vision featured a commune living together in a collection of structures designed by individual members or groups of people sharing a building. He imagined these dwellings to have no overall plan or pattern to them. One might look like a giant mushroom, one might be a geodesic dome, one might resemble a whale. Hell, one could be a replica of their current house. Oh, and one more thing; there would be lots and lots of dogs.

He received a nice round of applause, more restrained than some of the others. It wasn't because they didn't approve; by this time, most of the audience were so high they couldn't bring their hands together enough to clap.

What happened next depends on who you ask. It was easier for some to transition from highly structured presentations to leaderless open conversations than others. The visitors decided that they had visions of their own, deserving the same attentiveness and respect given to the others, even though they were making things up on the fly and seeking to impose them on the commune without having any stake in the outcome. Some were weird, and some were downright incoherent. Add alcohol to that, and comments became harsher, and tempers began to flare. Instead of listening and applauding, speakers interrupted each other.

Thomas turned to Hildy. *I think it's time we left.*

Janey heard it.

Froggie heard it.

Terry heard it.

Blossom heard it.

Hildy looked panic-stricken. She glanced around at the others and gave a helpless little shrug of apology, got up, and walked out with Thomas. One of the visitors yelled, *See you at the clubhouse, fuckface.*

One of the others had been holding forth about a rocket ship and didn't appreciate the interruption. *Hey, I'm trying to talk here.*

Nobody's interested, came the reply.

They began to fight. By most standards, it was pathetic. Both were so inebriated that they could barely stand up, let alone launch a decent punch. Froggie stood up and said, *the party's over, and everyone needs to go home.* Or it might have been Janey, or Terry or someone else. It wasn't Blossom. She was too busy snuggling up to Terry, who reciprocated and headed off to his room. Janey saw this and made a beeline for Froggie, fairly dragging him to his bedroom. Most of the other guests left, but two stayed behind, passed out in separate corners of the living room. They were gone by the time Blossom tiptoed out of Terry's bedroom.

Around noon, Hildy showed up and wordlessly began helping Terry and Blossom straighten out the mess. Nobody was making eye contact. Hildy took the silence as long as she could stand it, and then popped the question. *Where are Froggie and Janey?*

The silence from Terry and Blossom told her everything she needed to know. She fled in tears.

CHAPTER 35:

The Bikers

T he damage wasn't permanent. Blossom chased after Hildy and managed to get her side of the story straightened out. The reason she and Thomas left together was not what people assumed. They had driven together and she was his ride home. It was as simple as that. She managed to drop him off without driving into a fire hydrant and went back to her parents' house because it was closer than the commune. Nothing had happened between them. No sex, no infidelity.

Janey came down around 11:00, looking like hell. She rummaged around, attempting to clean up and wove her way back to Terry's bedroom, climbed into bed and passed out for another four hours. Froggie didn't emerge until 2:00, and when he did he claimed to have no memory of spending the night before with Janey. Blossom sat him down, gave him some coffee and told him what the others had told her.

I guess... Maybe... I kind of remember that.

Blossom's final counseling session was with Terry. She convinced him that the best thing to do was go back to his room, climb in bed with Janey as if nothing had happened, and take a nap. If he really was sick of her, at least wait until they were both sober before breaking up.

And where does that leave you and me?

We're friends, she told him.

Not?

I live alone, Terry.

Froggie cleaned himself up and drove over to Hildy's parents, unsure of his reception, but needing to face them. Her mom Phyllis came to the door and welcomed him in. She was gracious, but subdued.

I'll go get Hildy and then leave you two to talk.

It took Hildy twenty minutes to come downstairs. It was an awkward conversation. The easiest way to get through it was to blame it all on Janey. She was the one who misinterpreted Hildy departing with Thomas, and she was the one who wanted revenge on Terry by seducing Froggie. Whatever else may have happened, both Hildy and Froggie were victims. That was where they went, but to their credit, they didn't stay there. They had issues between them they needed to face, starting with Froggie's road trip. Froggie told her for the hundredth time how sorry he was for causing her such pain and anxiety, but he also said he had no regrets about the experience and wanted to be able to do other trips like it – except that he'd keep in touch. Hildy told him she was done taking drugs. Froggie wouldn't go that far, but he did promise to cut back on them, especially at large gatherings. He asked her if she was feeling out of tune with the commune and its values. She admitted she was, but that did not mean that she was falling in love with Thomas. Truth be told, she was beginning to see Thomas in a more positive light. Last night she began to see the commune through his eyes, and a lot of what she saw turned her off. He begged her to come back. The commune needed her almost as much as he did, and it wasn't as if the others were incapable of change. The best she could do was to say she would think about it.

It took a week, but in the end, she moved back. She slept in the same bed with Froggie, but they didn't have sex.

She went out a few times with Thomas, but only as friends.

So, what about Janey? Janey's behavior was something like Hildy's if you added drugs and sex back in. She spent some nights with Terry and some nights with a number of men in town. Always, in the end, she came back to the commune. She was very careful around Hildy and Froggie. At some point, the three of them sat down together, expressed regret and promised it would never happen again.

The commune began to function again, but it was a much more somber place. They had lost their swagger. They were living day to day, gathered together like a rack of pool balls waiting for something to happen. None of them guessed it would be the sudden appearance of Skullman and three fellow bikers on their way back to Anaheim from the Veterans Freedom Ride in Taunton, Massachusetts. After an exuberant reunion with Froggie, he introduced his friends: Hammer, Suzie Stinkeye, and Large Lizard (who went simply by Large.) Janey took one look at Large and began to pick a fight. He found her hilarious and utterly exotic.

Never met an artist before.

I've met more than my share of rednecks.

Guess that makes us even.

Before things could escalate, Froggie dragged Skullman off to the side and explained a bit about recent events at the commune and the agreement they had made not to host big parties, especially with strangers. It meant that, unfortunately, Skullman and his friends couldn't spend the night there. But he did have an alternative. It was a beautiful day and the overnight forecast was for clear skies and temps in low 50's. There was this abandoned YMCA camp a little outside of town, and they could camp there, along with Froggie and anyone else who decided to join them. Froggie would cook them a special meal back at the commune and deliver it to them. With any luck, most of the commune would come along. He hoped none of Skullman's friends would be offended. There was so much to talk about!

They spent the afternoon hanging around the commune trading stories. Even Janey began to warm up to them. By dinner time, Janey rode out to the camp on the back of Hammer's motorcycle. Large offered her a ride first, but there just wasn't much room behind him. Blossom and Terry drove out in the VW camper. Froggie and Hildy stayed back to cook. Hildy admitted that she could see why Froggie had hit it off with Skullman – not that it excused his lack of communication. She even went so far as to admit that she found herself liking him. She was concerned about them sleeping in the camp, but recognized that it was better than having them sleep at the commune. She thought about giving Thomas a heads-up. Froggie asked her what she'd do if he said no. She decided not to call. They cooked up a storm and brought enough food for twenty out to the camp. The food was unlike anything the bikers had ever tasted, and once they got over their hesitation they piled in and devoured everything in sight, praising Froggie to the skies for his new cooking abilities. Dessert was a pan of hash brownies, which Blossom decorated on the spot with frosting Froggie remembered to bring and some fresh flowers she gathered. Hildy politely declined, claiming she was full. As darkness fell, Hildy gathered up the pots and pans and assorted plates and random silverware and took them back to the commune, telling the group that she might or might not rejoin them, depending on how tired she felt. Nobody made a big deal about it.

After she left, Froggie went up to Janey and asked if they could use the piecepipe.

It's not mine, anymore, she told him. *Go right ahead.*

Do you want to explain it?

No. These are your friends. You tell them.

Froggie called for everyone's attention. He explained a

bit about the pipe, making sure to give Janey credit for making it. *Tonight, my friends, is a special occasion. Not only are we sharing the piecepipe with you, but I am supplying some of Froggie's Special Blend. Right now, this little baggie I'm holding is the only special blend on Earth. I hope you like it. After it makes the rounds, I'll tell you why I'm so happy that I can share it with you.*

This special blend was news to the commune. They began complaining, but Froggie's whole body seemed to be quivering with pleasure and excitement. There was no defensiveness at all. He fired up the pipe, but didn't inhale, insisting that Skullman be the first one to taste it. Skullman received the pipe solemnly and drew a deep breath slow as a snake ingesting a mouse. Even as he passed it along, a huge smile spread across his face. That response turned out to be universal. It was the smoothest marijuana any of them had ever tasted, and the smoothness extended into the high it produced. When it made the rounds back to Froggie, he pulled the last drag deep into his lungs and held it a long time.

Let me tell you about this blend, he said. The secret, he explained was that he infused the grass with the juice from a patch of pinesaps he had gathered when he first met Skullman. He told them about keeping them alive all the way back from Colorado and how he trusted Blossom to choose where to plant them. This was the first time he'd ever harvested a few and found just the right amount of juice to balance the harsher taste of the marijuana. There was more to it than that, of course. The grass was a very special crop he had growing in a hedgerow nobody knew about, and he had added some local mushrooms and a teaspoon of truffle oil to the mix before drying it in a special box hidden in yet another location that he would never reveal to anyone, so don't ask. Ever since developing it, he had fantasized about sharing it with Skullman, and, lo and behold, the man himself showed up at exactly the right time.

Is there any more?

That's it, I'm afraid. Next year, I hope I can make a bigger batch.

The party continued almost all night. It was everything the Vision Quest gathering could have been but wasn't. Blossom paired up with Hammer; Terry spent the night with Suzie; Janey ended up all over Large; and Froggie and Skullman kept the little campfire going and talked about the meaning of the Milky Way arcing majestically over them.

In the morning, there were no recriminations, no regrets, no secrets. The bikers packed up and went on their way. The commune members returned, mellowed out and connected more than ever before. Hildy had left hours earlier for the community college. When she returned, the vibe in the house assured her that everything was fine, including the fact that she hadn't returned. A new balance prevailed.

The last relationship to heal was between Janey and Hildy. Even it smoothed over after the bikers' visit and she heard about the various pairings and how Froggie behaved himself. Summer gradually yielded to Fall, and a new semester beckoned Hildy; her final one. She talked about how excited she was with Janey, but Janey had a hard time pretending to share in the excitement. She still harbored a lot of pain from her days at the School of Design and her decision to drop out. Hildy was disappointed at first, but then after talking with Froggie she got it. Her happiness was a reminder of a traumatic time for Janey.

The problem was that Janey couldn't drop it. She was becoming a real annoyance to everybody. Hildy was convinced that more was going on than bitterness over leaving school. After putting up with it as long as she could, Hildy finally confronted her.

What's going on?

I'm pregnant.

She didn't look happy about it. *How are you feeling?*

267

Like shit.

You mean, like physically? Or is it more than that? Do you want to have the baby?

I don't know. I think so.

Hildy almost asked if Janey knew who the father was, but realized that was not the way to phrase the question. *Have you told the father yet?*

Janey shook her head.

Forget the father, then. How do you feel about becoming a mother?

Janey struggled to answer. *Scared, for sure.*

I'll help you.

That got a smile. *We could call you Aunt Hildy.*

I would love that.

I just don't know how the others are going to react.

It's going to change things, that's for sure, Hildy said. She thought about all she could learn from Janey about raising a child. Maybe once the commune got used to caring for an infant, they'd all relax. Hildy recalled her babysitting days and how precious some of those memories were. She thought about how she and Froggie had essentially been raised in a kind of loose commune, sharing four parents. If she and Froggie had their own baby, it could play with Janey's, surrounded by a loving village of caretakers. Oh, boy. She and Froggie were going to have quite a talk tonight. She hoped he was ready for it, the poor dear, because she sure was. She began thinking about how their child would automatically inherit a lifetime's supply of outgrown clothes. She wondered if Janey knew how to sew. If she did, she could teach her; if not, well, they could learn together. Aunt Hildy. She liked the sound of that.

Froggie was off with Blossom, gathering moss and wild mushrooms by the creek. He probably wouldn't be back until dinner. After that, though, she'd have him all to herself.

After dinner, Hildy snagged Froggie and practically dragged him out the door. They walked in silence until they were far from the commune.

I heard a rumor today, she said. *I heard Janey is pregnant.*

Whoa! Who told you that?

Janey did.

Probably not a rumor, then. Did she say who the father is?

She wasn't ready.

How about the fact that she's pregnant? Is that private information?

I think so.

Then that's the way it should stay.

She looped her arm around him while they walked a little farther. She asked him what he was thinking.

I'm thinking about Terry, more than anything else. If he's the father, that's one thing. If he's not, that's a whole different thing. If she's not living with Terry, we don't have a separate room for her.

This was not what she hoped to hear. What she'd hoped for was more along the lines of him wondering if they should have a baby of their own. But she realized he was right. This was quite possibly going to be the end of the commune unless Janey fully moved back in with Terry or left the commune and found an apartment of her own.

Now you've gone quiet, he said.

I...

Just spit it out; I think I know what you're going to say.

I want to have a baby. Your baby. I've been thinking about it a lot, but when Janey told me that she was pregnant, it just kind of opened the floodgates of all these feelings I've been bottling up. Look, it doesn't have to be this month or anything.

I think nine months is the minimum.

That halted her. She looked at him and saw that he meant it kindly. *You know what I mean.*

I do.

The love in his voice was unmistakable. She still wanted to proceed carefully, though. *So, can we talk about it?*

I guess I'd like to wait until we know more about how this Janey thing is going to work out. I think I'm ready... Maybe... I might be ready to have a baby with you. But I'm not sure I'm ready to leave the commune or see it fall apart. I've always pictured us raising our kids communally. This really throws a pot of cold water on that idea. Just thinking practically.

They agreed to postpone their own discussion until Janey made some decisions, which Hildy thought would happen within a week or two. The important thing was that Froggie didn't rule out the option of having a child with her. The details were important, but the fact that it was almost a done deal was the most important of all.

Janey strung them along for almost three weeks before asking if they could meet at the Cardinal after Froggie finished cleaning up for the night. She didn't want to tell the others until she could think things through with them.

Hildy got there right at nine. Janey kept them waiting until a quarter after. When she shuffled in, she looked more stressed than they had ever seen her. The first thought running through Hildy's mind was that Janey had lost the baby. Or aborted it. She forced herself to block any ideas and wait for the news. The only thing she was sure of was that Janey was distraught.

She came right to the point. *The baby's father is you, Froggie.*

A stunned silence radiated out from them like frost spreading across the floor and up the windows.

Are you sure? Froggie asked. *I mean, there were others.*

I know, Janey said, *but the calendar doesn't lie. And I was real careful with birth control except for that one night.*

The night I don't even remember.

I'm so, so sorry. For both of you.

Hildy turned white as a ghost. *I can't take this,* she said.

Hildy, please!

She stood up and walked to the door. When she reached it she turned back. *You two lovebirds figure out what you want to do. I'm just a bystander at this point.*

Froggie began getting up.

Don't. When you make a decision, call my parents. No. Call your own parents. They deserve to hear it from you. I'd rather hear it from them.

She ran into town and asked Barney, who was working at the pharmacy, if she could use their phone. Her parents came to pick her up a few minutes later. Once she was home, she told them the news. Then she broke down sobbing and ran to her room.

CHAPTER 36:

The Fathers of the Bride

In order to make sense of what followed Janey's announcement that Froggie was the father of her child, you have to know something about the Hartzler family (Ray, Linda, and Froggie), the Bosch family (Stanley, Phyllis, and Hildy), and their relationship to Father Marcus Elliott, the rector of St. Alban's Episcopal Church in Sandusky. Father Marcus became rector there in 1960 and had stayed ever since, fending off all attempts by the Bishop to rotate him to a new parish after the typical span of five to seven years. He was new to St. Alban's when Ray and Linda asked him to marry them in 1961. Two years later, he married Stanley and Phyllis. Both couples had their first child within months of each other, and so it was that Father Marcus baptized little Ferdinand and Hildegaard on Pentecost Sunday in 1965. These were the first kids born to couples he had married, and Father Marcus took a special interest in them from that time forward.

Sixteen years later, Ferdinand (now Froggie) and Hildegaard (now Hildy) began living together in the commune to the dismay of both sets of parents. They also went through the discernment process that prepared them for confirmation as members of the St. Alban's.

The parents felt conflicted enough by this that they asked to meet with Father Marcus. They explained that they didn't know that their kids were having sex with each other, but it was a pretty safe bet. They wondered what Father Marcus thought about confirming kids who were sexually active outside of marriage. They were sure this wasn't sanctioned by the Book of Common Prayer. Father Marcus reassured them that the Episcopal Church saw itself more as a come as you are gathering than a pass a test before getting a license to drive club. They weren't sure if he was joking or not, but the tone of his voice made it clear that he had no reservations about confirming them. They let their fears about confirmation go. While they were in Father Marcus's office, they asked him about marriage. Would he feel free marrying a couple that were already having sex?

Marriage is a whole different matter, he told them in no uncertain terms. He explained it this way: as far as he was concerned, if someone declared that they wanted to join the Episcopal Church, all they had to do was say a few words in front of the congregation, make a pledge to donate to the parish, and they were in. If, on the other hand, a couple wanted to be married, they did need a license, and the Church as an institution had a lot of non-negotiable requirements. The first was that they needed a license from the State of Ohio. To get that, the couple had to certify that they were of age, weren't married to anyone else, weren't cousins or closer, and weren't idiots, morons or imbeciles. The Church had specific requirements on top of that. Ray asked for an example.

You mean, you've forgotten?

They looked at each other sheepishly.

You should know them by heart. You agreed to them in front of the whole parish.

Now they were in a real panic.

Father Marcus was a man of deep contradictions, simultaneously flexible and rigid, forgiving and unyielding, approachable, and fearsome. At one level, he was joking around about these requirements, but at another, he was the voice of God himself. After letting them stew a bit, he let them off the while nailing them to the foundation of the Church at the same time. He handed them copies of the Book of Common Prayer and told them to open it to page 424.

What the Church requires of all people wishing to be married is so important that it gets announced four times, he said. *First, I ask the bride for her consent to these requirements:*

Phyllis or Linda, will you have this man to be your husband; to live together in the covenant of marriage? Will you love him, comfort him, honor and keep him, in sickness and in health; and, forsaking all others, be faithful to him as long as you both shall live?

And before we can proceed, the Church requires you to say, I do. Assuming you do give your consent, I ask the groom for his consent to the same requirements:

Stanley or Ray, will you have this woman to be your wife; to live together in the covenant of marriage? Will you love her, comfort her, honor and keep her, in sickness and in health; and, forsaking all others, be faithful to her as long as you both shall live?

Ray Hartzler asked what happened to the obey part of the vows.

It's coming right up, Father Marcus assured him. He emphasized that this first bit of dialogue was between the priest (representing the Church) laying out the requirements and the couple agreeing to them. In other words, they were recognized as married by the State of Ohio, but not yet by the Episcopal Church. Having agreed to those requirements, the priest could legally perform the marriage according to the canons of the Church. But they weren't married yet. Before they could be, they had to pledge their vows to each other. In person. Face to face. In front of the priest, two official witnesses and everyone in attendance. His tone was light and friendly, but then it turned stern.

Since you seem to have forgotten these requirements, I'd like to hear you repeat the vows you made twenty years ago. Ray, since you were the wiseass who wanted to know about the obey your husband clause, you go first.

Ray looked like a defendant awaiting sentencing. He cleared his throat and did that which must be done.

In the Name of God, I, Ray, take you, Linda, to be my wife, to have and to hold from this day forward, for better for worse, for richer for poorer, in sickness and in health, to love and to cherish, until we are parted by death. This is my solemn vow.

Then it was Stanley's turn. He looked no better than Ray, but one glance at Father Marcus told him there was no getting out of it.

In the Name of God, I, Stanley, take you, Phyllis, to be my wife, to have and to hold from this day forward, for better for worse, for richer, for poorer, in sickness and in health, to love and to cherish, until we are parted by death. This is my solemn vow.

Father Marcus turned to the women and pointed out that their vows were identical to the men's except for one word: the infamous "obey" clause. It was one, short, simple word, tucked into the middle of things, which made it easy to skim over when you read it on the printed page. But it was quite a different matter when you had to say it aloud. Instead of vowing "to love and to cherish," the wife had to say "to love, to cherish, and to obey."

Wait a minute, said Phyllis. *I don't recall saying that. Do you, Linda?*

Linda couldn't remember, either way.

Father Marcus was enjoying himself a little more than a

priest should. He told them to relax; the obey clause had been removed a generation earlier. Their own mothers had pledged to obey their husbands, but they were off the hook. *I would like you to repeat them, however. Linda, you go first.*

In the Name of God, I, Linda, take you, Ray, to be my husband, to have and to hold from this day forward, for better for worse, for richer for poorer, in sickness and in health, to love and to cherish, until we are parted by death. This is my solemn vow.

She got through it without crying, but barely. Then it was Phyllis's turn.

In the Name of God, I, Phyllis, take you, Stanley, to be my husband, to have and to hold from this day forward, for better for worse, for richer for poorer, in sickness and in health, to love and to cherish, until we are parted by death. This is my solemn vow.

Phyllis did shed a tear, which she wiped away a little angrily. Why did he have to do that? But Father Marcus wasn't done with them yet. He suggested that – perhaps – this whole discussion with him really wasn't about Froggie and Hildy getting confirmed. Perhaps it was about them getting married. Was that possible?

Now he really had them in a panic. He assured them that their kids had not approached him with any plans to get married; he simply assumed that they would in the reasonably near future. They agreed with him.

I'm curious, said Father Marcus. *Now that you have been married and had children and are just at the cusp of them leaving home and probably getting married, how do these vows seem to you? We've already talked about taking out the obey clause, but are there other changes you'd like to see? Maybe some additional items?*

Phyllis brought up the intertwined topics of birth control, premarital sex, and abortion. Did the Church have official positions on those issues?

The priest countered with a question of his own: did she wish there were formal vows about those topics included in the marriage ceremony?

I don't think so, she replied, *but on the other hand, they sure come up a lot. I bet ninety percent of all couples end up talking about them, at the very least.*

Father Marcus thought she made a good point. He asked them to take a moment to picture their kids standing in front of the Church, making the following vows to each other:

I vow to use birth control until we are ready to have children, and never to demand, agree to, or have an abortion, no matter what deformities or genetic problems our child might have.

Linda suggested that they were better off without getting so specific. The others agreed. Father Marcus was relaxed and at ease now, acting as one of their friends rather than any authority figure. They got to talking about end of life issues, and the until we are parted by death clause. How about dementia? How about euthanasia? How about pulling the plug if your spouse is declared brain dead? They talked for another half hour without coming to any kind of consensus. Father Marcus said that the Church's official position was that there was no wiggle room on these end of life issues. As long as you were married, no matter how sick your spouse was, you were in it to the very end.

Could you get divorced in such a case? Stanley asked.

The look Phyllis gave him suggested that he would be sleeping on the couch that night. And with that look, they ended their session.

The conversation made a deep impression on them, even though they didn't talk about it afterward. Hildy and Froggie did get confirmed a couple of weeks later, and that was that. Life went on as before.

Until...

Until suddenly, Hildy showed up with the devastating news that Froggie had gotten this strange artist from New York pregnant. That made their earlier talk with Father Marcus seem preordained. They gathered around her and wept with her. She told them she didn't know what Froggie and Janey were going to do and didn't want to know, not from them, anyway. She told them how she had demanded that Froggie communicate with his parents and not with her. Linda and Ray assured her that was perfectly understandable and that they would let her know when he reached out to them.

Three days passed before Froggie called. Linda answered the phone. When she realized who it was, she let out a little gasp. *Oh, Froggie, what have you done? And what are you going to do?*

Can I come over and talk?

Of course, you can. You want Ray to be here, too?

Please.

You want to stay for dinner?

I don't think I could eat anything right now.

He arrived half an hour later and sat down with his parents.

We've heard Hildy's side; why don't you tell us what happened from your perspective? his father suggested.

Froggie told them everything. They took it in stoically, determined not to pass judgment, or get overly reactive. This was just information.

So now what? Linda asked. *What's Janey decided to do?*

She wants to keep the baby.

And how about you? Have you decided what you are going to do?

I'm the father, he replied, *and I'm going to stay with Janey and raise it with her.*

Linda drew in a sudden breath.

I didn't hear anything about getting married, Ray said.

And I didn't hear anything about being in love with her, Linda added.

I'm trying to do the right thing, he replied.

His parents exchanged a long look. His father took the lead. *You know, son, in matters like these, everyone who knows you or Hildy is going to have their own definition of the right thing. No matter what you decide, people are going to disagree with it. Your mother and I might disagree. If you want our opinions, we'll give them to you, but that doesn't mean they are the right thing for you and this Janey person. To my mind, the only two people who can determine what the right thing is are you and her.*

He looked to his wife for confirmation. He didn't get it.

But how about Hildy? she asked. *Don't you think she should get a say about what's right?*

No, sweetheart, I don't. This has to be between Froggie and Janey.

Froggie's mother turned to him. *Can you share with us what she's been thinking?*

He told them that Janey was absolutely, fundamentally opposed to abortion. No matter what else happened, she was going to deliver the baby. And she was not going to give it up for adoption. That was just as fundamental to her beliefs as the abortion issue. This was her baby, and she was going to raise it.

Is this a religious thing? Linda asked. *Is she a churchgoer?*

Froggie almost smiled at the idea of Janey going to Church. *She's pretty much an atheist, Mom.*

What about her parents? Were they religious?

To be honest with you, I don't know. She doesn't talk about them much.

Oh, dear. Do you know why?

Froggie hesitated.

Maybe that's a topic for later, his father suggested. *Does she want to get married to you? Is that what's going on?*

She's not a fan of marriage, he replied, *but she does want us to live together and raise our child as part of a growing family.*

You mean having other children as well? his mother gasped.

We're talking about it.

Linda began to cry.

Please, Mom. Don't. It's not something we've decided. Right now, it's all just talk. But we do want to be a family.

But not be legally married, his father said.

I'm afraid not.

His parents looked at each other.

What are we going to tell Phyllis and Stanley? Linda asked.

We're going to tell them the truth.

But how are we going to break this to Hildy?

We'll figure it out together. Right now, we need to concentrate on our son.

I suppose you're right, she said.

Ray lost a little of his warmth toward Froggie. *I've got to ask you again, son: do you love her?*

I like her. I respect her.

And how does she feel about you?

Pretty much the same. Look, we're not in love with each other, like head over heels in love, but we figure it could be like an arranged marriage. A lot of them work out. That's what she tells me, anyway. If nothing else, we want to try to make a go of it.

But no wedding vows? Ray demanded. *Nothing that says you'll stick by each other for the rest of your lives no matter how tough things get?*

It's just not like that with Janey and me.

On that note, that heartbreaking note, the visit ended. Froggie went back to the commune more shaken than he let on in front of his parents. His principled stand (as he conceived it) was tearing apart his extended family, returning grief for all the love they had showered on him his whole life. The pain he saw in his parents' eyes was unbearable, and he could only imagine how much more pain his decision would bring to his other parents, the Boschs. And to Hildy. *Oh, God. God in heaven, look over Hildy.*

In a town as small as Castilia, it was impossible not to cross paths with most anyone, but Froggie managed to keep away from the Boschs and the Hartzlers to the extent of only seeing them in passing, never having to speak with them. This went on for a month, then two months, then three. Finally, his mother reached out, saying that they wanted to see him; they meaning both sets of parents. They didn't want to be hurtful, but they would prefer it if he came without Janey. Hildy's parents weren't ready to meet her. Froggie was glad to hear that because Janey was not at all interested in meeting any of them, and this way, he didn't have to say it.

He came back to his parents' house for the inevitable first interaction with Hildy's parents. As far as he could see, they were more reluctant to be there than he was. Phyllis gave him a patently insincere smile. Stanley simply glared at him. His birth father looked embarrassed. This meeting was his mother's idea.

They sat in an icy silence that only increased everyone's discomfort.

We just wanted you to know that all of this deeply hurt us, but we are still your parents, and we will love you and care about you always, his mother said. *We don't want to keep hiding from you or worrying about bumping into you on the street and wondering what we should say. I imagine you feel somewhat the same.*

He just nodded.

Can you tell us, have you and Janey changed your minds about any of this?

He was amazed that she could even say her name. *We're pretty much going ahead with things,* he said.

So, not getting married but having the baby, his father said.

Yeah.

I have a question, his mother said. *Have you chosen a name yet?*

We don't even know whether it's a boy or a girl.

I mean the last name. Will your child carry our family name or Janey's?

He didn't know what to say; the topic hadn't come up. He didn't want to admit that they hadn't even thought about it. *We haven't decided,* he said.

What is Janey's last name? his father asked. *You haven't mentioned it.*

Janey didn't like talking about her folks, and Froggie was pretty sure she wouldn't want him to tell them. But how could he not? It's *Kiser,* he said. He spelled it out.

Phyllis let out a low moan. Something about having a name put to this intruder had cut her to the core.

Can I ask? Froggie said, desperate to stop the raw emotion emanating from her, *how Hildy is coping?*

It was the wrong thing to do. Stanley erupted in raw fury. *How Hildy is doing is none of your goddamned business.*

He doesn't mean it, his mother said.

I think we should go, Stanley said to his wife. Phyllis began to cry openly as he led her out.

I'm sorry, Froggie, I really am, his mother said. *I thought this would help.*

They listened to the sound of the car, starting up and pulling away.

I should probably go, too, Froggie said.

Linda was not quite ready to let him go. *We need to meet Janey. We need to get to know her if she's going to be your partner and mother of our grandchild. She's going to need a lot of support. You both are.*

Janey threw a fit when Froggie told her, but for once, Froggie held his ground. They got through that first get-together somehow, and the next time it was a bit easier. Janey confessed to Froggie that her own parents had been abusive both to each other and to her, so she feared that Froggie's parents would be the same. It didn't take long to see how different the Hartzlers were from her own parents, and she discovered how desperately she wanted parental figures who loved her. Soon, they were visiting her weekly, and then Janey took the huge step of driving out to their house to spend a day with Froggie's mother, soaking up advice about babies and how to care for them.

About the time Janey entered her final trimester, Froggie's parents visited the commune bearing troubling news about Hildy. She was getting married.

Janey looked over at Froggie, who wouldn't meet her eyes. That hurt, but what did she expect? She knew full well that Froggie still carried a torch for Hildy, and probably always would. Janey figured that Hildy meant for her marriage to hurt them. If that was the case, she'd accomplished just what she desired.

Who's she marrying? Froggie asked, eyes cast down.

Thomas Washburn.

Froggie looked like he'd been punched in the gut. It took him a moment to regain his inner balance. He looked up at his parents. *You know,* he said, each word laced with pain, *I can kind of see that.*

Janey looked like she'd tasted something green and sour. *You mean the guy who wanted to build a golf course?*

He's not a bad guy, Janey. Really. He'll be good to Hildy.

Froggie's mom cleared her throat. *She wants to see you,* she said—*both of you.*

They froze.

She's not going to yell or make you feel guilty or anything like that.

What, then? Janey asked.

She wants to bury the hatchet, put this behind her before she marries Thomas. To be honest, I think she wants your blessing.

Apparently, his mother had been talking regularly with Hildy, Froggie thought. That hurt, but so what? *So you're telling me the wedding hasn't happened yet?*

No, not yet. Pretty soon. A couple of weeks.

Which means she wants to see us real soon, Janey said, while Froggie sat there silently.

Tomorrow or the next day, if possible.

Where?

Not here, Froggie's mom said. *We offered our place. It'll be just the three of you, nobody else.*

She's not...

What?

She's not going to be inviting us, is she? I don't think I could handle that.

No, said Froggie's mom. It was a short word filled with

compassion.

Froggie finally stirred. *Are you going to be there?*

It was his father who answered. *Stanley and I will be walking her down the aisle. Together.*

Janey twitched at the news.

His father saw it but said nothing.

Do the Boschs still hate me?

No.

But they're not quite ready to see you, yet, his mother added, gently. *You know, with Janey. I hope you understand.*

Yeah, they said in unison.

Can I ask? What do you think about this wedding?

Froggie's mom took a moment to gather her thoughts. *We're scared, to be honest. We think it's too soon, but we're going to support her decision and be there for them in any way we can.*

Just the way we are for you, Ray added.

Janey's eyes grew dark as she remembered how stressful her first meeting with them had been, and how warmly they probably greeted this Thomas Washburn guy when they met him. Froggie surprised her by putting his hand over hers. For once, he knew exactly what she was thinking.

Two days later, they drove up in Froggie's wreck of a car to the house. The car was noisy; the couple was silent. Hildy was already there to greet them. She seemed determined to make it as easy as possible. *Hello, guys.*

They fell into their roles immediately. *Hi, Hildy.*

Hi.

Come on in, she said, playing the role of hostess, graciously welcoming them to the house where she had grown up just as much as Froggie had.

They sat down on three chairs in the living room.

This is awkward for all of us, I'm sure.

They nodded solemnly.

I can't say that I'm not still hurt. I'll carry some of that forever, I suspect. But I would like for us to be friends again. Not like before, of course, but friends.

We'd like that, too, Janey told her.

The two women looked at Froggie, waiting for his agreement. *Everyone at the commune misses you,* he said.

And I miss them. You can tell them that.

They'd love it if you felt like visiting.

Perhaps after the wedding, she said diplomatically. *And the honeymoon, of course.*

They didn't ask for details.

How's the pregnancy going?

Fine, Janey said. It came out more abruptly than she'd planned.

The doctor says everything checks out, Froggie added.

Do you know if it's going to be a boy or a girl?

Janey began to stiffen.

Not yet, Froggie said before she could start telling Hildy that that was none of her damned business.

Janey let it go. *Yeah. We chose not to know. Let it be a surprise.*

Hildy's careful façade began to crumble. It was just for a moment, and she was able to pull herself back together. *I have a request.*

They waited.

When the child comes, can I be part of its life?

They waited some more.

Can I be, like, Aunt Hildy?

Froggie looked over at Janey and answered for both of them. *We'd love that.*

Two weeks later, Thomas Washburn married Hildegaard Bosch in a lavish celebration at St. Alban's Episcopal Church with Father Marcus Elliott presiding. The next day they flew to Bermuda for two weeks of sun and surf and snorkeling.

Janey gave birth to a beautiful baby boy on January 11, 1984. His parents named him Elroy Hartzler, using Froggie's last name. This pleased Froggie's parents and made it easier for Janey to keep the news from her own parents.

The day Janey came home to the commune with little Elroy, Hildy came to visit. *Oh, aren't you the cutest little cabbage! You don't know me yet, pumpkin, but I'm your Aunt Hildy and I'm going to love you to pieces. Just you wait and see.*

EPILOGUE

[April 2006 – a few weeks after the raid]

Arne and I were ensconced in a booth at the Buckeye Bar, honoring a tradition we had established early on in our friendship: celebrating the first loss of the season for the Indians. It came on opening night, which made it especially noteworthy. I was feeling put out because it happened while I was driving back from Castilia and I had to listen to it on the radio. Usually, Bucky would give us a pair of decent seats. Arne and I would enjoy the game and then go have a couple of beers downtown while our host stayed back at the stadium doing his job. Poor bastard. Imagine having to write about the Cleveland Indians year after year after year.

"Here's a thought for you, Arne," I said.

"Don't."

"No, hear me out. What if there was a big shakeup at the paper and we had to change jobs. I'm just talking about us reporters. Whose beat would you choose – assuming you had to choose. And let's say we drew straws and you went first, so you could pick anyone's. Which would you choose?"

Arne narrowed his eyes. "This is either a set up or a joke."

"Hey, it's the beginning of a new losing season. Why can't it be both?"

Arne looked over at Stan, who was pretending to clean the top of the bar with a look of abject boredom. "I wouldn't want to be him," he said.

"He's not an option," I reminded him. "And just how low do you want to set the bar, anyway?"

"I know, I'd ..." He cut himself off. "Okay, here's a second rule. You have to choose a different beat, but you only have to cover it for a year. Then you go back to your former job."

"Like a sabbatical."

"Yeah, exactly."

That brought up an interesting thought. "Why don't reporters get sabbaticals?"

"We don't need them," he said.

"I don't see why not. Every one of us is getting burned out."

"Not you, surely."

I gave him my best grimace, the one I practice in front of the mirror.

"Whoa!" He leaned forward. "Mouse, if I didn't know you better, I'd think you were being serious."

"Nah, it's nothing. Just bummed about the Indians."

"Look, if you don't want to talk about it, that's fine. I am your friend, though. You know you can tell me anything."

I couldn't resist. "If I tell you what's going on, you've got to promise me you won't laugh and you won't tell another soul."

"I won't tell another soul."

I let him stew there, refusing to ignore his partial answer. "I'm being stalked by a woman who says she's obsessed with me."

"Now I know you're joking."

"Not at all."

"So, how is she stalking you?"

"Anonymous love letters. Flowers delivered to my apartment. Phone calls where all I hear is deep breathing."

"Jesus."

"No, I don't think so. I'm pretty sure it's a woman."

"Jerk." He took a good pull on his beer. "You're sure?"

I nodded.

"Well, let me ask you this, assuming that it's real and not one of our buddies who's getting back at you for some stunt you pulled months ago: how do you feel about being stalked?"

"It's kind of creepy."

He waggled his hand. "That's one way of looking at it."

"How else should I look at it?"

"Some guys would be thrilled. Or at least complimented. I suppose some might get positively paranoid, but I don't see you going that route. Aren't you at least intrigued?"

"Nope. I just wish it would stop."

He sighed. "Sometimes, I think Peter is right about you. Deep down inside, you're not a reporter. You've got no curiosity."

I hung my head, drawing it out.

"When did it start?"

"A month ago."

"Hmm. Try to think back. What changed in your life a month ago? Did you join a club or go to a reunion or bump into an old friend? Anything like that?"

"I can't think of a thing."

"How about your apartment complex?"

"I suppose. People come and go there all the time."

"But nothing stands out?"

"Not really."

He shook his head in puzzlement. "Most likely an internal affair. I got it! Jane Smillens."

"That's not even funny," I snapped.

"I guess you're right. I have noticed you spending time with her. What's that about?"

"I've been telling her about my friend Dr. Tennyson and she's been wanting to meet him."

"He's that professor you told me about, right? Have you gone to see him?"

"A week ago."

"And how was that?"

"Mixed, to be honest. He's not in great shape, and he's got this fulltime nurse watching over him. Name's Debbie."

"Aha! She's your stalker."

"I only just met her."

"So the timing's all wrong."

"Not to mention the woman," I said. "She's a grandmother."

"Just your type."

"More like yours, grandpa."

Arne was beginning to lose interest in this imaginary stalker. "So, you've gone to see Dr. Tennyson and you've been talking to Jane about him. What's going on?"

I told him about Jane's interest in all the pesticides Stanhope was producing and their effect on the soil. "*Glyphosate* is the key, according to her. She wanted me to ask him about that."

"What did he say?"

"Well, that's a whole story in itself. You see, I bring it up and before I know it, nurse Debbie is getting into this long discussion about using MowDown™ on her lawn to kill the dandelions."

"Wow, Mouse, that must have been fascinating."

"You'd be surprised. That's one of the things I like about Dr. Tennyson the most. He can take any subject at all and turn it into the most interesting topic you've ever heard of."

That got a laugh. "No wonder you're friends. He's just like you."

I let the compliment slide because I didn't want him to see how much it meant to me. "One thing I realized afterward is that Debbie is a walking, talking, breathing embodiment of my ideal reader."

"But not dating material?"

"Stop it."

"Why? I seem to be getting under your skin, buddy. Feeling defensive for some reason? Or are we still talking about this supposed stalker? You say Debbie is out because the timing is wrong. Could she be a nurse? You been to the doctor or hanging out in hospitals lately?"

That's the problem with talking to Arne. I end up getting caught in my own stories, and before I know it, he's the one who's playing me rather than vice versa. I was halfway beginning to think I did have a stalker. I had to fight back and I had to do it quickly. "I did have a dream about her," I told him. "It was about dandelions, not roses. I was thinking about this whole apocalyptic vision of Stanhope taking over the world so that there was only one crop able to grow anywhere on Earth, but that crop was dandelions. And there she was, standing in the middle of this immense field of them with one of those old hand pumps spraying MowDown™ on them and saying, 'Thank God for Stanhope. Where would we be without them?"

"That doesn't make any sense. You just said that Stanhope was the reason there weren't any crops other than dandelions."

"That's dreams for you."

He shuddered. "More like a nightmare."

"How much have I told you about my little excursion to Castilia?"

"Nothing, really."

"I'll tell you what: if you want to find a group of people who really hate Stanhope, that's the place to be. Forget Cincinnati. Forget Peter and his holy war to take them on. This little, unknown town is ground zero when it comes to what's really happening on that front."

I started telling him about what I experienced. At some point we took a break to hit the men's room and get another pitcher of beer. By the time we got to the bottom of that one, I was begging him to drive out there and see it for himself.

"You're forgetting we're under the gun here," he said. "In case you haven't noticed, Peter's getting so cranked up I'm afraid he's going to bring a gun to our next staff meeting."

"Ah, screw him. Come with me to Castilia. Let's go tomorrow. We can call in sick. It would do you good."

"The way we're going, we're going to be calling in sick, anyway."

"So, what have you got to lose?"

"My job?"

The last thing I remember from that night was insisting he had nothing to worry about in terms of his job. "Castilia, my friend, is the biggest story in Ohio."

To be continued.

CLEVELAND QUARTET

Book One:

The Biggest Story in Ohio

Can the aging hippies of the Bite This Commune thwart the plans of the worst polluter in America to build a chemical plant in their backyard?

Not a chance...

Unless a pair of rogue reporters from Cleveland start digging into the story. Then --just maybe -- there's spark of hope.

That's the local story.

A similar drama is playing out around the world, as modern, industrialized agriculture destroys the fertility of the soil we depend on to grow our food.

Book Two:

In the Land of the Nematodes

Tadpole, a mysterious bit character from Book One, comes to prominence, further linking the Bite This Commune to Stanhope Chemicals. Dr. Tennyson leads Mouse and Arne deeper into the history of chemical and biological warfare and how it has been applied to modern agriculture. Froggie starts an organic trout farm. The commune becomes self-sustaining and middle-aged without losing any of its quirkiness.

Book Three:

The Flaming Trout Festival

Corporate espionage enters the picture and leads to the botched FBI raid on the commune that started the events of Book One. Land developers from New Jersey bring new twists to the plans of Stanhope Chemicals and the Bite This Commune. Mouse becomes increasingly frustrated with the limitations of his job and begins exploring options to report on the environment. Tadpole's plans to attack Stanhope Chemicals threatens to destroy commercial fishing on the Great Lakes. Lampreys become a major topic.

Book Four:

Mouse, Reporting from Lake Erie

Mouse reports on the lamprey eradication project by the Fish and Wildlife Commission as it poisons the Vermillion River, during which he finally comes face to face with Tadpole. Dr. Tennyson joins forces with the Bite This Commune. Things come to a head at the Cleveland Plain Speaker with major implications for both Mouse and Arne.

ACKNOWLEDGMENTS

Looking back on the long, winding path this novel took from first idea to finished product, I am astonished at how many people became involved at one point or another.

I have to start with my wife Pat. It's not easy being married to a compulsive writer. She has put up with a lot of moodiness and neglect all these years, understanding that I am what I am even if she doesn't understand it. I love you deeply.

Nobody has been as involved throughout my entire writing life as Doug Harper. Not even close. Poor Doug has read and believed in a string of novels preceding this one, novels I ended up abandoning. I'm amazed that he has hung in there all these years.

My primary source of inspiration and guidance in all matters of science is David Shupe. He is an inspired teacher and true friend. Don't blame him for whatever I got wrong. Give him credit for introducing me to most of the topics I cover in this and the succeeding books in the series.

Another major influence in my thinking and development as a writer is my dear friend Ken Gowdy, a biblical scholar and spiritual guide. I can safely say that I never would have finished this novel without his continued support and understanding.

I haven't hung out with other writers very much. And shame on me. But I am happy to list the following writing companions: Joe Helgerson, Ric James, Kevin Fenton, Joan Mickelson, Deb Jones, Gene Tierney, and Jim Miles. Each and every one of you has made me a better writer.

Finally, there is a group of friends and relatives who showed up at just the right time(s) when I needed support: Polly Schaffner, Pi Luna, Hans Bucher, Philip Schaffner, Kate Moss, Paul and Esther Bucher, Shirley Gowdy, Kathleen Cassen Mickelson, Jim and Kendra Golden, Mark Salling, Clyde Thompson, Mark Maronde, Jim Frazier, Mary Harty, Ernesto Ferrer Nunes, Linda Lehmann, and a special callout and thank you to William Gillis, whose wonderful photo of a farm graces the front cover. And one final shoutout to Beth Flavell, my final volunteer proofreader.

CAST OF CHARACTERS

STANHOPE CHEMICALS, INTERNATIONAL

Ronnie Haskins: Senior Executive Vice President, North America Operations, Stanhope Chemicals, International

Shira Beck: Chief Legal Officer

Robert Harris: VP, Government Relations

Scott Ranhovsky: Chief Acquisitions Officer

Duncan Gabardine: VP, Digital Security

Ginny Powell: VP, Media Relations

[Terrance Courtney: senior Senator Ohio]

[Benjamin Wicker: Congressman, Ohio District 6]

[Maeve Waldock: lawyer in Cincinnati]

THE CLEVELAND PLAIN SPEAKER

Peter Zenger: Editor

Dorothy Dreyfus: Peter Zenger's secretary

Mouse: reporter, people who aren't newsworthy

Arne Price: reporter, race relations, politics

Jane Smillens: reporter, science

Lenny Kellerman: reporter, economics

Terry Trowbridge: reporter, crime

Tom: reporter, politics

Sarah: reporter, politics

Trisha: reporter, politics

Dr. Jeremiah Tennyson: environmental activist. Mouse's friend.

Debbie Bohmeyer: Dr. Tennyson's nurse

Eliska and Katerina Svoboda: owners of Dvorak Bakery

CASTILIA / SANDUSKY OHIO

Bite This Commune

Froggie: chef, unofficial leader

Janey: sculptor and artist

Elroy: Froggie's son ("the first born")

Blossom: earth mother, food artist

Terry: leather artist, saddle maker

Skullman: biker, recovering addict

Townspeople

Hildegaard Bosch: real estate agent

Phyllis Bosch: Hildy's mother

Stanley Bosch: Hildy's father

Ray Hartzler: Froggie's father

Linda Hartzler: Froggie's mother

Elliott Washburn: Pres., First Bank of Castalia

Clarissa Washburn: Elliott's wife

Thomas Washburn: son of Elliott and Clarissa

Franklin Bucher: attorney

Christine Nichols: owner Cardinal Café

Father Marcus Elliott: Episcopal Priest

Fred Williams: farmer

AUTHOR BIO

I am not a scientist. I lack the training for it as well as the temperament. What I share with scientists is a sense of awe at the complexity and beauty of the natural world and a drive to understand it as best I can. My formal background is in English Literature, especially in the study of narrative or dramatic structure.

How do stories work? How do ordinary people confront their own ignorance of how the world works? What happens to individuals and groups when the world changes either physically (think climate change and environmental degradation), intellectually (think evolution, quantum mechanics, bio-engineering), or technologically (think computers, the internet, scanning electron microscopes, space telescopes?)

Nobody can understand it all, and even if they could, half of what they understand today would be outdated tomorrow. This reality is cause for deep fear and pessimism.

It is equally cause for humor, compassion, resilience, and hope.

STAY IN TOUCH

The three best ways to stay in touch are...

Greg Schaffner author page on Amazon.com

My website: www.gregschaffnerauthor.com

My email list: [sign up at the website]

I will be regularly updating and expanding my website as I proceed to make final revisions and release the other books of the Cleveland Quartet. One feature I plan to add is an updated bibliography of books I am reading for source material on the latest scientific findings and theories.

Made in the USA
Monee, IL
28 February 2021

61551752R00177